Edouard Rod, Bradley Gilman

Pastor Naudié's Young Wife

Edouard Rod, Bradley Gilman

Pastor Naudié's Young Wife

ISBN/EAN: 9783337715687

Printed in Europe, USA, Canada, Australia, Japan

Cover: Foto ©Raphael Reischuk / pixelio.de

More available books at **www.hansebooks.com**

PASTOR NAUDIÉ'S YOUNG WIFE

BY

ÉDOUARD ROD

TRANSLATED BY BRADLEY GILMAN

BOSTON
LITTLE, BROWN, AND COMPANY
1899

TO MY FRIEND

ALBERT BONNARD

INTRODUCTION

ÉDOUARD ROD belongs more to the country of Calvin and Amiel than to the country of Hugo and Molière. He is a Swiss by temperament quite as much as by birth. The sombre beauty of Alpine slopes permeates his books ; and, dark as are the valley paths along which he sometimes leads his readers, those readers can never lose, from the background of their consciousness, the awed sense of snowy heights far above them, where dwell purity and majesty and peace.

Behind the deserved success which has now come to Rod, there are many years of patient toil ; prolonged effort has combined with his inborn powers of perception and analysis, to place him where he now stands, in the foremost rank of living fiction-writers in France. He was born in 1857, at Nyon, near Geneva. He

Introduction

studied in Switzerland and in Germany. His independence of judgment was shown by the pamphlet which he put forth in 1879, "À propos de L'Assommoir," in which he earnestly defended Émile Zola, at that time assailed on every hand by the most violent denunciations. His championship of Zola brought Rod unconsciously under the influence of that writer's style; but in 1885 he had regained his poise, and "La Course à la Mort," published during that year, shows his growing individuality. During several years he was at the head of "La Revue Contemporaine." Until recently he has occupied the Chair of Literature in the University of Geneva; but this post he has now given up, in order to devote himself more fully to the special field of fiction.

Rod has published, in all, about fifteen volumes. His "Nouvelles Romandes" and his "Scènes de la Vie Cosmopolite" are short stories. "Études sur le XIXième Siècle," "Les Idées Morales du Temps Présent" and "Essai sur Goethe" are works of a critical nature. His most distinctive writings, however, are his novels,—"La Course à la Mort,"

Introduction

" Le Sens de la Vie," " Les Trois Cœurs," " La
Sacrifiée," " Le Dernier Refuge," " La Vie
Privée de Michel Teissier," " La Seconde
Vie de Michel Teissier," " Le Silence," " Les
Roches Blanches," " La Haut," and, latest in
the list, " Le Ménage du Pasteur Naudié."
" Les Roches Blanches " has been translated
into English, under the title " The White
Rocks;" and " Le Ménage du Pasteur Naudie "
is presented, in this volume, under the title
" Pastor Naudié's Young Wife."

An examination of these books shows Rod
in his twofold character of philosopher and
literary artist. He is not a philosophic pedant,
crammed with the systems of Plato, Aristotle,
Kant, and Hegel, but a student and analyst
of human life, as he finds it manifested around
him to-day. Rod's readers must not expect
to find him elaborating a comprehensive theory of the good and evil of the world; indeed, they must not expect to find him always
consistent with himself. He is too emotional,
too fanciful and spontaneous, to be exclusively
a philosopher. In a private letter which he
recently wrote to a friend, speaking of a certain

Introduction

suggested reform, he said: "It can surely do no harm, for the world's affairs already go as badly as possible." That remark is not the fruit of calm, philosophic judgment; it is, rather, the passing mood of an artistic, impressionable nature, which feels deeply the burden of human woe. Jules Lemaître complains, in "Les Contemporaires," that Rod has no reason to feel so badly about the woes of life, since his own worldly conditions are very comfortable. Such a criticism errs, in that it fails to take account of the delicate sensibility of a nature like Rod's, which feels the pressure of life keenly, and carries, by its power of sympathy, other men's burdens as if they were its own.

The man who could write "Le Sens de la Vie" is more or less a theologian, vehemently as he would probably repudiate that term. More than this, he is even a religious man. If Carlyle's broad definition of religion in "Heroes and Hero Worship" is sound, then Édouard Rod must be classed among those who interpret life religiously. His natural inclinations take him frequently into the atmosphere of clerical life; and his mind is never

Introduction

more alert, his words never more eloquent, than
when he is discussing the fundamental problems of theology and religion. Certainly he
is far removed from that superficial, frivolous
spirit, which is so often condescendingly attributed to the French character by English
and American critics, and is attributed by
French critics, with equal soundness, to the
American character. The reader will see that
the author of " La Sacrifiée " and " La Vie
Privée de Michel Teissier " and " Les Roches
Blanches " takes life very seriously, even sadly.
To the hasty reader he may seem gloomy and
pessimistic, but his sadness has its root in a
genuine faith ; and he is gloomy, because he
sees, in human life, truth so often on the scaf-
fold, and wrong so often on the throne. Yet,
behind that very gloom and indignation, is faith
in eternal truth and everlasting right, else the
ethical chord in his heart would not vibrate so
readily and so intensely. Outward pessimism
often implies an inward idealism ; scorn of ex-
isting conventional codes of morals and religion
frequently grows out of a profound reverence
for absolute standards of human conduct ; and

Introduction

this condition of mind and heart is closely akin
to theism, and even to Christianity.

Centuries ago, a wise observer of human
life said that if only he might be allowed to
write the songs of a people, he cared not who
framed its laws. This observation has com-
mended itself to the judgment of reflective
minds through all the succeeding centuries.
But one would be justified, in our time, if he
retained the spirit and altered the letter of that
ancient saying, thereby making it read, " If
only I might write the novels of a people, I
care not who frames its laws." For laws and
statutes are only the results, the products, of a
people's growth ; whereas novels are the fore-
runners and guides of that growth.

The writer of fiction, in our day, is a pioneer
of thought ; he is teacher and preacher, theologian and sociologist, all in one. And he has
the incalculable advantage over other guides
and reformers of human conduct, that he offers
his lessons, his criticisms, his exhortations, in
a form which gives them easy entrance into
human hearts ; he incarnates his opinions ; he
breathes into an abstract idea the breath of life,

Introduction

and it becomes a living soul, and walks among men, to be either hated and shunned by them, or loved and emulated by them, according as its creator, the novelist, has willed.

This high office — of moulding public thought and conduct, by works of fiction, rather than merely registering the public will, by laws — is one that is shared by all novelists, though in varying degrees. Some of them [1] make themselves, consciously, leaders; others teach more unconsciously, more indirectly; but on all, in some measure, fall grave responsibilities. Whether they will it or not, they must picture human character and conduct, again and again, as they believe it ought to be. Though they may try to sink their moral convictions in the unmoral artist-instinct, nevertheless the coloring of their adjectives and adverbs usually betrays them.

Édouard Rod's earlier writings, like the earlier writings of Dickens, Stevenson, and many other novelists, were tentative and transitional. With sure, yet by no means slow steps, he has made his way into his proper field of work, the delineation of human character in real life; here he finds the fittest conditions for the exercise of his best powers. His style is so simple and clear, that the reader hardly stops to ask if he has one. Benjamin Wells, in his "Century of French Fiction," speaks of him as "a subtly delicate genius;" and Edmund Gosse has said of him, "Whether in criticism or in fiction, his work always demands attention." Nearly all the characters in Rod's novels are drawn from the middle classes of society. Of wit and humor there is little. He does not throw his own emotions into the scale, laughing and weeping with the joys and sorrows of his men and women; he is too busily and seriously engaged in analyzing their actions and their motives. There is, in his pages, no seeking after novelty of material, no straining after "local color." He is an anatomist of the human heart, writing for readers of intellectual tastes like his own.

This latest of Monsieur Rod's novels, "Pastor Naudié's Young Wife," appeared in the May and June numbers of "Le Revue des deux Mondes" of 1898. Its title was "Le Ménage du Pasteur Naudié." It is a

Introduction

study of life in the historic town of La Rochelle, and is wholesome in its moral atmosphere, even reminding some critics of Mrs. Humphry Ward's novels. The author throws a shaft of light down into that obscure old Protestant bourgeois community, as it is sometimes thrown down through the water, upon the sea-bed; and every living creature, within the circle of illumination, stands as clearly defined as do the figures in one of Meissonier's pictures. Even the characters that move about in the shadowy penumbra just outside the circle, are in good outline and proportion; and the reader feels, as he finishes the book, like asking the author to shift slightly the angle of his shaft of light, to bring these minor characters out into the illuminated circle, and then, in another volume, tell us about the detailed workings of Monsieur Lanthelme's mind, and what Monsieur Merlin really thought about himself when alone at his own fireside. This is the remarkable effect of Édouard Rod's books. Even the dim secondary characters are so true to life that they arouse a vivid interest, and one wishes to follow them to their homes and haunts, and learn more about them.

Introduction

Monsieur Rod is only forty-two years old, and his hand has gained steadily in strength and skill from the first; doubtless the quality of his work will improve still more, as the years pass; as Alphonse Gaulin has said, we are justified in expecting from him, in the near future, a masterpiece. Certainly, as his work becomes more widely known, he will find many readers; for the human heart is the most fruitful and most interesting of themes; and, however we may yield to the encroachments of material things, however we may bow to the tyranny of outward circumstances, yet, in the last resort, we recognize the truth of those words, so often upon Édouard Rod's lips, and so deeply engraved upon his heart, — "L'Âme seule importe."

BRADLEY GILMAN.

Pastor Naudié's Young Wife

❦

PART FIRST

CHAPTER I

MONSIEUR NAUDIÉ stood shivering in the dim light of the cold April morning. Then he set down his small handbag on the seat of a second-class carriage. Next he began walking with long strides up and down the platform, stamping from time to time, to warm his feet. "It would be a good plan," said he, talking to himself, "if this station of La Rochelle, now so small and dark and inconvenient, were entirely rebuilt."

At that moment he heard some one call him by name.

"Ah, Monsieur Defos!" he replied, with a salute.

The two men shook hands. Monsieur Naudié, tall, rather slender, narrow-chested, shivered underneath an overcoat which would have been warm enough a little farther south, but was not warm enough, in this latitude, for a night on the steam-cars. His companion had red cheeks, broad shoulders, and full whiskers; and his profile, with its large curved nose, indicated a strong will. He luxuriated in a thick fur coat; and, as he promenaded up and down, he seemed very much at home; indeed, he acted as if he owned the earth itself.

"So you are off on a journey, my dear sir?" he inquired.

"Yes," replied Monsieur Naudié, "I am going to Montauban."

Then he added, straightening up, with an involuntary gesture of pride, " The Faculty celebrate to-morrow the fiftieth anniversary of my father's election to the Board of Instruction."

"Ah! to be sure!" said Monsieur Defos; " I read about that in the *Signal*. It will be a happy day for your family, my dear sir; and for us also, and for all of us, because we are all proud of your father. Doubtless you will remain with him several days."

"Hardly that! I must be back by Sunday, for my sermon."

"I have had it in mind, my dear pastor, to write to you and ask you to dine with us, one of these days, quite informally. How would Tuesday suit you?"

This invitation caused Monsieur Naudié some surprise, because, during his residence of twelve years in La Rochelle, he had not dined more than four or five times with Defos, and always under such circumstances as the transient visit of a missionary, or the sitting of the convention. He accepted, however, with thanks; and then inquired, though in a hesitating way, as if he hardly dared question so grand a personage, "I believe you have, at present, all your family with you?"

"Yes," replied Monsieur Defos. "My second son is on a vacation; we shall keep him a fortnight. You know my niece has been with us, also, for some time."

"To be sure, I have met Miss Defos several times, in the dwellings of the sick and at committee meetings. It gives one pleasure to see a young girl so earnest, so bent upon doing good."

While the clergyman thus spoke, his companion's keen hard eye was directed toward him, with a penetration that almost wounded; it seemed to be seeking some concealed thought behind the spoken words. But Monsieur Naudié expressed, with entire simplicity, his sincere approbation. Monsieur Defos could not read in his eyes anything different from what he expressed in his speech.

"Yes, yes," he remarked, rather dryly, "it is a good thing to have her busy."

The railway officials were now closing the doors of the carriages. The two men found themselves obliged to separate, — one climbing up into a compartment of the first-class, marked " Reserved," while the other found a seat in a carriage already occupied by four other travellers. The train at once started. As it issued from the station, a few rays of yellowish light entered at the car windows, despite the smoke of the engine. Monsieur Naudié snuggled up into a corner, wondering within himself at the possible reason Monsieur Defos could have for giving him this invitation. Surely he must have some purpose ; he was a man who never acted without one. Monsieur Defos was a man of mark, as much by his wealth as by his family and his own self-assertion. His name — which appeared for the first time, in the Protestant registries of 1616 — was connected with several events in the history of La Rochelle. He was a descendant of that David Defos, mentioned so often in Mervault's *Journal,* who was one of the sheriffs of the year 1627 ; he served his fellow-citizens on several important missions, at the beginning of the siege, but lost their confidence by his luke-

warmness in following plain instructions against
the judge, Raphael Colin; he regained favor,
however, later; and he dared take to task,
with haughty dignity, Anne of Austria, when
she visited the conquered and depopulated
town. The persecutions which preceded the
Edict of Nantes by no means served to drive
the members of the Defos family from the
city; for their name is again to be found
among those youth of La Rochelle who, during the war with Holland, served with dis-
tinction under a chief of their own faith, —
later a renegade, — Baron de Chatelaillon.
Privateersmen of the eighteenth century, as
they were, participating in several of those
undertakings which failed to establish French
colonial rule, the members of the Defos family
were almost ruined by the Revolution. In
1789, when the National Assembly was preparing a new division of the country into de-
partments, one of them took upon himself the
mission of expressing the old-time individual-
ism of La Rochelle, by publishing a " Memoir
concerning the Rise, the History, and the Interests of the Province of Aunis;" this was an
open protest against the reuniting of Aunis
and Saintonge. When public peace was restored, they revived the ancient maritime and

commercial enterprise of their family. Their business house, " Wood and Coal," established in the early years of the Restoration, quickly brought them the old-time prosperity. This is the important business house which Monsieur Georges Defos, the real head of the family, conducted with success. Although he was, at one and the same time, a member of the Consistory and president of several boards, he devoted a part of his time to caring for the affairs of the Reformed Church. Experienced merchant that he was, at once energetic and adroit in the battle of commercial life, he was also a thoroughgoing Christian. His religion, although entirely genuine, did not prevent him from keeping abreast of the times ; for God has put the world into the hands of the men of strong will. With his upright exact nature, and with his dry rigid character, this man was incapable of doing a wrong to any one, especially if it were for his own advantage. Instead of struggling between opposing motives, it usually happened that his scrupulous conscience and his egotistic soul gave to each other mutual support. As the head of the family, he was rigid, autocratic, unsympathetic, and moody ; but at the same time he was well-intentioned, regardful of the rights of each of its members, capable of great devotion to the common interests. As an employer, his extreme severity did not prevent him from exercising a watchful care over the welfare of his workmen. In return for the sacrifices which he willingly made for improving their houses, their food, and the conditions of their old age, he demanded of them their best efforts, entire regularity in the performance of their tasks, and even in their observance of religious duties. Indeed, in his mechanical view of life, religion was an important part of the complete equipment of a good house. God, in this man's system, seemed to occupy an elevated position, much like a superior magistrate. He believed that every person owed to God a portion of his energy about equal to that which a loyal citizen owes to the state. He was, then, a member of the Consistory, as he was of the Council General; or, rather, he would have been a member, if the electors of his department had allowed it. Nobody could harmonize more closely than could he the claims of time and of eternity; rendering, with sternest justice, unto God that which belonged to God, unto Cæsar that which belonged to Cæsar, and perhaps — for new epochs demand new methods — rendering unto Mammon that which belonged to Mammon.

Meditating upon the invitation given by Monsieur Defos, the good clergyman ended by deciding that it was due to the celebration at Montauban, and that he owed it to the reflected glow which came to him from his father's honors; and this solution aroused in him not the slightest bitterness, but a slight feeling of scorn for the man whom he had just left. Then, soothed by the movements of the train, his reverie turned toward objects of more immediate interest to himself: he thought about his father, whom he had not seen for three years; about his brothers, now scattered abroad over the world; and about his children, whose care weighed upon him without ceasing.

In eight years of married life Monsieur Simeon Naudié had had six children; the two eldest were welcomed with joy, the two following, with increasing anxiety, and the two last, with resignation. The mother, good woman that she was, stood up strongly against the trials of life, trusted in God, and conducted, without any show of excessive economy, a very large household on a very small income. Whenever they grew anxious about the future, they comforted each other by recalling the blessings promised to large families. Has not God said " Increase and multiply"? He cares for the birds of the air. He caused the manna to rain down upon the children of Israel. . . . While waiting for the manna, Madame Naudié found a way of providing food, by repeating from time to time the miracle of the bread and the fishes, with respect to clothes, shoes, and other necessaries. But, one year, the croup settled down upon their little nest ; three were attacked, two died. Madame Naudié was in a delicate condition for the seventh time, and the premature birth of this child caused the death of the mother. Monsieur Naudié was thus left alone with his four little ones, shattered by this tragic sequence of sad experiences. The difficulties with which he found himself all at once overtaken did not allow him to resign himself to fruitless grief. He bore up under his sorrow with that calm dignity, that serene fortitude, which Christians sometimes show. Nobody suspected — such were the dignity and the discretion of his manner — the store of energy which he was compelled to expend from the first, which he must needs put forth as a mournful tribute, month after month and year after year, as each day brought with it its train of cares.

Pastor Naudié's Young Wife

On this very day there was added to him a new burden of care. Abraham, his only boy, a lad of thirteen years, strong, indolent, wilful, and wayward, had barely escaped expulsion from school, because of a bad book which he had loaned to his companions. Urgent supplications availed to change into temporary suspension the decree of expulsion which had been at first pronounced; but Monsieur Naudié could still hear the irritated tones of the master, as he stood for a long time unyielding, urging the welfare of the class; and the pastor's conscience reproached him, as he recalled the weak arguments he had used, — the boy's future compromised, his shame recoiling upon his family, and the scandal of the affair, all the greater because of its occurrence in a clergyman's son. This last argument had been effective. Monsieur Naudié, however, recognized it as an unsound plea. " What, then," he reflected; " if the son of my neighbor had been guilty of a similar fault, he would have found justice inflexible toward him, that justice which has in this case conceded a point to my profession. That is not right; it is dangerous. I ought to have allowed them to carry out the deserved decision. But, then, what could I have done with Abraham? What would have become of him?" He tried to excuse himself for this little misuse of his pastoral influence, and succeeded in satisfying his conscience only by looking upon himself as a widower in straitened circumstances, and as a father overburdened with cares. Absorbed in these disagreeable reflections, he gave scarcely any attention to the day which was breaking over the plains of Saintonge. It was only as he arrived at Rocheport that he roused himself. His fellow-passengers alighted. He scanned the travellers crowded upon the platform, and at once recognized the broad shoulders, the perennially young appearance, and the dark brown beard of his brother William, whom he immediately summoned by a signal.

William Naudié, the eldest of the numerous family, was, as his father remarked, its "dry fruit." Variable as a vapor, fantastic, imaginative, Bohemian in taste, he had begun his career by studying law, then had turned to medicine, afterward had made an attempt at literature, and, finally, after various youthful follies, had become stranded in the customhouse. For three years he had been living in Rocheport, amid the changing horde of functionaries, civil or military. A sceptic, and a cynic at times, he saw very little of any of his family except Simeon, whose house he occasionally visited for a Sunday ; at such times he took great pleasure in attacking theology, and to the best of his ability undermining it ; if his arguments clashed with those of the pastor, he was especially delighted.

William entered the train, seated himself in front of his brother, and, first of all, asked about the children. The narration of Abraham's escapade, instead of arousing his indignation, only drew from him an indulgent exclamation, " Ah, the scapegrace ! "

" Besides, I believe," explained Simeon, " that this was only heedlessness. Abraham is by no means a wicked boy. But he makes me despair of him, by reason of his idleness, by the readiness with which he follows a bad example, and by his morbid love of vagabond ways. Now that he is no longer under surveillance he slips away to the wharves, plays or fights with the boys there, and returns much disordered. Indeed, after several reproofs, he has gone out in the fishing-boats without troubling himself as to our anxiety. Neither admonitions nor punishments avail anything."

" He will end, perhaps," said William, " by becoming a sailor. It is an occupation which is as good as any."

Pastor Naudié's Young Wife

Instead of taking up this line of thought, Monsieur Naudié began to sound the praises of Esther, his eldest daughter; a wise little housewife of fifteen years, industrious, frugal, devoted, she took charge of the house as if she were a grown woman, and seemed to have only one aim, to help the others.

"Such a daughter as that," said he, "is a blessing."

"Doubtless you are correct," replied William, "but perhaps she, for her part, would prefer a little more pleasure."

"She has what she gives. Is not that the higher joy?"

"When one has satisfied his own hunger, he tosses a few crumbs to the birds," said William.

Again, as before, Simeon let the whimsical suggestion pass unchallenged. Then the conversation turned to the next day's celebration; an occasion which would bring together at least a part of the scattered members of the family.

"Which of our number are we likely to meet to-morrow?" asked William; "do you know?"

"First of all, Marcel, now that he is here in Europe."

"I dare say," remarked William, "despite all the tales about his conversions among the Bassoutas."

" Our brother," continued Simeon, " is a faithful servant of the good cause. I never think of him without admiring his courage and devotion."

" For my part, I am in favor of leaving the savages to enjoy their idols. Freedom for all, I say. Then, there is Paul ; what about him ? "

" Oh, yes, Paul! " exclaimed Simeon, without saying anything more.

In the veins of this brother the old Huguenot blood ran fiercely and fanatically. From his childhood up he had shown an inclination for a sort of passionate mòrbid mysticism. Even at the age of seven he was one day observed standing and waving his arms ; when asked why he did this, he answered, " To fly away to heaven, to the Saviour." When he was studying with his brothers at Montauban, and afterward at Paris, he grew indignant at the follies of Protestantism. Before he was consecrated he abruptly broke with the official church in order to enter the service of one of the evangelizing societies, whose propaganda was carried on often with more zeal than discretion. Several years later he entered upon evangelistic work in Auvergne, making use of all the customary methods of saving souls, such as healing by prayer, distributing aid to the neophytes, and frequently disturbing the peace of the villages; often he was hooted after, sometimes he suffered physical violence, but he never ceased his labors.

"See how inconsistent you are!" said William. "You approve Marcel and you blame Paul. Oh, but you do blame him; don't deny it! And the two are really doing the same work."

"Allow me!" replied Simeon, vehemently; "there is a world of difference; besides, whatever you may think, I do not blame Paul. I know that his purposes are excellent."

"Not at all," exclaimed William. "He has no excellent purposes. He has only pride; a boundless vanity. He is proud of being better than the common run of men, proud of being the only person who comprehends the plans of Deity, proud of being the representative of God, of taking part in his plans, of speaking, and especially of condemning, in his name. I shall never forget a certain sermon which he gave me once; he gave it to me in Scriptural phraseology. 'We are the peculiar children of God, who have been chosen and set apart —' Oh, the imbecile!"

At heart, Simeon agreed with his brother;

but he disliked to agree with him openly for fear of strengthening in him the spirit of scepticism. He therefore began talking about such matters as he knew concerning their other brothers. James, the next to the youngest, now teaching in Russia, could not possibly come. No more could Auguste, the youngest, who had gone to Southern Africa, where he had amassed riches. As for the sisters, one of them, Louise, married to a Scotch clergyman, was not able to leave her husband. The other, Sophie, who was teaching in America, could not take so long and so expensive a journey.

"We shall be reduced to our poor 'Antigone,'" remarked William.

He referred in this way to their eldest sister, Angelica, a tender creature, now growing gray and wrinkled, disciplined and patient, very sweet, yet firm, who was utterly sacrificed to her father, a very old man, for whom she cared as if he were an infant, submitting to all his despotic vagaries, humoring all his caprices, and acting, at one and the same time, as his governess, his secretary, and his nurse. She was one of those admirable creatures who seem to be born for self-sacrifice; so good that their virtues are overlooked, so necessary

to others that their services are undervalued —
like unseen flowers of the field, whose fra-
grance fills the air.

The two brothers conversed, after this fashion, as far as Bordeaux; where a change of
cars turned their thoughts into other channels.
After a short delay they resumed their journey
upon the line of the Midi, and felt inclined to
chat a little more cheerfully. Over the level,
fertile country the sun poured its joyous flood
of light, and high in air a few luminous clouds
floated across the blue sky. Two clearly outlined ranges of hills stood out in bluish tints
against the horizon, on the right and on the
left; they were dotted with groups of trees,
which looked like yew or cypress. Several
antique villages were passed, with crumbling
old houses grouped around a church whose
buttresses seemed to stretch out toward them
as if to afford them protection. Or, again,
they noted some tower, toppling under its
weight of years, a ruin of dislodged stones,
among which the roots of ivy twined themselves, like perpetual youth twining about de-
crepit old age. Poplars and willows looked
down upon the sluggish currents of the streams;
some of them leaning over in fantastic atti-
tudes, with their trunks covered by leafy twigs.

Others were stunted, and seemed to thrust out their broken branches like clenched fists, threatening but powerless.

As their journey carried them more and more into regions which were familiar, the two brothers felt, growing upon them, that indefinable softening of spirit which comes to one as he revisits the land of his birth, and returns to that corner of the earth to which he is tied by the strong cords of heredity and early association.   This feeling became even more touching and more intense when they reached the banks of the Tarn, upon whose waves they had floated in the olden time, and dreamed their earliest dreams.   The stream meandered, as in their youth, across the open plain, reflecting in some places the green color of the abundant foliage on its banks, and again showing gray with the grayish tint of the fallow land.   Along its margin were scattered, at intervals, little brown houses, from whose gardens the rich efflorescence of peach-trees burst forth, as if it were keeping a festival in the springtime, as if it were the harvest of the winter.

Drawn together and brought into sympathy by a common instinct, the brothers began to tell the beads of the rosary of memory ; again they were children ; an unseen, tender hand lifted the burden which life had laid upon their shoulders, and, during this blessed moment of retrospect, they breathed again with keen enjoyment.

"Don't you remember, William, when I went a-fishing, down there, near the Albacedes mill ? "

"Well, you never caught anything."

"Oh, yes, but I did. Why, don't you know that trout, — the trout that weighed two pounds ? "

"And the lesson that father gave us, about gormandizing ! All the time eating it himself! Ah, his example was clearer than his precepts, was n't it ? "

"Oh, his precepts ! They were more difficult than algebra. Lucky for us, Angelica was there to explain them to us."

"Then, those other lectures, my dear fellow ! About all I recall of those days is the inscription which I one day discovered in the waste-heap: 'Sister Clara is very eager to leave the convent because . . .' How that did appeal to our imagination ! "

"However," sighed Simeon, "we have never known anything better than those delightful old days."

While they chatted in this way, the village

drew near, — the old, bare village with its weather-beaten brick walls rooted deeply in the earth, and with its gloomy tower from whose belfry the flight of the hours was announced in solemn tones. The tower was scarred by Catholic bullets, and seemed to stand as a defiant memorial of battles and sieges, awaiting always the coming of some enemy, ready to resist, and protect its sanctity. The two men, who had not set eyes upon it for many years, saluted it with deep feeling, and were barely able to speak. Then, as they looked out of the window, they perceived upon the platform their father awaiting them. There he stood, straight and robust, under the weight of his seventy-five years, really grand, with his long white patriarchal beard, and with a stern beauty of countenance which recalled some of Da Vinci's meditative old men. Standing at his left was Angelica, in the attentive attitude now habitual with her, a genial smile irradiating her gentle but worn face. At his right, Marcel could be seen, the living image of his father, a bit reduced in size, with beard a trifle less profuse, and of a bright blond tint, the color seeming to be burnt in by the heat of the tropics. Paul, the evangelist, whose presence there surprised the new-comers, kept a position a few paces distant from the little group, as if with deliberate intention. He seemed to belong to a different order of beings, with his spare form, thin cheeks, angular features, close-shaven square chin, and nose like the beak of some night-bird.

They greeted one another, and all embraced, with the exception of Paul, whose thin lips hardly separated enough to utter a welcome; then they exchanged a thousand broken phrases and confused ejaculations. Passers-by saluted them; they recognized countenances of the olden time. And as they walked out of the railway station, Simeon exclaimed, as if he had been a school-boy coming home for a holiday, " Ah, how good it is to be back again! How delightful to return home once more!"

CHAPTER II

THE Naudié family were quite as much at home in Montauban as were the Defos family in La Rochelle. As early as the dawn of the Reformation their name was to be seen in the town records. A Naudié was among those first converts to the new faith who, after concealing their heretical beliefs for a long time, dared to make them manifest at the burial of one of their number, on the 13th of January, 1560, under the very eyes of the consuls, who, although a little timid, were very favorably disposed. From this date onward, the name of Naudié figured, like a red line worked into the fabric of all the stirring events which characterized the turbulent town during two centuries, — threatening resolutions, rebellions, temporary discouragements, heroism, intrigues, exaltation. One of the three ministers who dared counsel resistance, when Montluc appeared, and the military leaders urged capitulation, was named Jacques Naudié. During the siege which followed, another Naudié received an important order, as may be seen by referring to the forty-ninth folio of the *Rhymed*

Pastor Naudié's Young Wife

Records of Montauban's Misfortune; where, we are told, of three banners which were raised for the more efficient leadership of the people, one was put in charge of a certain " Naudié."

A Naudié (perhaps the same man) was consul in 1593, when it became necessary to take action upon the murder of the noble captains who were imprisoned by the citizens, to indemnify their widows, and to make full reparation. Another member of the family took part in the siege of 1621, and afterward married Martha Carnus, a heroine of twenty-two years, who, under the eye of Louis XIII., spiked one of the cannon of the constable of Luynes.   After the town capitulated, and the Protestant party was finally defeated, the Naudiés shared the lot of their fellow-believers, constant and faithful, tossed about in alternations of hope and despair. Their family registry records an incident very characteristic of these sad years.   In 1775 Jean Naudié had four dragoons quartered at his house.   He soon found himself unable to satisfy their demands ; and he went to ask of the king's agent that he be excused from this duty.

"On one condition," replied this officer : " you must promise that you will live and die in the Catholic faith."

Pastor Naudié's Young Wife

" I cannot do that," said Jean Naudié.

" Why not, inasmuch as the king commands it ? "

" If the sultan were to quarter in my house twenty janissaries, would I then be compelled to turn Turk ? "

In the middle of the eighteenth century a Naudié was one of those " pastors of the desert," as they were called ; oppressed persons who wandered about with no secure retreat, holding services in caves and forests, hunted by the so-called " Faithful," as if they had been wild beasts. At about the same time a branch of the family — the only one that became firmly established — repudiated its former policy of antagonism, made a fortune in some dye-works, and yielded to the temptation of worldly ease. One of these people expresses regret, in his will, that he fell back into this disgraceful reconciliation with the others, and that he embraced or pretended to embrace the Catholic faith. Three generations later, the decline of business in Montauban checked their prosperity so completely that Abraham Naudié, reared in luxury, found himself unable to live except upon his modest salary as professor of theology, and by some slender rentals, and his house of Villebourbon.

Pastor Naudié's Young Wife

This house was an old structure, facing the quai; and was built, for the larger part, over the cellars and vaults where, in old times, the fugitive dyers worked. The huge apartments of this ancient mansion were fitted up with furniture which was very old-fashioned but extremely beautiful. Here the theologian dwelt, and never gave a thought to his careful, painstaking wife, whose entire life (her children were now grown up and gone out into the world) was devoted to sparing him all sensations; his daughter Angelica also wore out her life in the same effort. As for his sons, their hold on life was very slender, and they were in a fair way to perish before they were able to explain to him their perplexities. He was thus left free to develop himself, like one of those mighty oaks which sometimes stand in a clearing, surrounded at some distance by saplings. And, for a third of a century, he was justly looked upon as one of the grandest types of Protestantism in his generation.

This man was at home upon the dim frontiers of thought, and he often illumined them by his own brilliant ideas. He was a strong writer, tending to fine-spun logical processes, put forth in a rather obscure style, and he often expressed his thought in images and symbols.

Pastor Naudié's Young Wife

There could be no question but that he had exercised a great influence over his contemporaries; and, among his many volumes on exegesis, ecclesiastical history, and morals, some had really made their mark in the world. In a word, Abraham Naudié was a theologian of a unique kind; mystical, zealous, bold, independent, he never began upon any subject without shaking it thoroughly in the sieve of his critical reason; and often reason seemed about to triumph, but, at the appeal of religion, suddenly betook itself to flight. Thus the unexpected inconsistencies in his logic were indications of the spiritual duel which went on between his loyalty to the faith and his free spirit of inquiry; and these inconsistencies often disconcerted even his most devoted admirers. After he published his " History of the Apostle Peter," he was thought to lean toward Rome; and there was considerable solicitude felt in the higher circles of the Reformed Church; but, later, in a " Study of the Christian Humanists," he stood forth as the zealous defender of the Reformation, in history; and this attitude was again taken by him, in his ringing " Reply to Jean Janssen." Between these two publications he issued " Dialogues upon Actual Questions;" and this work made some people fear lest he should fall into free thought; but, on the other hand, he had expressly opposed free thought, in his " Essay on Faith."   During all these years, this apparent instability on his part served to bring upon him many reproaches ; but, at the end of his career, when his system appeared in its entirety, there was clearly present in it a firm, consistent unity of thought.   Despite its temporary contradictions and turnings and unexpected teachings, its audacities and its timidities, it really formed one completed circle, and a very large circle, within which rested much careful, fruitful meditation ; and this system moved straight on toward truth, without halting at any obstacles, yet commenting wisely on the transitory appearances of things.   Among all his readers there were a few of his more penetrating pupils who saw that if the implications of his thought were carried out logically, he adhered to Protestantism more by tradition than by conviction.   The ties of a revered past held him to the beliefs of his ancestors, despite the leaps of his imagination and the bold advances of his logic.

The vexations, the controversies, and the enmities which this man had sustained during his long career were forgotten in the joyous festival which now had come to him.   Sur-

Pastor Naudié's Young Wife

rounded by his colleagues, his pupils, by delegates of Protestant Faculties, by theologians and philosophers, Abraham Naudié was almost overwhelmed by the showers of addresses, telegrams, resolutions presented in leather cases, and diplomas on vellum, naming him, *honoris causa*, for professorships in a dozen universities of two worlds. At times he seemed to totter under the weight of so many eulogies; his feelings made his lips tremble or his eyes moisten. Then he quickly recovered himself, and, standing firmly erect, grasped his long beard, as was his wont, and smiled with an air of irony. And this smile was, doubtless, his revenge for the bitter memories of attacks and abuse heaped upon him in former years, because of his earnest search for truth.

A long day of receptions could not exhaust either his freshness or his brilliancy. In the evening a banquet was given in his honor; and when he rose to respond to the many complimentary speeches, he stood firmly, confidently, and spoke with a brilliancy of improvisation which the university never before had witnessed. With that mingling of reserve and good-fellowship, of genius and simplicity, which always characterized him, Abraham Naudié reviewed the events of the century as he had witnessed them and taken part in them, a period of time in which his own life had been an episode, and to which his thought had been a valued contribution. Meanwhile his admirers, his friends, his sons, were grouped about him, and they felt at times as if they were lifted to the summit of a mountain, breathing the rarefied air of a great height, and looking down upon the manœuvres of a vast army scattered over the plain below.

"My earliest recollections," he said, "date from the famine of 1817. I committed at that time my first piece of foolishness. I split with a knife a sieve which was used in our house for sifting or bolting wheat. That was the time when Louis XVIII. made his mistake about the desires of his people and about his rôle of constitutional monarch. And from that time on I have moved from folly to folly, keeping pace with the century, which moved from error to error."

They were all marshalled in order, all the errors, with the illusions, hopes, expectations which led up to them, the enthusiasms which upheld them, and the deceptions and regrets which inevitably followed. The doctrinaires of the Restoration, the Utopians of 1848, the republicans of the second empire, the socialists of the third republic, as also those of imperial Ge: any, — all these could be seen, called up by certain words which gave them life; the dreamers, the rationalists, the philosophers, the charlatans, men of theories and men of action, poets, savants, and adventurers, — all this train of chimera-hunters, these gamblers in futures, these venders of empty hopes. And always close by them, as they passed in review, seemed to pass also one who studied them and judged them, — the grand old man, who resembled, as he stood there, the traditional figure of Time; and picturesquely did he unite his recital of simple daily deeds with narration of more sonorous exploits, which he deftly labelled "vanities," and passed quickly over.

"I recollect," continued he, "an ascent which I made of the Alps, in July, 1830, with a friend, who became later a pharmacist in Montpellier. Standing on a lofty peak, we saw the sun rise, and we likened ourselves to Charles X.; and the vapors which strove against it seemed to represent the masses of the people rising to attack the monarchy."

At last, after he had thus run through the enormous book, whose final pages his finger could not turn, the old professor gathered up all his observations and reflections, to direct them, with the gaze of a prophet, toward the mystery of the future.

" This much I have said, friends; I have observed many events, plain, unpretentious man as I am. Now, although my sight has become dim with age, I still love to look around me. And what do I see? Alas! a most chaotic state of affairs. Among the upper classes an enormous industrial and commercial development, with wealth accumulated to a point of undervaluing it; while, among the lower classes, misery pesters and threatens nations who prepare for war (while they swear that they wish for peace); and peoples hungry for order and union. I observe learned men who make many discoveries — discoveries which are merely the application of the commonest principles — and these discoveries and inventions pretend to make life easier, but really complicate it, without meeting one of the deeper needs of the soul. What will be the outcome of it all? I cannot say. You will see it, you young men who are to move forward into the future. As for me, whom you have so honored here to-day, my life is bound up in the past; and I know not exactly why, but I long to arm and equip you for the strife which is before you. But there! I find, at the bottom of all my experience, as an old man, this plain counsel, — Be men of high ideals! for they are the men whom God loves, they are the men whom he leads toward the best things. And it is to all such that I drink this glass of good wine which you have placed in my hand."

Thus spake old Abraham Naudié. From him, on all sides, his sons radiated, like shafts of light kindled by his brilliancy. Paul alone, thin, shrivelled, seemed to show restlessness and dissatisfaction. Evangelist that he was, this picture of the century was altogether too coldly philosophical, neglected too much the factor of divine intervention, and was wholly lacking in tirades against Rome. Among the listeners there were doubtless many, who, if they had reflected, would have agreed with him. But, intoxicated by the address, by its suggestiveness, and by their respect for the speaker, they did not reflect; and, forgetting their contentions and their sects and parties, they applauded to the echo the wise old man whose range of view transcended their horizon.

The next day the last remaining delegates went away during the forenoon, and the patriarch with his four sons came together for a quiet family dinner before they separated. All of them resembled their father, and seemed like more or less perfect copies of a model too lofty to be quite equalled, however closely it might be approached. The paternal imagination was reproduced in Marcel, the missionary; though a little brutalized, as if it lacked in him the regulative power of reflection. William had his father's irony, but with less delicacy, and his spontaneity, though not in so abundant a measure. If you studied Paul, you sooner or later saw, in the length of his profile, despite its dryness and sharpness, a certain family resemblance. As for Simeon, who was almost as large as his father, though more slender, and with black beard a little thinner and shorter, he was, after all, his father's living image; he had less of genius, but more sweetness. He had a dull olive complexion; his features were as regular as those of a medal, and his great dark eyes gleamed with fire. A few tufts of black hair, shot through with silver, fringed his bald head; his forehead was expansive, lofty, broad, striking, and was lined with veins which swelled and throbbed under the pressure of a great thought. He had the forehead of a poet, the forehead of a prophet; which had made people credit him, during his studies, with being the intellectual heir of his father; but it concealed, however, only mediocre faculties and average intelligence, combined with honesty and patience and courage.

After this last meal together, they took coffee in the library. Their father dozed, comfortably installed in his big armchair, and smoking his pipe of Marseilles clay with its long reed stem. Angelica distributed the cups and offered the sugar, with that quiet gentle way which always gave to her movements an air of great serenity. She paused in front of Simeon and asked, "Are you really going this afternoon, my dear brother? Can you not allow yourself one more holiday?"

"It is impossible," replied Simeon. "I have my sermon to look after. Besides, I have been three days on this journey, and you know that I never dare to remain away longer than that."

William broke in: "Oh yes! the children! See what comes of having a lot of children! There is no such thing as freedom."

"You have scarcely mentioned them to us," said Angelica. "We have had so little time for personal conversation during this entire celebration. So tell us the news!"

Pastor Naudié's Young Wife

Abraham Naudié was following the conversation without seeming to, for he half opened his eyes and asked in a sleepy voice, "What has become . . . of my . . . godson?"

"Ah, your godson," replied Simeon, who hardly desired at such a time to speak of the disgraceful doings of the boy, "your godson gives me a great deal of trouble. I don't know whether he is merely heedless or is really vicious; in either case he is a hard child to manage."

"Probably you are too easy with him," suggested Paul, always ready to blame somebody.

Marcel was more kindly disposed, and added, "Probably his sisters spoil him."

"I do as well as I can," said Simeon, "and so do his sisters. Oh, they don't resemble him in the least. They are good little girls, especially Esther, who has had considerable experience. Bertha is the only one at all troublesome . . ."

With the tender sympathy of her heart Angelica divined thoughts which her brother had not expressed; and she exclaimed, "My poor dear brother, you have indeed a great deal of care."

"There is no doubt," said Simeon, "that the position of a widower, with four little ones, brings cares; but, I assure you, God helps me greatly."

At this point Abraham Naudié asked, out of his half-asleep state, "You have never thought . . . of marrying again?"

Simeon smiled. "I marry again? At my age? With four children?"

The old man shook off the ashes from his pipe and went on: "Why not? It is precisely when one has such burdens as yours that he ought not to remain alone. At the dawn of life, it is well to pause, before entering into the married state; but when once the fire has been kindled on the hearth, a woman is needed to care for it. The older your girls grow, the more need they have of a mother."

"I have always believed," said Paul, "that for the man who has pledged himself to the service of God, the family is, or soon becomes, a hindrance. A man must not parcel himself out. With children and a wife, that takes up too large a part of a man's heart."

Abraham Naudié had never been able to urge his views with calmness. Even the most tactful opposition roused him to fury. His face became purple; he glared at Paul with a look of irritation, and thundered, in that formidable voice which he used in his lectures when confuting the sophistries of Renan or Strauss: "There is nothing better than the family, nothing more sound or sacred. God does not wish to keep anybody out of it. Every man has a right to the love of wife and to the affection of children, just as he has a right to the air or to the light. The hearthstone is blessed. It quiets the storms of the soul, as also those of the heart; it is the condition necessary for pure reflections. Do you not know Schleiermacher's charming apologue? So long as man was alone with nature, the Eternal towered far above him, and spoke to him in various ways; but man did not understand, and made no reply. Eden was beautiful, like unto a radiance of glory let down from heaven; but man had no clear perception of nature, and his own soul revealed nothing to him. However, oppressed by the solitude, he trained the animals to bear him company. Then the Eternal saw that man, in so far as he was alone, could not gain a true apprehenison of the universe; for that reason he gave to him a companion similar to himself. Immediately joy throbbed in the breast of Adam, his eyes were opened, and he really saw the world. In the flesh of his flesh and bone of his bone he discovered humanity, and he discovered the universe; he now became capable of understanding the voice of the

Eternal, and of replying to him; and even his extremest violation of the sacred commandments was not sufficient to sever the tie which united him to the Eternal. Such is our history; the history of us all. Nothing exists for the man who is alone, and he can see nothing in its true meaning; because, if he would comprehend the Eternal, if he would understand religion, he must first find humanity; and this he can find only in love and by love."

Paul sat listening and gnawing his lips; his manner indicated that he utterly disagreed; he refrained, however, from replying.

"I look upon this matter as our father does," said Marcel, who always took hold of ideas on their practical side. "A solitary man is an incomplete being. Whatever his functions may be, it is necessary that he have a companion, a woman, if he is to attain his full stature and reach his limit of effort."

"But," interposed William, "where will you find a woman capable of assuming . . . ?"

Angelica did not suffer him to finish his remark. "My dear brother," she exclaimed with warmth, "you know nothing about women."

Then she continued: "Or, at least, you have no idea of the rich stores of devotion which the best of them hold in reserve. And be assured of this, that the very difficulty of undertaking grave household cares would be, to many women, a prospect more alluring than any prospects of personal selfish happiness. What could any woman imagine that would be nobler than to act as mother to orphan children ? "

" I am convinced," said Simeon, " that there are such women, but I have never met one."

William maliciously went a step beyond. " Simeon never will find this pearl, my good Angelica," said he. " Why, then, do you urge him to look for her? "

Angelica replied, with tender gravity and with an air of conviction, " God sends his angels whithersoever it pleases him."

" So, then," William went on, " a good wife will be a gift from God? "

" Most assuredly ! " replied Angelica. " Everything that comes to us is a gift from God."

William gave way to his mischievous inclinations, and said : " How about the bad wives? There are such creatures to be found, you must admit. Where do they come from ? "

They had reason to suppose that their father was fast asleep, for he had stopped smoking, and his eyes were closed ; but at this point in the conversation he opened his eyes, and murmured, as if in a dream: "Problem! Problem! We know nothing . . . and yet we must believe."

This brief speech ended the discussion. Abraham Naudié made good use of the momentary silence which followed, by going to sleep again; his calm features, his abundant head of hair, like a crown, and his long white beard sweeping down over his breast, — these suggested the emperor in the legend, who waits through the centuries for the solemn hour of his awakening.

Angelica approached her father softly, to pick up the pipe which had dropped from his lips; and Marcel murmured, "Poor father!"

One tender, anxious thought was in all their minds, but nobody else expressed it.

Little by little, however, they roused themselves, and began to talk together in a low voice. Marcel, when asked his opinion about the new countries whither he had carried the gospel, went on in such a way that you would have taken him for a political economist rather than a missionary. He was more interested in the destiny of our civilized races than concerned for the salvation of savage tribes. And it was easy to see that his thought was simply this, — to conquer the dark continent for the good of European races; to give them more room, and establish their sway for all time.

"God is in it," he exclaimed, with suppressed exaltation of soul. "That is the place to call forth courage and energy. The outcasts of our land have only to follow us; there they shall find what is here denied them, — bread which they have vainly sought, freedom which they love, and gold for which they have longed."

Paul did not like this zeal, which seemed to him materialistic and almost blasphemous. He remarked that, according to this view of Marcel's, the Christian races ought not to dream of carrying light to their ignorant fellow-creatures, but rather of seizing their lands and their wealth.

Simeon must have been reflecting that life in those warm countries is probably easier for everybody; he said in a low voice, as if speaking to himself, and desiring to express only a part of his thought, "It must be a good place for those who emigrate young."

And Marcel carried out his idea: "Or for those who have suffered, or those who are eager for an active life, or those who are glad to forget the past."

CHAPTER III

SIMEON NAUDIÉ returned at night to La Rochelle, and could get only a short sleep. The noises in the house disturbed him. He was aware that only a brief period of time remained, in which he must look over the notes of his sermon; and he hastened downstairs to ask his daughters for his usual morning cup of tea. Esther, his eldest, was the only one up. She wore a blue wrapper, simple and tasteful; and she was almost pretty, with her frank eyes which rarely smiled, her rather large mouth, pure and serious, and her luxuriant chestnut hair with its golden gleams, hanging in a large braid down her back. Large for her years, as she was, she stood up bravely under the double burden of her rapid growth and her hand-to-hand struggle with the trials of the household. This continuous strain, shutting her out from all relaxation, gave her an air of severity and almost sulkiness; and it encased her in an armor of reserve and even coldness, which quite concealed her really alert nature and passionate temperament. Her sisters, her brother, and even her father never read the secrets of her silent heart. To them she was simply somebody to be consulted, somebody to be given control of affairs, somebody to whom one could run in time of danger; a person whose devotion was accepted by them unconsciously, because the habit of accepting it had become firmly rooted.

As she attended to her father's wants, Esther informed herself regarding the journey and the celebrations. He, in his turn, asked what had transpired during his absence. Nothing, except a violent quarrel between Abraham and Bertha. When Simeon asked his daughter the cause of this quarrel, she only shrugged her shoulders and said, "Oh, nothing!"

At that moment Bertha entered. She came in like a whirlwind. She was thirteen years old; but even at that age she showed a passionate, tempestuous nature. There were gleams of fire in her great black eyes; her very hair seemed to vibrate with energy as it tossed upon her delicate shoulders, and the clear-cut lines of her features were as restless as ripples on the sea. Sometimes she was indolent and sometimes active; at times she was fitful, wilful, sulky, and would bury herself through entire days in savage taciturnity; then suddenly she would overflow with spirits, and show strong affection. She was like a little Fate, holding momentous mysteries. Standing in the doorway, the full memory of the scene the evening before came over her, as she had dwelt upon it and amplified it; and she exclaimed, holding out her hands with a theatrical gesture, "Papa, papa, just think what . . ."

Monsieur Naudié hastened to break in upon her, with that quiet, firm manner which alone he opposed to the violent outbursts of his daughter. "No, Bertha, you know I do not take sides in your wrangles. You are always both wrong."

He went out, and Bertha's gaze followed him, with a tragic expression in it; then she seated herself before her cup of tea and buried her head in her hands in an attitude of despair. Esther looked on; all this fury was incomprehensible to her rational nature, and she was scornful of it.

Before he went into his study, Monsieur Naudié entered again his children's rooms, in order to embrace little Zelia, whom the nurse was dressing. The little fresh rosy child, with her blond head and her vivacious ways, brought light into the household; indeed, she was the only one who really lived a child's life. All in the house conspired to purvey joy for her, freedom from care, and many of those little indulgences of which their own lives had felt the lack. In return, she scattered gayety around her with her prattle; affection welled up from her tender heart, as did the fresh kisses to her lips. These were the ornaments of childhood, which can arise only from a sweet, pure nature. Between her father and herself there was an especial sympathy, which was almost strange. When he held her on his lap, he seemed to become young again; she seemed to understand him and to be able to console him. She kissed her hands to him, as he entered; he took her up in his arms, and made ready to listen to her narration of all the mighty events in her little life; but, at that moment, a noise in an adjoining room attracted his attention. Almost at the same instant he heard footsteps on the staircase. He at once suspected that Abraham was in full flight; and he tried to call to him from the upper landing, "Abraham! Abraham! Where are you going?"

The sound of a hastily closed door was all the reply he got. He threw open a window. The fugitive had disappeared under a row of arches; there was no possibility of calling him back.

Pastor Naudié's Young Wife

Monsieur Naudié was much troubled by this incident; it reawakened in him all the anxieties which his wilful boy had caused him. He could not, although pressed for time, quite settle down to his work; and, with a troubled and heavy spirit, he walked up and down the floor of his study. This was a room with an alcove, and was furnished with a desk, a round table, and a few chairs, including one or two straw armchairs, covered with Indian saddle-cloth. Three or four hundred volumes, chiefly bound in cloth, rested on some white wooden shelves. A few dark-toned lithographs, after Ary Scheffer and Paul Delaroche, adorned the walls; while upon the mantel, between two vases of very ordinary make, mused an exquisite Penseroso in bronze, a present from a group of grateful pupils. The two windows of the room — two fine old mullioned windows, obscured by white curtains — opened upon the Rue de Merciers; the houses of this quaint old street seemed, each, to have an individuality of its own, and, in their widely varying styles, served very well to indicate the varying stages of the town's history. There, first of all, at the head of the street, stood the modest dwelling of Jean Guiton, having no other ornament than a plate upon which was inscribed the fatal date of the last mayor. Three or four houses with more imposing façades came next; these bore several tasteful ideas sketched over the doorways; then some grotesque figures were scattered, haphazard, among the window-spaces of the first floors, and other figures and foliage were added in abundance, quite up to the large gargoyles near the roofs. In such buildings as these, where they have been rebuilt or too zealously restored, the purer classical taste triumphs, with its acanthus motives, even to its corbellings of four or five constructions in slate. These are the very ancient structures, upon which have fallen all the missiles of many sieges, which date back of the religious wars and even back of the rise of the Reformation. Rigid, heavy, massive, with here and there in front a round window, like the eye of a Cyclops, they have the appearance of poor old men, infirm, worn, yet obstinately refusing to give up; and one finds himself sometimes standing before them with a certain respect, such as he might feel for old workmen worn out by toil, for old peasants broken by hard work. Monsieur Naudié was proud of this outlook upon the street, so suggestive of the valiant little town's vigorous yet often desolate past, an expression of the architecture and the spirit of olden days. Many a time he forgot himself, as he stood and gazed at it, and lived in fancy through those heroic days when newly ennobled governors went forth from the city-hall; then, a few steps beyond, where the thirty-seven pastors, influential and venerated, shared with them the honor of steering, upon its quartz sea, the golden vessel which bore the noble device *Servator rectore Deo.*

On this day, however, these memorials of struggle and glory stirred not at all the pastor's emotions. His glance wandered aimlessly up and down the street, or fell unheedingly among the corridors and arches. He was thinking about that boy of his, to whom he was able to give so little attention, when only the strictest surveillance could suffice to correct his wilful nature; indeed, the counsel of his father and sister seemed to go in at one ear and out at the other.

A distant clock struck eight; the sound recalled Monsieur Naudié to the exigencies of the present, and he seated himself at his desk where the notes of his sermon awaited him. Before he had set out on his journey, he had selected — as he sometimes did, in case of need — from his old sermons; and this material he now began to look over.

Pastor Naudié's Young Wife

The sermon selected dated from the days of his seminary course, and was composed, according to good homiletical rules, upon the sixth chapter of St. Matthew. "No man can serve two masters; for either he will hate the one and love the other, or else he will hold to the one and despise the other: ye cannot serve God and mammon." The skeleton of this discourse, written out on the first page, was extremely simple, and capable of being worked out very easily.

Exordium. — Our life belongs to two different masters, whose service is incompatible the one with the other; between these two we are free to choose, and we are obliged to choose. Who are these two masters? God and mammon (that is, the world).

I. That which we call "the service of the world," its insatiable demands, its hollowness, the pain it causes us, the hopelessness to which it brings us.

II. That which we call the "service of God," its blessedness, its comfort and peace, its promises.

Peroration. — Why hesitate? God is the one who must be loved, if the seductive snares of the world are to be avoided. Rewards of those who make this choice, both in this life and in the life beyond.

Pastor Naudié's Young Wife

These developments of the theme were enriched with Biblical citations and by a few excellent figures of rhetoric. When he read over this discourse, in the hurry of his departure on the journey, Monsieur Naudié did not notice its weak points; now they struck him suddenly and forcibly. He compared its abstract mode of thought, its absolute affirmations, and its simple conclusions, with his experience of life and the incidents which had come to him personally. And, looked at in this way, the discourse seemed to him unsound; it seemed to him built upon false foundations; and he regretted selecting it. "Alas!" exclaimed he, as he turned the yellow pages, covered with his youthful handwriting, "the reality of things gives, each day, cruel contradictions to these fallacious theories. Jesus, who drove the traders from the temple, was single-minded in his lofty service of God; but with the rest of us, practically, the service of God and mammon is intermingled. The higher things succumb. Even those men whose lives are consecrated to the service of God allow their high resolves to be vitiated by unworthy aims and interests. Indeed, my own life is invaded and weakened by just such things, for I am even now conceding to these same temporal interests a portion of my life, when I am on the point of going to preach in God's house. Dare I affirm that my father, high-minded as he is, has been wholly and absolutely free from every possible worldly consideration and earthly ambition? Paul certainly showed a considerable element of pride mixed with his apostolic zeal; and Marcel, who started out under a grand burst of devotion, seems to be quite as solicitous for the advances of secular civilized life as for those of his religious faith. Everywhere around me I see men, even the most upright of them, living in tacit compromise between laws of life which Christ pronounced antagonistic, incompatible. For me to preach to them about ceasing this compromise with sin, as I have written it here in my childish sermon, why, it is a waste of time, a throwing away of the brief hour which they set apart for listening to me. The only appeal that can reach them is some truth more prosaic, closer to them, more practical, less abstract. Alas! as I try to teach them what they ought to be, I must not forget what they are."

These reflections led Monsieur Naudié to make sundry corrections in the material of his sermon; and he was busily engaged in these alterations when Esther opened the door slightly, in order to say, "Come, father! It is time to go ; we are all ready."

"Very well. Go along, and I will follow," he said ; and in a few moments he was walking rapidly after them.

The congregation was thin. About a hundred faithful ones sat waiting on the benches. The huge hall was devoid of decoration, from floor to ceiling, except the garnet-colored velvet of the pulpit, and the black tablets on which were indicated the order of services for the day.

However, Monsieur Naudié's sole rival for the attention of his auditors was the bright spring-time sun ; the "Dissenters" had not yet taken root in La Rochelle ; this church was the only home of the old-time respectability of the town, the sole asylum of that ancient faith which made heroic magistrates, which kindled a spirit of devotion in navigators and traders, and armed for defence even the women themselves. Moreover, these faithful attendants on public worship were not all of as fervent a spirit as could be desired ; there were rich merchants, hard-working, economical ; absorbed in their business affairs, watchful of any wasteful expenditure ; many of them responded to the summons of the church bells with lukewarm convictions, led by the feeling that it is the proper thing to appear cultivated and to come into harmony with a probably existent God, and to sing in the fine choir which is placed near the organ. Some of these people have descended in a direct line from the honored conquerors of Richelieu; these form a kind of sacred band, holding their convictions strongly, always suspicious of some persecution, and cherishing, deep in their hearts, underneath the lethargy of indifference, hatred of Rome and the Pope and the Jesuits. Here and there, throughout the congregation, you might note a few humble peasant women, their dark skins showing plainly against the whiteness of their laces, heaped up into mountainous head-dresses. Occasionally a sailor might be seen, in his pea-jacket; and perhaps some old man, following attentively the reading of the Word, as he turned over the worn leaves of an old Bible with his great rough fingers.

During the singing of the first hymn, Monsieur Naudié ran his eyes over the congregation. At first he looked for his three daughters,—Esther attentive, Bertha patient, and Zelia alert and watchful, much like a bird in a cage. Then he noticed several other persons. There was Monsieur Lanthelme, professor of philosophy at the academy; a little old round-shouldered man, his face sparkling with maliciousness; perhaps at that very moment preparing one of those acrid speeches with which, on every possible occasion, he lashed both enemies and friends. There, also, was Monsieur Merlin, the attorney; an exceedingly shrewd person, who piqued himself on his literary tastes, read the most modern fashionable poetry, and wrote several treatises against immoral literature, at the same time collecting with pious zeal some very remarkable specimens of this kind. There, too, was the Dehodecq family, which stood, with the Defos family, first in the community; it filled completely one of the long benches, even though not all its members were present. At the moment when the pastor's eyes rested on this group, at the instant when he was reflecting upon their quiet, earnest demeanor, and upon their Christian conduct, vigorous but unobtrusive, his attention was distracted by the late arrival of the Defos family.

Monsieur Defos made himself, everywhere, very much at home. From the very way in which he entered and looked about him, and from the way in which he advanced to his

Pastor Naudié's Young Wife

seat, an acute observer might see that when he came into the house of the Lord, he came in as an allied monarch, who did it for the sake of courtesy. His wife was no less majestic. She was quite as corpulent as he, but with coarser features; and she tossed back her head, allowing her double chin to roll about on a lace collar. Her small piercing eyes passed swiftly over the assembly, in a sharp glance of inspection, and her umbrella resounded upon the floor with all the authority of a beadle who precedes a procession. Behind her walked their pretty niece, Jane; small, dainty, graceful, with a humming-bird perched upon her hat, she seemed like a vireo or warbler skipping along behind two geese. Their two sons brought up the rear. David, the elder, was already heavy and coarse, although he had barely passed his thirtieth year. Henry was very different; he was smaller, more slender, with a timid gait, and an air at once restless and self-absorbed; his pale face, with its mobile features, was surrounded with a beard so refractory and unkempt that it seemed to be wholly neglected.

Monsieur Naudié could not look upon these people without applying to them at once his recent reflections. Did not Monsieur Defos exemplify, by every act, the ease with which one may harmonize the service of the two masters? Accustomed as he was to be seen of men, held by the faithful as an exemplary Christian, he looked upon his salvation as a matter of business, and upon his business as his salvation. Monsieur Naudié said to himself, while the last stanza of the hymn was being sung, that if one wished to speak convincingly to such people, if he wished to draw them for a moment from their earthly thoughts, and encourage within them the divine spark, he would need the eloquence of an apostle or a reformer. And the good pastor felt, on the instant, coming over him, a breath of the holy indignation of Jesus against self-satisfied souls, and was stirred to exclaim at once against such pharisaic hearts. His conscience roused itself at the thought of their compromises, though a few moments before he had accepted it all as unavoidable; and, in the twinking of an eye, he saw and accepted the high idealism of his youthful sermon. He preached it almost word for word as he had written it in the former time, expressing all its faith and consecration and high purpose. His manner, which ordinarily was slow and dull, grew animated; the fervor of his tones gave life to his figures of speech;

he made vigorous gestures; his earnestness was almost fascinating.

Accordingly, the faithful, passing out of church, spoke to one another about the "excellent discourse." Even Monsieur Lanthelme, whose commendations usually carried a hidden sting, said to Monsieur Dehodecq, as he met him at the entrance, "Anybody can see that our pastor has been at Montauban; his father has lent him a few bright ideas."

As for Monsieur Defos, he had not the slightest notion that the sermon applied to him. His family walked out in front of him, and he stood for a moment listening to Monsieur Merlin, who informed him (lowering his voice) that he had just received from Brusselles a most shocking romance. He was not, however, at all interested in such nonsense, and brusquely left the attorney at the moment when Monsieur Naudié came out. He at once joined him, and felicitated him on the merit of his sermon.

"You have given us an excellent discourse, pastor," said he; "it is, unhappily, only too true, in the case of many persons. I am glad to see that your journey did not fatigue you. The *Signal* referred to the celebration. You must have experienced many pleasant emotions. You will give us an account of them day after to-morrow, for we may count on seeing you then, may we not?   At half-past six."

As Monsieur Naudié re-entered his house, he said to himself: "Ah, it is utterly useless to speak the exact truth.   To-day, as in the days of the Master, there are those who have ears, but hear not."

But scarcely had he entered his doorway, before he found himself dominated by the cares of the world, like those whom he had rebuked for their religious lukewarmness, and that too without being aware of it.   His son Abraham entered, with garments torn, having been wrangling with some cabin-boys on the wharves.   Esther at once showed much so-licitude, turning him round and round in front of her, and trying to make the edges of the torn and tattered garments meet.   At the same time she gave her father a glance such as a doctor might have given when asked to revive a dead man.

"There will be no way of mending them, papa.   It will be necessary to purchase new ones.   And they were his Sunday clothes, too."

She expressed in her tones all the anguish of a young housekeeper who has reached the end of her resources.   From force of habit Mon-sieur Naudié comforted her, and reminded her that things always were straightened out, with the help of God, in due time.   But presently, when he reflected that the trip to Montauban had emptied his pocket-book, he felt greatly vexed.   "So much the worse for him," he said. "Let him wait!"

And, raising his voice, he began to scold Abraham.

Like the sermon to the faithful, all reprimands fell harmless upon this terrible youngster, who took the reproofs with great calmness, at the same time turning and twisting between his fingers the shreds hanging from his torn jacket.   However, as the dinner was waiting, they all seated themselves at the table; in an irritated tone Monsieur Naudié said, crossing his hands before him on his plate, " The blessing, Zelia ! "

The child lisped in a soft little voice, " We thank thee, Lord, for the blessings which thou hast given us. Amen ! " And the repast began, in a constrained way.

CHAPTER IV

MONSIEUR NAUDIÉ, when he accepted Monsieur Defos's invitation, had no idea that he had been for some time the subject of unceasing anxieties and continuous debate in the councillor-general's family. So it was with his usual serenity of manner that he presented himself at the house. Esther had picked out a shirt for him whose wristbands were not too much worn, made a few needed repairs on his frock coat, and tied with her deft fingers his fine white cravat. After which, stepping back a foot or two, to judge the better, she said, with one of her rare smiles, " There ! I say that you are very handsome."

In point of fact Monsieur Naudié seemed almost a young man; his noble forehead, his fine black eyes, and his full silky beard almost justified his daughter's frank admiration.

" Child ! " said he, with a little shrug of his shoulders.

All the family assisted at his departure, as if he had been starting for a long journey. Bertha, who was a bit of a gourmand, said,

Pastor Naudié's Young Wife

"You will have some good things to eat, papa."

"But we," said Esther, facetiously, "will eat potatoes with white sauce."

Abraham made a wry face.

"I confess, children," said Monsieur Naudié, "that I would prefer to stay with you."

He looked at Zelia, whom to-day he would not be able to take upon his knees at dessert, and she piped up in the voice of a spoiled child, "Papa, you ought to stay with us; you ought, you ought."

He lifted her up to embrace her. "Up! Up! There! What a nice little girl!"

Then, as the time was passing, he sallied forth, and in a few minutes was in front of the old Defos mansion, which stood in the broad, dignified Rue Reaumur; a street which was occupied, in the days of great colonial activity, by rich and rather ostentatious merchants.

A liveried attendant ushered him into a spacious parlor, wainscoted in the fashion of Louis XV., filled with beautiful furniture of antique pattern, and adorned with various kinds of costly bric-à-brac. A number of pictures hung on the walls, among them several which the master of the house loved to point out with a satirical air, as belonging to "The

Pastor Naudié's Young Wife

School of La Rochelle." Two Algerian landscapes by Fromentin, and a St. John by Bouguereau, he held in high estimation. Monsieur Naudié felt a little distrust, as he noticed the coldness and even hostility with which Madame Defos rose to receive him, in all her glacial majesty. Then the condescending good-nature of her husband offset this a little, yet without putting him entirely at his ease. The two sons, who were seated back to back at the hearth, saluted him; but David's greeting was without any warmth, and Henry's was quiet and reserved. Jane, who entered a moment later, came and gave him her hand with a frank and gracious air, raising to his face her beautiful eyes, which seemed to hold some hidden mystery.

In the midst of all this cumbrous luxury, among these rich, heavy, impassive tradespeople, the young girl in her tasteful tailormade gown, with collar and necktie like a man's, with her slender, graceful figure and attractive ways, seemed like a beautiful misplaced statuette on a shelf with a lot of coarse kitchen pottery. She was of another race, of quite another species. She was small, dainty, refined; there was a tint of peach-blossoms on her cheeks; her features were delicate, as if drawn by an artist; they showed a fascinating irregularity, and were so mobile that they varied her expression unceasingly; her hair was dark and was caught up in loops, and beneath the symmetrical arch of her brows were her great oval eyes, Oriental eyes, where one saw at times fleeting suggestions of an unknown world.

After Jane entered there was a moment or two of constrained silence. A few listless remarks were dropped, at long intervals, until the time came for seating themselves at the table. This constraint continued until the dinner was fairly begun. At length Jane mentioned the festivities at Montauban, and Monsieur Naudié conquered his shyness enough to give a detailed account of them. A gleam of the paternal glory still lingered upon his forehead. He spoke with animation; he repeated his father's address; he narrated incidents of which the old sage had been the central figure; and all this without divining the diverse feelings of his listeners. Jane hung upon his every word, compelling her pretty mobile face into an expression of severe gravity. Madame Defos's thin lips grew even thinner, and the rigid curve of her mouth expressed her displeasure at hearing Monsieur Naudié speak so freely and boldly, without showing any awe at the grandeur of his surroundings, — either at the magnificence of the massive candelabra, or the majesty of the mistress of the house. David and his father listened with mingled respect and distrust; the goodness of Abraham Naudié seemed to them a trifle contemptible. Besides, if they showed any particular admiration for men of reflection and meditation, it was solely for what they might get out of them in the form of practical activity; and the hasty glance which they gave to the inner life of the old philosopher made very clear to them that metaphysics was a useless article. Henry, on the contrary, brightened up, and his features grew animated. Several times he was on the point of saying something, but refrained. Finally, as Monsieur Naudié recounted the recent testimonials of admiration which had come to his father from the most distant places, he exclaimed, with an emotion which contrasted with the simple character of his words, " All that is but justice, pastor, for your father is an admirable thinker." And then he added, in an undertone, " At least in the larger part of his writings."

This unexpected reservation of course called for explanation. Monsieur Naudié supposed that the young man, in the fervor of his approaching consecration, took exceptions to some of his father's more radical progressive ideas. But Henry glanced around, with a startled air, as if he regretted having raised so complex a question; then, as all were waiting, he spoke again, trying to modify a little his thought.

" Of course his work is so abundant that a person can choose from it what he likes; for my own part I admire most in him the boldness of his logic, the honesty of his reasoning. He is one of those who follow out their thought to its utmost conclusions, without having any regard for consequences. That is true of all his books, but especially of his ' Dialogues on Real Problems.' "

Henry's voice trembled, for he was afraid of his own boldness. Then Monsieur Naudié, surprised, said : " That book is not the one rated most highly by my father; he wrote it during one of those periods of doubt and distress which are not always spared to the most faithful. He calls it the fruit of his temptation. Many times he has described to me his anguish during this period, out of which the goodness of God at length lifted him."

Monsieur Defos was restless under the course of conversation which his second son was carrying on, and he looked at him and frowned; but the young man would not heed the admonition of this frown. For doubt rested heavily upon his heart, as it had formerly rested on the heart of Abraham Naudié. He hardly admitted to himself, as yet, that the foundations of his faith were shaken; he suffered, though, already; and he felt it as a gnawing need, this desire to speak of matters which filled his breast with mystery and with passion. This fervor of soul, throbbing and impetuous, held back in its wild impulses by a strong will, all this stormy inner life was wholly unsuspected and quite incomprehensible, so far as his immediate family was concerned.

He said: "The book bears the marks of his sufferings; that is what gives it its value. It seems to me to have a flavor like the first chapters of St. Augustine. Will you allow me, pastor, to express my ideas fully and freely?"

His voice grew stronger, warmer, and more resonant, in the midst of the unsympathetic silence around him. "I believe that it is in just such books as this one that your father has expressed his real religious faith, that which gives him his glory; I mean his faith in

Pastor Naudié's Young Wife

Truth, far higher, far more fruitful than any acceptance of established dogmas can ever be. If he afterward returned to more orthodox beliefs, he did it by submitting his thought to the domination of his will,—excellent lesson for those who boast themselves of their intellect. But, in spite of that backward step, his vision always transcends the horizon with which he seeks to surround himself, always goes beyond it, always rises high . . ."

"Henry!" interrupted Monsieur Defos.

The young man glanced at his father, whose great threatening eyes were levelled full at him, hesitated a moment, then with a sigh drew back, saying, " I mean to say, simply, that Monsieur Abraham Naudié is one of those thinkers who sacrifice nothing to conventionalities."

" I assure you," said Monsieur Naudié, " that my father is a man whose faith is very simple and very vital."

Henry made no reply; perhaps he was doubtful about the effect of his words on his own conscience; for, at this period of his life, it seemed to him obscure and full of contradictions.

The conversation changed ; it became commonplace again. A few bits of gossip crept in. The talk did not reach a higher level after they went into the parlor ; there Madame Defos, still unapproachable, served the coffee, refusing, with a curt gesture, her niece's aid. Then Monsieur Defos, with an air of familiarity, took Monsieur Naudié's arm, saying, " Come along, pastor, and smoke a cigar with me in my study ! "

" I don't smoke," said Monsieur Naudié, " but I will be glad to go with you."

The two men went out, and the others remained.

" So you do not smoke," remarked Monsieur Defos, choosing a cigar very carefully. He lighted one, pointed his guest to an armchair, installed himself in another, and continued, —

" The papers that speak of your father and his habits of life, mention that he is a confirmed smoker."

" Yes, the fact is that my father clings closely to his pipe ; he says that it clears his mind. For myself, I have no such excuse ; so I have given up the habit."

Then followed a pause. Monsieur Naudié waited. Monsieur Defos, judging that it was not worth while to prolong these preliminaries, cleared his throat and began: " This is the first time, pastor, that we have had the pleasure of receiving you into our family circle, although we have known one another . . . well, a dozen years, I think."

"It is twelve years since I came to La Rochelle."

"So wags the world; people live opposite each other, meet each other, come to know each other, and yet really see very little of each other." There was a slight hesitation in Monsieur Defos's speech, as if he were hunting for the right words. He went on.

"In order to have you here, certain circumstances were necessary, very peculiar . . . eh . . . which I . . . eh . . . wish you to be acquainted with. But . . . but, first, some explanations are needed. Do you know the history of my niece?"

"In a general way I do. I have heard it said that . . ."

Monsieur Defos interrupted him sharply. "I fancy that there has been more or less gossip about her; for people always meddle with what does not concern them. Now, these are the exact facts. My oldest brother, David,— in our family the eldest always has taken the Christian name of our illustrious ancestor,— had an adventurous spirit and an undisciplined nature; my second son, alas! somewhat re-sembles him. This brother of mine, David, being unable to get on harmoniously with my father,—who never allowed any resistance to his wishes,—left home at an early age, and went to the Indies. He rarely sent us news of himself, and never came back to this country. However, he announced to us his marriage with an Anglo-Indian, and, in the course of time, at intervals came news of the birth of several children. We may take for granted that he was prosperous, for, at this present time, the fortune which he left goes beyond the figure of two millions."

Monsieur Defos stopped a moment, to watch the effect of this information upon the other; but although he waited, his words produced no visible result. The good pastor was so simple and pure of heart, so devoid of greed and self-interest, that wealth was like a remote sun, too distant to dazzle. It was therefore out of mere courtesy that Monsieur Naudié repeated, in a tone which he compelled to express admi-ration, "Ah, two millions!"

"Yes; two millions, and even beyond that."

Then Monsieur Defos continued his story. "It is now seven years since a plague of cholera swept over that district; and it carried off, pastor, nearly all that happy flourishing family. The ways of God are inscrutable. Of them all two children survived : these were their youngest, my niece Jane, then fourteen years old ; and one of their sons, Harold, at that time nineteen. Possibly you may know that my journey to the Indies was made in order to arrange their affairs, which gave me a great deal of trouble ; but, with God's help, I was able to get them all into good shape."

Monsieur Defos here turned aside, for a few moments, to award himself the praise for his disinterestedness which the circumstances warranted ; because, without any object but that of assisting his niece and nephew, he had undertaken a long journey, set aside his own interests, and given up four months of his laborious existence. Perhaps, however, his action would have been seen to be less admirable if he pushed a little farther his examination of his conscience, for, after all, despite appearances, his self-sacrifice was really an offering to the golden calf ; certainly he would not have exerted himself so much and so readily for relatives who had been left in less fortunate circumstances. But Monsieur Defos never penetrated to the depths of the soul where such discoveries are made. It was with entire good faith that he thought of his journey to the Indies as one of those acts by which, as the Gospel expresses it, a man lays up "treasures in heaven, where neither moth nor rust doth corrupt."

So it was with utter sincerity that once more, for the duration of a quarter of a minute, he went on praising himself for this check which he had drawn on the uncertain bank of eternity.

After this, Monsieur Naudié waiting meanwhile, he continued: "My nephew Harold wished to become an artist. I did the best I could to turn him away from a career which is no career at all; but he would not listen to me. He is not my son; he possesses a fortune large enough to lift him above the usual exigencies of life. I have decided that I cannot push my opposition to his 'vocation' any farther, without going beyond my limits of duty; so I have given in. He is at present travelling. Occasionally he paints, but his pictures don't sell, and never will. They are too fine."

The scornful face of Monsieur Defos told his opinion of his nephew's work. Then he went on: "As for my niece, I thought, at first, of bringing her up with my own family; but I reflected that, having two sons, I would thus lead to malicious public opinion to credit me —

as it often has done, unjustly — with deliberate selfish calculation.   I placed her, then, in England, at an excellent school.   Each year she divides her vacations between her only maternal aunt, who lives in London, and my family. In this way we have her with us four or five weeks, and thus we are able to keep in touch with her as she grows up."

Up to this point, Monsieur Defos spoke with the freedom and ease of a man who knows just what he intends to say ; his task now grew more delicate ; he showed signs of being ill at ease, and shuffled his big feet about over the flower-pattern on the carpet.

"My dear pastor," said he, speaking now more slowly, "I will not conceal from you the fact that she has caused us some surprises and even some anxieties ; not, indeed, that we have anything of a serious nature with which to charge her, but hers is a nature — how shall I express it ? — uncertain, unstable, which will doubtless become steadier with years, when she shall have some aim, some task, and various duties ; all those things which give steadiness to life, things which thus far have been lacking in her experience.   In her first vacations her only idea was to play the roughest games, and she greatly regretted that she was not a boy.

Pastor Naudié's Young Wife

The next year we hardly recognized her as the same person; she spent all her time reading the poets; several times we missed her from the house, and found her on the border of the lake, declaiming verses, in the midst of a storm. Afterward, it was music to which she was passionately devoted,—would you believe it? she even had a notion of going upon the stage; luckily that whim passed quickly out of her head."

Here Monsieur Defos's speech became more and more hesitating. He had now reached an incident about which he had been anxious for a long time; and the recollection of it partly explained his present state of mind. During the girl's stay in London she had become infatuated with a popular singer, and, with the connivance of a sentimental governess, she had had a rendezvous in one of the churches; quite a romance it all was, but without any serious results; still, it was rather disturbing to her friends, because it showed how capricious and wilful her nature was.

Monsieur Defos was almost on the point of narrating this episode, which touched rather unpleasantly the self-respect of his family; but he suddenly changed his mind, and decided to pass it over in silence. So he added: "A short time ago my wife was saying, 'Heaven alone knows what will become of that child !' But our fears have been lightened, my dear pastor. God has not suffered us to undergo any serious shame. The girl has become wiser, much more so than we had dared to hope. The turbulence of her nature seems to be tranquillized ; she has now become much interested in religious matters, and the only possible thing which we could object to is that she has gone into this new experience a little too earnestly."

At this point Monsieur Defos recalled the sermon of the day before, and added with a slight accent of scorn, " But that is a fault that leans toward the side of virtue ; you showed us, yesterday, that it was impossible to be too zealous in the service of the Lord."

Monsieur Naudié reddened, as he recalled, also, other sentiments which he had uttered. These long explanations of his host puzzled him ; he could not understand why he had been so fully taken into the family counsels. Now, as Monsieur Defos remained silent, and evidently awaited a reply, he said a few words in praise of his great care of the girl, and felicitated her upon being the object of it.

Without replying to the complimentary words, Monsieur Defos said : " And now, my dear pastor, I wish to ask you a question which, after all that I have been saying, may be not wholly unsuspected by you. Have you ever considered the possibility of a second marriage for yourself?"

This time Monsieur Naudié understood; but it came with such a shock that at first he could not find words to express his surprise, and he repeated blankly, "Me? For me?"

"Surely it cannot be possible," said Monsieur Defos, good-naturedly, "that such an idea has never occurred to you, or that none of your friends and neighbors has suggested such a contingency?"

By a great effort Monsieur Naudié held back the flood of commingled emotions which these words set loose within him; and he appeared outwardly calm, smiled as if he had been listening to a fairy-tale, and replied in all simplicity: "Why, yes, my friend, it is an idea which sometimes has occurred to me; both my father and my sister have had the same idea, also. But I am no longer young, I have four children; these are conditions which make a second marriage very difficult. I believe that only some very serious-minded woman, knowing enough of life to know the cost of devotion, would be likely to accept them."

Monsieur Defos appeared to weigh these

words carefully. "I see," said he, "that you are not opposed, on principle, to the idea of second marriages. And you have doubtless divined the drift of my question? It is, in short, this : that my niece, Mademoiselle Jane Defos, has taken into her head the idea of marrying you. The fact that I speak thus to you about it ought to be evidence that I have ceased to regard her idea as an altogether absurd caprice. Indeed, on the whole, I am inclined to favor her wish. Now, my dear pastor, I trust that I shall give no offence if I add that I bring this peculiar affair to your notice only after much hesitation, and only after having overcome considerable opposition; for I shall not conceal from you that Madame Defos has been extremely reluctant to give her consent; it is the first time, in thirty years of married life, that we have found ourselves in disagreement. Besides, so far as I am concerned, I have not had the time to think over all the moral advantages which such a plan offers. It has been enough for me that it has seemed inevitable; that was what weighed me down."

Monsieur Defos spoke as if the only possible objections must be on the side of his family, and that Monsieur Naudié must, of course, be only too ready.

Pastor Naudié's Young Wife

The pastor was injured in his feelings; and he said: "These advantages of which you speak,—I must confess that I do not yet see them. Mademoiselle Defos is very young and very rich. Youth and wealth are excellent things; they are not, perhaps, in this case the things most desirable."

"As to that matter of wealth," said Monsieur Defos, warmly, "you forget that it might be, perhaps, an injury to a young girl who was very nice and yet . . . yet very . . . romantic. A young girl is never sure of being sought for herself alone, and she therefore becomes distrustful; she is suspicious of all suitors, she doubts everybody who comes near her. And that is not all. My niece, as I have already told you, is very devout, very seriously inclined; she would like to have the wealth which has fallen to her put to good use, good Christian use. More than that, she feels deeply the need of consecrating herself to some noble work. She had a plan of becoming a nurse; if she gave it up, it was because the sight of physical suffering made her ill herself. Then she cast about for some other mission, and believes that she has found it; and what nobler task can there be, really, than the bringing up of motherless children?"

These words recalled to Monsieur Naudié

the saying of his sister Angelica and of his father, both of whom were always so frank and sincere before the mystery of life; did their words presage the coming of an unknown, whose soft touch would comfort his little ones? And was Jane the one? Then he murmured, "These are noble sentiments."

"Without question," said Monsieur Defos. "It is because I have understood and weighed them that I have come to approve my niece's course; and for other reasons, also, my dear pastor, as I have told you frankly. If these plans come to nothing, we shall be unable to keep her with us, she tells us. . . ."

Monsieur Naudié hastened to ask: "She will leave us?"

The other went on: "She will go away to England, and then what will become of her? Everything is to be feared for a nature as wilful as hers, at least until the time when she shall have gained that stability which is given by duties and affections. It is upon these duties that I count to make her more reasonable and serious; it is her immaturity of mind, I judge, which dismays you. As for any difference in fortune . . ."

Monsieur Naudié interrupted. "I am far poorer than you suspect."

Pastor Naudié's Young Wife

Monsieur Defos looked at him, as if estimating his worth, and then shrugged his shoulders. "That is not the question," said he. "To be sure, my niece will bring to you wealth, but you, for your part, have your profession, — the noblest there is, — your name, your father's name, and your family's record. You are one of us, my dear pastor; you belong, as we do, to a kind of aristocracy. Two centuries of persecution, of earnest effort, of honesty, of loyalty to the faith, — these are titles of nobility. Which do you suppose I would prefer, — to give my niece to a man like you, or to see her follow in the footsteps of her brother and become the victim of some adventurer? Her fortune, my dear pastor, — ah! it is a great peril for her. Marriage is the only safe course for her. She has chosen you. I approve her choice; and it becomes my duty to ask your hand for her, since you have certainly had no idea of asking her hand of me."

At these words Monsieur Defos allowed himself to smile in a friendly way. Monsieur Naudié did not reply. A dull pain seemed to overwhelm him, as it might overwhelm some poor traveller, who sees a mirage rise before him and prepares to approach it, although greatly in doubt as to its reality. Presently he murmured, "All this is so unexpected and so very serious."

"Doubtless it is," said Monsieur Defos, complacently; "but I do not expect you to give me an immediate response. Take time to think it over! Come and see us. You ought to have some idea of my niece's character. However, try to decide the matter as soon as you can, before all the gossip arises which your visits are likely to cause. Nothing is more disagreeable than to offer to Mrs. Grundy a vague and mysterious state of affairs. So far as other things are concerned, I am sure that you will quickly and wisely rectify the objections which you have named."

Thereupon he laid aside his cigar, which he had taken care not to light, and said: "Now, my dear pastor, let us return to the parlor, if you wish. Our conversation has been a little protracted."

The return to the family circle was very trying for Monsieur Naudié. The four persons grouped in the parlor waited without speaking a word. He had the feeling that the glances, there awaiting him, sought to probe the secret of his soul, which as yet was confused and obscure even to himself. Instinctively his gaze sought Mademoiselle Defos.

She had arranged herself in a dim corner. Although he could scarcely distinguish her features, she appeared to him quite different from what she was an hour before, when she had counted for nothing in his life. Then he glanced at Madame Defos, who was sitting upright upon her chair, with an irritated and almost threatening air. David concealed his ill feeling a little better, and Henry seemed less interested, yet a trifle cynical.

Then this feeling pressed heavily upon Monsieur Naudié's heart: " They all are passing judgment upon me, they are condemning me." And he asked himself, " What shall I do ? " And for the first time perhaps in his life he acted without reflection; he obeyed, almost in spite of himself, the inspiration which came to him. With a resolute step he advanced toward Jane, and said loudly enough for all to hear: " Mademoiselle, your uncle has just told me several things which greatly stir me. I cannot express how deeply I am touched by your kind attitude toward me ; but I am sure that you will find, as I do, that a question as serious as this ought not to be settled hastily. You will reflect more upon it, mademoiselle. There are matters upon which it is highly important that you should be fully informed. As for myself, I have too many duties and too many responsibilities to reach a decision without careful consideration, indeed, without having asked the guidance of God."

This was said with such dignity that the distrustful faces began to unbend, — all except Madame Defos, who glowered even more deeply. Then Monsieur Naudié said " Goodnight," and went out; leaving a favorable impression on at least one of those present, — Henry, whose place in the family was not yet fully established.

CHAPTER V

A FEW days afterward Monsieur Naudié was taking a walk with his children, for exercise. Abraham, who was bored by these family promenades, diverted himself by running about like a young dog, shouting loudly in the fashion of a teamster; or, if one of his sisters left the group for an instant, he took advantage of this to pinch and strike her. Monsieur Naudié turned to the boy, and uttered a sentence, which from repeated use had about lost its meaning: "See here, Abraham! you are unendurable to-day."

He was holding Zelia's hand, and her little legs toiled bravely to keep up with him. She twittered like a little bird about all sorts of things, in a most inconsequent way. As for the pastor, he was preoccupied, silent, turning over in his mind the insoluble problem which the interview with Monsieur Defos had brought to him,—a problem upon which he could not reach any satisfactory decision. For, with all his heart, he longed for the happiness of which he had obtained a glimpse; and yet in his heart there was a voice — each day becoming feebler — which held such happiness in contempt. In truth, hope and cheer seemed to float in the balmy air, and in the clear sunshine which flooded the dear familiar scene, and in the springtime, heralded as it was by the buds of the grand old elms, whose branches hung low, in benediction, over the grass-plots of the lawns.

The sea, not far away, hidden behind a hedge of tamarinds, kept up its ceaseless roar, yet not in anger. On the other side were the groves, and ducks, and well-kept roads of the Charruyer Park. Farther on, toward the town, the ancient tower of La Lanterne raised high its eight-sided steeple, and the little tower where formerly the signal fires were lighted behind the ogive windows. At the approaches of the Casino the sea showed itself, smooth and blue, swept away by the low tide behind the black ruins of the Richelieu dyke. These antique objects, like the ancient elms, and like nature herself, seemed to become young again in the springtime, and even the vault of heaven seemed full of joy.

Monsieur Naudié's heart was much stirred, and he murmured, " It would be so good to be a little bit happy."

Esther and Bertha walked in front of him,

holding hands, and, in low voices, engaged in confidential talk. They were too warm in their winter cloaks, which were very simple and rather worn. They turned around to wait for their father. He finished his thought with, " They, too, will be happier."

And then the distrustful voice within him said, " Who knows ? "

" My ! there are the Defos family," exclaimed Esther, suddenly.

It was true. Monsieur and Madame Defos were coming toward them, madame leading ; the two looking like heavy cuirassiers, moving their imposing persons forward with some difficulty. At their side glided Jane, with airy grace, as if she had been a pretty little skiff, only asking to run before the wind. Instead of passing with coolness and rigidity, they stopped and exchanged greetings. Madame Defos, with mistrustful glance at the young girls, and with her hard mouth much compressed, expressed to Monsieur Naudié the pleasure which his visits would give them. At this, Jane reddened a little, and began to caress Zelia's cheek.

When the Defos family had departed, Esther, after a moment's reflection, exclaimed, " Then you are going again to their house, papa ? "

Pastor Naudié's Young Wife

Monsieur Naudié was taken unawares, and replied nervously and almost deceitfully, " Of course, I ought to make my return call, after going there to dinner." The young girl compared this response with Madame Defos's words, and remained silent. Her father was surely hiding something from her; but what?

She could not divine; but an obscure impression linked Jane with the problem, for she said, " Mademoiselle Defos is very friendly to me at the Philharmonic Society, but this is the first time her uncle has spoken to us in this way."

" Monsieur Defos is a very kindly man, I assure you," said Monsieur Naudié. " He is merely a little cold on the outside; that is all."

Then he put on an air of indifference, and added, " As for the young girl, she is altogether a charming creature."

" They say," remarked Esther, " that she is engaged to her cousin the student."

Monsieur Naudié knew perfectly well that this was a false scent. Yet he was no less keenly aware of a sharp pain, which seemed suddenly to grip his throat; and then, as he paused, astonished at the strange association of ideas, by some unknown law, he seemed to see passing suddenly before his eyes, as plainly as though he were reading it upon the yellowed pages of his large Bible, those warning words from the Book of Proverbs : " She shall hinder thee from pondering on the way of life ; her paths are deceitful ; thou knowest not whither they shall lead thee."

The illusion was so strong that he stopped, and passed his hand across his forehead. But already the words, graven upon his mind by an unseen hand, grew dim ; and he began to reproach himself for allowing such a base suggestion to tarnish the thought of one who seemed to be a person of great sweetness and nobility of soul.

Quite unconsciously his hand clasped Zelia's little hand too tightly, and she disengaged it. Then Bertha summoned him, to show him Abraham, who, profiting by this little distraction, had slipped away toward the harbor.

A series of incidents, which are sometimes signs of destiny, brought Monsieur Naudié and Jane together. A number of times they met each other on committees and in the homes of the poor and the sick. Everywhere Jane appeared like a sunbeam, with a most trustful smile. Her charity, fresh as her own youth, gracious as her own beauty, was not at all like the harsh charity which places its benevolent deeds on account in the savings-bank of heaven. She was a cheerful consoler of sorrows, and she sowed her kind deeds broadcast unconsciously, with a readiness and eagerness which far exceeded the ordinary chary giving of doles; and Monsieur Naudié noted it and admired it. Each time that they met, their interviews were more prolonged and their conversation more intimate; after having consoled the sick upon their couches, or the poor, whose restless eyes followed their every movement, they conversed with each other and walked together, talking over such and such a hopeless paralytic, or such and such a widow whose sorrow was very heavy.

Monsieur Naudié had not quite confessed to himself his leaning toward these prearranged meetings. He grew suddenly red as he said to himself, " If I go to-day to this house of sorrow, rather than to that other one, it is because I am more likely to find her at the bedside." He did it, nevertheless. He even forgot some of his own calculations, as he marvelled at the frequency of their meetings; and he came to see, or almost to see, that in these meetings there was an indication of the approval of heaven.

Pastor Naudié's Young Wife

Two or three visits to the house of Monsieur Defos — which he concealed from his children — strengthened the invisible ties. But, although he was drawn by an irresistible loadstone, he reached no decision, and always found in the path of his growing passion his unsatisfied conscience, bristling with scruples, easily heaping up new obstacles. Feeble and specious, his heart said: "Why not? God permits it. Every man has a right to his share of happiness. The children, too, will be happier. Do they not need a mother?"

Then conscience replied quickly: "You are but slightly acquainted with her; you know nothing about her except that she pleases you; you do wrong to place your future in her hands. She is too rich, too young, too beautiful; you will be too happy." And this word "happy" resounded continually in his heart, with soothing echoes, and aroused all those melodious chords which make sweet music.

"If only," he thought, "I were able to write to her, or able to speak to her all that I feel and think, without the presence of that frigid aunt! Then I could learn to know her better; I would be able to take some decisive step."

Then his conscience stopped him. "Avoid such an opportunity! It is a snare."

" Seek it ! " responded his insidious heart ; " and whatever the result may be, you will have at least one happy hour in your impoverished life."

Jane wrote to him,—not a complex maze of doubts, but scattered fragments of partial confessions ; and she was surprised. Of an active temperament, instinctively knowing how to subordinate her will to the service of her wishes, and keeping always before her the one object whose pursuit absorbed her utterly, she was quite unable to understand his hesitations and misgivings. Already certain peculiar sentiments began to mingle with the romantic exaltation which she had mistaken for love. In spite of the chill which had come to her feminine vanity, and in spite of her impatience, she was determined to succeed. Her infallible instinct warned her that there was one thing — her aunt's unsympathetic presence when Monsieur Naudié came — which arrested the words as they hung upon his lips, words which a word or a look from her would have drawn from him, in spite of himself, in one of those moments when men are so weak and confiding. She wished to put an end to this delay.

" It is a long time since we saw you in the Rue Reaumur," said she to him one day, as

they were issuing from a humble home of affliction; "you have given us up. Won't you
come to-morrow at about four o'clock?"

She was aware that her aunt would be out
at that hour; but she was careful not to
say so; and Monsieur Naudié presented himself the next day, at the hour named, never sus-
pecting that this visit would be at all different
from other visits. It happened that at about
this time a new coat was brought home, which
he had ordered several days before, without
mentioning it to Esther. She was not a little
surprised at this bit of unusual indulgence, and
especially at seeing him quite eager to put this
on, and upon a working-day too. So she could
not forbear asking him where he was going.

Her question annoyed him; he gave an
evasive answer; he said he was going to pay a
visit; then he hurried and went out, to avoid
any further questions. Esther's question,
simple as it was, showed him the necessity of
arriving at some conclusion, under penalty of
arousing local gossip; certainly his going and
coming could not remain much longer unnoticed. And he found himself more perplexed than ever. As he passed under the
arches of the Rue Chef-de-Ville, he encountered
his colleague, Monsieur Fridolin, a little thin

man, with a head like a bird, a smooth chin, alert, talkative, a man gifted with much wordy eloquence and untiring activity. Some articles had been recently published, attacking the Protestants. Monsieur Fridolin was much excited, and began to quote one which seemed to him directed against himself; then he detailed the reply which he intended to make to it, and spoke of other letters which he would send to other papers, if the campaign were kept up.

Monsieur Naudié listened in an absent sort of way, his thoughts being far from these quarrels, which he hated anyway, and he finally tried to end the interview by saying: "These controversies are to be regretted and are unfruitful; for my part, I cannot but feel that it would be far better not to reply to such unjust attacks. Silence is about the best weapon that has ever been discovered against calumny, and honesty always wins in the long run."

As he said this, he held out his hand to his colleague, to say good-by; but, in place of taking it, the other seized him by the arm, and began to walk along with him, talking and gesticulating excitedly. "Silence is not a weapon," exclaimed the hot little man; "it is a surrender. Injustice is done to those who remain silent. It is best to defend one's self, when one has right and justice on his side. The world is full of people who would like to revive the dragonnades."

Monsieur Naudié was by no means desirous that his friend should see whither he was going. So, instead of turning to the right into the Rue Reaumur, he turned to the left, and came presently into a shipyard. Monsieur Fridolin talked continuously, as they walked among the old hulks, and in a few moments the two retraced their steps, and came back along the street.

Time was passing, and Monsieur Naudié, filled with impatience, and unwilling to keep Jane waiting longer, finally stopped short before Monsieur Defos's house, saying: " I am going in here. If you would like to continue this subject, at some other time, I shall be most happy."

" Ah ! You are going to call on Monsieur Defos. Yes ! He is a very remarkable man, is n't he ? And madame ! what a good creature she is ! "

Then he departed ; and Monsieur Naudié, as he pulled the bell, reflected, " He too, doubtless, wonders what I am doing here." At that moment the butler let him in, looking at him, as he did so, with some interest. And the perplexed pastor again said to himself, " And this man, also, wonders at my frequent visits."

The parlor was vacant. He stood waiting before the " Jean " of Monsieur Bouguereau, with its beautiful tints set off by its heavy gold frame. " Yes, most certainly it is necessary," said he, " to reach some decision, and not delay any longer." Yet, though he had pondered so long over the matter, he was no further advanced toward a decision than on the first day he dined there. Still, his heart spoke more and more loudly, and the thought of never seeing Jane again sent a chill through his very marrow.

Soon Jane entered, and put out her hand. " My aunt has gone to Rocheport," she said, " and I am the only one here to welcome you."

This was the situation so longed for and yet so dreaded. Monsieur Naudié was conscious of the same tumult within his breast, which had so nearly overcome him when Monsieur Defos first broached this matter. However, he commanded himself, and replied, as he sat down opposite the young girl : " Ah, then I may take advantage of this occasion to say one or two things, frankly, which I think you ought to know. Thus I shall be able to return, toward you, that full confidence which you have evinced toward me."

His voice did not seem very steady. Despite the purpose which his opening words implied, he did not seem to get hold of the ideas which he wished to express. He coughed like an embarrassed orator. Jane, for her part, sat with her head gracefully inclined to one side, looking at him from time to time through her long eyelashes; and so pretty and bewitching was she that he could hardly keep from falling at her feet like a young passionate lover of twenty years. But he believed that he ought to act in keeping with his age and profession.

He began again: "I will not rehearse the difficulties of the task which you have so generously taken on yourself. I am sure that you have carefully weighed them all. Is that not so?"

Jane murmured very sweetly in reply, "There are no difficulties which cannot be overcome with patience and love."

In picturing to himself beforehand this tranquil and yet decisive interview, which he had hardly dared wish for, Monsieur Naudié had told himself that he must make clear the great difficulties of the new position; but now this reply of Jane's seemed to show, so plainly, that she had gone over the whole ground candidly herself, that he exclaimed, in an ingenuous burst of trustfulness, "Oh, I know that you will conquer them all, since it is by sheer goodness, devotion, and the spirit of self-sacrifice that you are led to come to me . . . to us, I mean; but this sacrifice which you are making,—do you realize what it means for a person of your youth?"

"Is it a sacrifice?" asked she, raising her eyes. "I am alone in the world. I am, indeed, in the greatest loneliness possible, since I am rich. You have no idea of the calculating adventurers I have already perceived about me; not my uncle, by any means!—he is a good man,—but many others. Even at the boarding-school I was not treated like the others. I came to mistrust all sympathy which was shown me; I became suspicious. It will be much the same everywhere else in life."

A contradictory smile was outlined upon her lips as she spoke. "You know very well that the sacrifice is not so very great. What I shall give up will be only the jealousies and intrigues and shams of the world."

"I know that the world has its burdens and

its sins," said Monsieur Naudié; "but it has
also — it must have — its pleasures also. You
do not consider that side now, mademoiselle;
but some day, perhaps, you will regret giving
it all up? If only I could believe that in exchange for these deprivations I would bring
you a little happiness; but how can you wish
me to cherish such an illusion? I know well
how much you will have to give up. Alas!
what will you receive in its place? And
here I come to a real difficulty, — a difficulty
so real that any right-minded person ought
not to think of ignoring it. I almost fear to
point it out to you in its full meaning, it is
such an impassable abyss."

This image of the abyss was undoubtedly a
remnant of Monsieur Naudié's habitual form
of oratorical expression. The sad vibrations
of his voice, and his keen anguish, were expressed vividly on his handsome face, and glo-
rified it.

"It is life, with its hard experiences, that has
created this abyss. They are two lives, yours
and mine, — your young life passed in goodness,
gayety, freedom from care; my years of heavy
cares and disappointments and obstacles and
sorrows. You do not realize what life can
become for two hearts that are in accord, two

souls in harmony, according as it is kindly or cruel. Ah, you cannot realize how life's lessons may be transmuted in such a fashion that they speak, each in its own language, and yet never, never are fully understood. Ah, I know that you have been put to a great test; but you were only a child, and God will not allow the souls of little children to be torn with sorrow. Their wounds heal quickly; they preserve their hopefulness and their strength."

Jane sat listening, in an attentive posture. Monsieur Naudié perceived that his words touched her. With his many years of bearing heavy unshared griefs, he now yielded to the weak, unworthy desire to which men at times do yield, of laying bare their hungry worn hearts to some woman, who must either pity or love them; he yielded to the burning desire, which souls often feel, to come forth from their solitude when a kindly gesture invites them.

" Between the happy people, mademoiselle, and the unhappy, there is a world of difference. For my part, I have never been among the happy. And now it is too late to alter my way of life. You see, I do not even know how to be happy. I have known, with Job, the days of adversity. You, who have gotten through them in your early years, God grant that you may never know them again! Why should I draw you within the circle of my life? Why should I overshadow you with my dark experience? More than all this, between the beloved ones who depend upon me for support, and the Master to whom I have consecrated my best effort, where shall I find leisure in which to search for happiness, or, alas, leisure to give it? Your goodness has aroused a thirst in my heart, and already I begin to rebuke myself. Here below, all that I can do, all that I ought to wish, is for the welfare of my little family. Oh yes, for them I would deeply desire happiness. You will bring it to them, I am sure. But, in order to accept it for them, it would be needful for me to forget all that I have been saying, and other things, also, which I have not said; it were needful for me to be another man, younger, better, more worthy . . . Ah, there is the barrier, mademoiselle, the great one; and when you consider it carefully, you see that no amount of well-wishing and good intentions can surmount it. You will continue to be happy. As for me, I will pursue my journey to the end, faithful to my duty and destiny, as I have accepted it, not complaining, since the Lord has ordered it. Our acquaintance will remain in my soul as a beautiful boundless dream, a sweet dream, from which I have awakened."

Who shall analyze the close sympathy between our words, and the ideas and feelings which they serve to express? Monsieur Naudié intended to speak, doubtless, in all sincerity; for he thought all that he had uttered. However, his sincerity was not entire, for an inner voice warned him that he was pleading at cross purposes. He knew, with a mysterious and unavowed certainty, that at each of his words Jane became more and more his; he knew that at a signal all his destiny was to be changed, that destiny of which he had been declaring himself the slave. And that signal, — he was waiting for it.

For a moment silence settled over them, — silence heavy with thoughts which could not be expressed, shadowy sentiments which guide vacillating wills and pave the way for deeds. Then the young girl spoke. "Do you think to teach me something by talking thus? What, indeed, is the bearing of all this? Yes, what does it signify, since I know it already, since I accept it, since — " her voice grew faint, as she added, "since I love you!"

The word vibrated and lingered like a sound which will not die out; and Monsieur Naudié's eyes filled with tears. As she glanced furtively at him, Jane saw how overwhelmed he was with emotion, and she resolved to go on. She began to speak again, with a steadier voice, and partly smiling : " You can surely see that there is no obstacle, none at all. We will both speak the same language, that of happiness ; you will learn it ; it is easy, the world is full of happiness ; why should not joy come from God as well as sorrow? See, it is he who sends you, at last, your own just reward, and it is I who bring it to you."

She arose and drew near to him with outstretched hands, waiting for one cry of love, for a kiss. But, although at this moment all that there was of the man in Monsieur Naudié was stirred and upheaved, yet the habit of his profession was stronger. Scarcely did he dare to press against his lips the dainty hands, full of caresses, which she offered him, and he sobbed almost as if praying : "I thank you, oh, I thank you, for saying this to me. Yes, you are right ; happiness comes from God ; it should be accepted just as it comes to us. I accept mine, and bless you for it. And how great will be the happiness of those whom I love, whom you love already ! "

His words no longer quite fitted his thought.

Pastor Naudié's Young Wife

If he had spoken according to his heart, Monsieur Naudié would have said that his love was already too strong, and his thirst for happiness too eager. And as he released Jane's hands, and went on murmuring phrases in which God was frequently referred to, the young girl, without yet being conscious of it, began to despise him because he was not more overcome by passion, because he did not more completely forget himself.

PART SECOND

CHAPTER I

ALL in due time came the first anniversary of Monsieur Naudié's marriage. It was decided to have a family dinner; and, in addition to the Defos family, William Naudié came also, leaving his work, at Rocheport, all the more willingly because of some little disagreement which had arisen. The Fridolins too were invited, as also Monsieur Lanthelme, whose sarcastic manner always amused Jane. Monsieur Naudié arose early, went into his study, which was exquisitely furnished in the English fashion, and busied himself at his day's letter-writing. This charming study opened out upon a garden where grew an old and majestic cedar-tree; and there, beside a little pond, Zelia often passed considerable time watching the gold-fish. The Naudié family had now taken up their residence a short distance from the Defos family, in one of those grand mansions in the Rue Reaumur, whose large parlors have carefully preserved their old-fashioned wainscoting, and handed it over to us moderns like a souvenir of the grace and beauty of the past century.

Monsieur Naudié opened a dozen letters. Some of them asked assistance; alas! he received so many of this kind that he could not even reply to them. One of the other letters, which seemed to amuse him, came from his brother Paul; the evangelist explained that he wished to buy a barn, for his meetings, in a certain Auvergne village, where the property-owners had refused to rent him any of their buildings, and he hoped that his brother would assist him in this plan. "My enemies," he wrote, "shall be put to shame, and shall be compelled to confess that the Lord is with us; and, in spite of their evil intentions, the Word shall resound at their very doors."

"No! no!" exclaimed the pastor, in a loud voice, as if his brother were actually present, listening to him, "nothing for this mischievous proselyting; there are other and more worthy needs."

Then he sat thinking how little he was able to bestow, in relief of distress. For a moment it came to him how small a part of his income he was allowed to devote to charity; four house-servants, a carriage, two horses, and a multitude of whimsical indulgences, — what was there left for the poor? His family accounts were about as hard to balance as in the old days of his straitened circumstances; only, the columns were now a little longer. He gave a great deal of time to the conduct of his affairs, and when he stopped to reflect upon it, he reproached himself for letting them take him so much from his duties. However, he did not reflect very often. He was caught up into a whirlwind of passion, following about this fascinating, absorbing little being, his wife, whom he knew no better now than before, and whom he adored more than ever. At this very moment she filled his thought, and she so completely stifled the pain aroused by these flooding letters, that he was really not much disturbed by them, but turned constantly to her. While his eye paused for a moment, in glancing through their plaintive pages, he was conscious of one unending refrain in his heart, " I love her, I love her, oh, how dearly I love her!" Then at intervals another voice would speak, — the voice which ·had struggled with him before, — and it murmured, deep in his soul: " You love her? Why do you love her?"

Pastor Naudié's Young Wife

There was a rap at the door. Monsieur Defos entered, on his way to his office, to say that Henry, whom they had expected that day, had been delayed and would not be with them. "Without him," said he, "we shall be thirteen at table, and, as you know, I am a little superstitious; so will you try to find a fourteenth?"

"Yes, I will try," replied Monsieur Naudié, smiling; "or perhaps the children need not come to dine with us." Then he insisted that his visitor should be seated for a moment, as he had at that moment some advice to ask of him.

"The trouble is this," said he. "There are those houses at Bordeaux; our income is derived in part from them, they represent a full quarter of my wife's fortune. Now, they give me a good deal of anxiety."

"How so?" inquired Monsieur Defos. "Why, they are an excellent investment, one of the best possible, one of the safest that I could make for my niece; as much as five per cent, at least."

The other answered quietly, "Yes, without doubt. Five per cent, on condition that the occupants pay as they agree; but what if they do not pay?"

"Do not pay?" exclaimed Monsieur Defos,

opening his eyes wide, staring and threatening. "Why, they must be made to pay. Thank Heaven, there are still good laws to protect owners. And your agent? You have not dismissed him, I hope?"

"No, I have retained him."

"Very good! He is a strong, capable man. You have only to leave it to him."

Monsieur Naudié's face assumed a careworn expression, and he drew his hand thoughtfully through his beard, as he said, "But I cannot drive those people out into the street when they are out of work, or are suffering from sickness; I really cannot do it."

"Of course you cannot; and you have no need to. Leave all that to your agent; he will attend to it."

"And I shall be responsible, nevertheless."

Monsieur Defos raised his left hand and let it fall, with a gesture of contempt, upon his knee. "You are too much influenced by sentiment," he said.

"Listen!" said Monsieur Naudié. "You yourself, when you were acquainting me with my wife's affairs, had a great deal to say about the usefulness of this investment, in the aid it gave these poor people to find good dwellings at small cost."

Pastor Naudié's Young Wife

"Ah, yes; and are not your tenants given reasonable terms, better than most others? All the more reason, then, that they should pay their rents promptly."

Monsieur Naudié remained silent, because he did not care to speak about this pitiless kind of charity.

"See here, my dear friend!" replied Monsieur Defos, with his grand air. "If you indulge any more in this weak sentimentality, you are lost. It is a hard thing to be a millionaire. The only way to carry on such a business successfully and comfortably is to hold strictly by the law. The law is the one standard which ought to guide our actions. My principle is, *Never overstep the law! Always make it serve your interests!* I commend that same principle to you. It is simple, effective; it solves all difficulties. I don't see why the enforcement of law should shock a Christian man. Jesus himself said, 'Render unto Cæsar that which is Cæsar's!'"

Again Monsieur Naudié was hurt by this rigid, literal, and savage application of justice. "I am not Cæsar," said he, with a touch of irony.

"No more am I," exclaimed Monsieur Defos; "but . . ."

He did not finish this sentence; the word "but," spoken with a brusque tone, and accompanied by a gesture of the arms, showed clearly that, in his opinion, justice needed not to be tempered by any mercy.

"Now, I cannot reason in that way," said Monsieur Naudié. "To me it seems impossible to compare the relations in which these poor people stand to us, with the relations in which we stand to God. The two are not parallel."

"All right, then, sell your houses! that is the best thing you can do. I am at your orders."

Monsieur Naudié was about to accept the offer with joy; but it suddenly occurred to him that such a change would probably deliver his poor tenants into the hands of this dreadful man. It would simply be a new way of hiding himself behind another person, another way of shifting responsibility off his own shoulders. "Thank you!" he replied, in a listless way; "I will think it over, and we will speak of it again later."

Monsieur Defos looked at his watch, and arose, saying, "Very well, just as you wish; this evening, perhaps."

As soon as his visitor had gone out, Mon-

sieur Naudié set busily at work on his corre-
spondence. Presently his butler, Frederic, a
tall, withered, dignified-looking individual, appeared at the door. A farmer had come to
beg the pastor to hasten as quickly as possible
to Marcilly, where a dying widow needed his
services. Frederic's scornful air said very
plainly that in his opinion the pastor ought
not to be disturbed in any such way.

"I will go at once," said Monsieur Naudié.
Then, hesitating, he added, "Have the horses
hitched up!"

Usually he avoided using the carriage; its
luxurious presence weighed upon him and
caused him regret; but to-day his wish to
return quickly overcame his scruples. Wish-
ing to recall to his wife the memories of the
day just commencing, he went out into the
garden to gather some roses for her; then he
returned and knocked gently at her door, but
she made no response. So he entered. She
was still asleep, with the easy sleep of a happy
child, charmingly beautiful in the careless dis-
order of her dishevelled black hair. Oh, to
awaken her by stealing the kisses which seemed
to blossom, like flowers, upon her parted red
lips! But he dared not, for he never gave
himself up to the free expression of his emo-

tions toward his wife ; he concealed them from her, just as he concealed her little deceits from himself. He contented himself, therefore, with gazing at her a moment, holding the bouquet in his hand ; then he spread the roses out over the coverlid, and with a troubled heart went out quietly.

The children, who were starting for school, had paused beside the carriage ; they embraced him ; then he entered the carriage, and the sound of its wheels upon the pavement went echoing through the silent street, with its row of dignified sombre old mansions on either side.

The village of Marcilly is the only one of the adjoining Protestant districts which has been restored to the parish of La Rochelle. The two pastors took turns in visiting it, each fortnight. In former days Monsieur Naudié was accustomed to go his rounds on foot, partly for the exercise, and partly to save the expense of a carriage. He walked then with a strong, steady gait ; carrying his coat on his arm, and with his forehead perspiring under his thick, heavy hat, he strode vigorously along the path which wound among the fields, and was bordered by young trees bending gracefully under the pressure of the west wind. It is a bare, melancholy landscape. Here and there, hidden away in a group of trees, or grouped around some old church, you will see, rising, the low roofs of squat-looking houses, gray like the tilled fields which the sun and wind have dried up. At times you will see windmills, with their sails fluttering in the breeze, and groves of great rugged trees, and, occasionally, a row of tall, slender poplars. On the right and on the left the sea appears, as a continuation of the level plain, intersected by the dark line of the island of Ré, — a black mark on a blank page. An exhalation of sadness seems to be continually rising from this desolate landscape, and a harsh wind blows continuously across it. Yet, in the spring mornings, the birds sing among the trees and among the fields of young wheat. After two hours of rapid walking, the pastor could reach Marcilly. The square tower of the ancient church, with steeple dismantled in some old fray, sent forth peals of welcome by its bell, calling upon the worshippers of another faith to come to service.

Monsieur Naudié entered a narrow lane, at the right, which led to a humble temple of the Reformed Protestant Church. Within, there was a small square hall, principally occupied by a low platform.   The pastor seemed to be a part of the congregation ; and he felt that he was talking to them as individuals, standing thus in their very midst.   He was fond of the plain peculiar people gathered here, — the two or three gaunt old men, and the silent old women, in queer caps ; their troubles seemed to him much like his own.   They were hardly more burdened by their daily cares than was he; their families, which were almost always numerous, gave them no greater trials than did his own ; the little beings which they had brought into life are like grains of seed, which sprout and bud under a little sun and rain ; they struggle and grow, nourished by their powerful neighbor, and quickly become useful, and soon are scattered abroad.   As he spoke to these people, and listened to them and observed them, the pastor had sometimes seen a peculiar phase of the hard problem of pauperism.   Poverty here was different from that in the cities; it was not so oppressive ; it seemed not so much an enemy as an educator ; for it abounded in wise counsels, it tended to develop sympathy, and it taught that each day was to be accepted, just as it came, just as the earth and the seasons made it.

Thus Monsieur Naudié used to reflect, in

the old days of his own straitened circumstances.
Now, as he followed the familiar road, and as
he entered the well-known place of worship,
his impressions were different.   His hearers did
not look upon him in quite the same way;
something seemed to separate him from them.
Moreover, his terms of service at Marcilly
seemed to him more and more like drudgery,
which he avoided as often as he honestly could.
To-day, rocked and lulled by the regular movements of the carriage, his view cut off by the
bulky form of the driver, he paid no attention
to the scenery, which was flooded with the
clear light of a summer morning, and he revolved various shadowy unquiet thoughts in
his mind.

A sad scene soon drove away, for a while,
his own personal cares.   It was a woman, still
young, in the midst of squalor, resting on a
couch, without power of recognition, and almost
without breathing, so near to death that already
the barrier of unconsciousness shut her off from
this life.   Three children, of tender age, were
huddled in a frightened way in a corner, an
abandoned brood, poor little creatures, cower-
ing in the presence of a sorrow which they
could not understand.

Monsieur Naudié tried to question them.

" Are you all alone ? Is there nobody here ?
Has n't the doctor come ? " But they could
make no reply. They gazed at him with
troubled eyes, and stood before him as if
petrified.

" Poor little creatures ! " he said, caressing
them. Then he leaned over the sick woman,
trying to make out what last wishes she might
have at the bottom of her heart. Her dim
eyes seemed to express some desire, but her
lips moved not.

" God will care for them, be sure of that,"
he said tenderly. " You have done right to
call me. Whatever I can do, shall be done.
Now I will pray with you." A great pity
filled his soul for these unfortunates, smitten
thus by the hand of that One whose ways we
know not. And at the same time he thought
of his own little ones and of their dead
mother ; and these memories made his sympathy all the stronger, more intelligent, and
more delicate, and strengthened his desire to
help them.

He prayed, although the poor woman seemed
to take no notice ; then he reassured her, and
again comforted the children. As he was about
to go, a little girl held him back, and a little
tearful voice begged him, " Don't go ! not yet ! "

Pastor Naudié's Young Wife

Several moments passed thus, in prayer and waiting; and Monsieur Naudié thought of Jane, who doubtless was waiting for him, and would reproach him for his delay; or, alas! would she reproach him? The arrival of a neighbor finally allowed him to depart. As he laid three gold pieces on the table, the neighbor exclaimed, "Ah, anybody can see that you are rich."

He promised to return, and climbed into his carriage. As he went his rounds, the country-people, the very ones who had formerly seemed so near to him, seemed to evince a new attitude of respect; a respect such as the poor show toward the rich, but not what they should have toward a servant of God. Their glances followed him, and behind his back they exchanged remarks secretly upon his equipage, his improved condition, and upon his good luck.

Ah, but he had not bettered himself. There were cares weighing upon him now which once had not troubled him, cares which seemed to keep him far from God; and the great happiness, which he had thought within his grasp, diminished from day to day. The ecstasy of devotion and piety which Jane had at first shown, had not survived three months of married life. The duties which she had taken upon herself so lightly she had repudiated with equal readiness. At the first difference arising between herself and the children, she had ceased to love them; she took no more interest in the poor and the afflicted; she did not care for her husband, she cared only for herself. One of those sudden changes which had made her cold, critical uncle uneasy, had transformed her into a self-absorbed, frivolous creature, excessively solicitous about the insignificant things of life, capricious, fitful; yet her beautiful quiet eyes held out the same promises of goodness, and she seemed to glow with the love of loving, and of the joy of living. She was like a superb block of marble, out of which a clumsy sculptor had failed to carve a masterpiece, or like a heavy mass of common stone which no chisel could ever ennoble; she was like a mysterious stream, whose unfathomable waters sent forth both flecks of gold and bitter poison.

Already Monsieur Naudié meditated much upon her, growing critical over petty details which heightened his unwise and almost unnatural infatuation. Had he not to-day done wrong in leaving her without saying good-bye, and especially in staying away so long? Would she have wished him to go out without telling her, on such an anniversary day as this? Indeed, how much did she care for the anniversary? Perhaps it caused her regret, and perhaps her careless hands would not trouble to gather up the roses which he had scattered about her.

But even while he surrendered himself to such childish reflections, Monsieur Naudié was haunted by more serious thoughts; for he murmured softly, again and again, "Oh, how I do love her! Oh, I love her too much," and he repeated, as if he were censuring himself, "Yes, I love her far too much."

At the same time he perceived with impatience that the carriage was not moving fast, and he called to the driver: "Go faster, please! We shall be too late for breakfast."

At the same moment, the whole situation passed rapidly before his mind. He compared the misery which he had just seen with his own abundance, and the sympathy which cut into his heart with the actions of those who made life so bitter for the poor. He explored the depths of his soul, and trembled, as he found it possessed of one sole idea, one sole desire; he recalled the verse in Proverbs which had been such a mysterious warning to him; and a dull fear took possession of him.

CHAPTER II

AS the carriage bowled along toward home,
Monsieur Naudié's reflections pressed
upon him more and more heavily. Patient as
he was in most respects, to-day he felt urged
by a feverish haste to return to his household;
and his heart quickened its beating, through a
vague anxiety as to what was there awaiting
him. The carriage, meanwhile, rolled through
the Dauphine gate and crossed the city at a
rapid pace. Several persons of his acquaintance gave him respectful salutations, turned
around to gaze after his equipage, and afterward exchanged comments with one another,
or stood silent and thoughtful. The town
had not yet, in fact, gotten over talking about
his marriage; people could not forget in a
moment the many years during which Monsieur Naudié had been a familiar figure in the
old streets and among the antique arches,
wrapped closely in his threadbare old frock-
coat, or with his thin overcoat buttoned tightly
about him. Now that he had become a
capitalist, people remarked in the usual exag-
gerated way, "We shall never see him except

Pastor Naudié's Young Wife

in a coach." And the public eye was levelled at him and his new surroundings, with a little of that cruel curiosity which predicts misfortune, counts on dangers ahead, and prophesies evils to come. In front of the Café François, Monsieur Naudié's carriage encountered Monsieur Dehodecq and Monsieur Lanthelme, who were sauntering together along the sidewalk. They saluted him, paused in their conversation, glanced significantly at each other, and Monsieur Dehodecq said: " Happily as that affair has turned out, and charming as is their home, yet the pastor was guilty of great rashness. We may venture to say that, of course, strictly between ourselves."

" Why do you think that ? " asked Monsieur Lanthelme, who had always a way peculiar to himself of defending his pastor ; namely, by tearing him in pieces leisurely, as if he held in his claws an unusually choice morsel.

" Why, just think of it ! " said Monsieur Dehodecq. " At his age ! There can be no doubt, can there, that she is at least fifteen years younger than he is. And then, such a difference in their conditions ! Why, he always lived in a state closely approaching destitution."

Monsieur Lanthelme wriggled uneasily at

these words. Monsieur Dehodecq went on: "It was a great match. He captured her, we grant that, but he had good luck. Only think what risks a pastor runs when he plunges into an affair of that sort! It is useless to say, 'Oh, he is a man like other men.' The consequences of an act like his are of the greatest importance, in his position; and his responsibilities are equally great."

Monsieur Lanthelme's little eyes glowed brightly in his red face. He was an outspoken freethinker, who went to church only to find fault with the sermons; he hated theologians, and never lost an opportunity to have a rap at them. "Pooh!" said he, "the famous Strauss married a public singer."

"Is it possible?" exclaimed Monsieur Dehodecq.

"Entirely so. It is true he ended by divorcing her, but only after they had lived very happily together for several years. Of course he could n't see into the future. His letters to an intimate friend have been published. They are excellent reading, you may be sure."

He hugely enjoyed his companion's astonishment, and he returned to the subject. "May Heaven keep Monsieur Naudié from any such

Pastor Naudié's Young Wife

fate! The thing that I like about him is that his prosperity has n't spoiled him one bit. He puts just as much work into his sermons as ever, and they are no worse than they used to be. A case like his is worthy of all praise. He reminds me of a friend of mine, whose conditions were somewhat like his. He preached better, but he was n't so successful in resisting the temptations of fortune. He had remained unmarried, in the most prudent fashion. Then one fine day — he was not much younger than Monsieur Naudié — he found, directly in his path, a dowry. Yes! an enormous one. You see, a young girl, an orphan like Mademoiselle Defos, had vowed that she would marry a minister and only a minister; for there are people who have such whims. No sooner were they married than she put on the pastoral robe, though she did n't go into the pulpit. The Consistory filed a protest. But it did no good! She presided over committees, started numerous beneficent schemes, and wrote some doctrinal treatises of a controversial nature. As to theology, I never could see why they shut women out; their qualifications are singularly adapted to its requirements; they have a certain illusive spirit, you know. Well, what was the husband doing all this time? Why, he was attending to the business affairs of the household; and doing it well too, I must admit. He had given attention to the parable of the talents, and had made his multiply."

Here Monsieur Lanthelme broke out into a bitter kind of laugh, enjoying his own maliciousness. Monsieur Dehodecq had been listening, with that close, labored attention which he gave to everything.

"That is an accusation," said he, reflectively, "which could be urged against us also, quite as easily as it could be urged against Monsieur Naudié, if he turned out badly. But such circumstances as his are very rare. Out of the six or seven hundred pastors among our clergy, how many do you suppose you could find who had made rich marriages? Three or four, at the most."

"Without counting, however," said Monsieur Lanthelme, "those whom marriage has simply lifted above the level of need. Oh, you need n't be so eager to defend them, I 'm not inclined to blame them. How do you suppose they manage to support themselves with a salary of about four hundred dollars? Certainly a wife with a dowry is more needful for them than for any other profession. They have cares of all sorts, with their large families."

Pastor Naudié's Young Wife

Monsieur Dehodecq remained silent, weighing seriously these bantering words, quite unconscious of the disguised malice. Presently he said with a long breath, " Well, Monsieur Naudié is safe under cover now."

Excited by the love of controversy, Monsieur Lanthelme retorted : " Safe under cover, yes ; but safe from what ? From poverty only. His children have a plenty to eat, and so does his horse. But . . . are there no other dangers ? "

" What, for example ? "

" Oh, my dear friend, you ask me too much. The future alone can reveal. Marriage is a fairly good bulwark, but it does n't guarantee one against all accidents."

Meanwhile, Monsieur Naudié, as soon as he reached home, went in search of Jane ; he was nervous, and was eager to wish her " many happy returns of the day." She was in her boudoir, adjoining the large parlor and opening also upon the garden ; a tiny room, which she reserved for her own occupancy. It was padded and cushioned with modern stuffs, so that its antique flavor was gone. It had nothing of antiquity about it, except its mullioned windows, which were crowded with English vases and foreign books. Jane was arrayed in a white tea-gown, her finely cut features and her pretty little head rising up from a sea of lace. She seemed to be busy arranging some papers at a wooden desk brought from England, the key to which she alone possessed. This private desk was looked upon by her husband with that kind of dull uneasiness which one often feels, as he looks upon some mysterious symbols, or at silent lips, or on illegible writing. As she heard him enter, the young wife turned slowly, without laying down the " portrait album " which she held in her hand. Monsieur Naudié kissed her upon the forehead; but the words which he was eager to utter died upon his lips, as he noticed the photograph before her. It was that of a young man, handsome, with large mustaches, eager eyes, and features of a Roman type. He had a melodramatic air, with arms crossed under a kind of Spanish cloak, and forehead concealed by a sombrero; he had taken the kind of pose which is usually taken under similar circumstances by much admired artists, pianists, singers, actors, and acrobats. Below, under some notes of music, could be read this verse, scrawled by a clumsy hand, *Vorrei poterti dar quel po' che resta . . .*

With his right arm Monsieur Naudié encircled lightly his wife's graceful form; for an instant he struggled with himself; then, over-come, he took with his left hand a corner of the picture, lifted it, Jane still retaining her hold, and asked, " What is this thing ? "

The young wife smiled; her eyes wandered from the picture to her husband, as if she were drawing a mischievous comparison between the two faces, so different from each other.

" That ? " said she.   " That is Beltram."

" Beltram ? "

" You don't seem to know the name. Oh, my dear friend, you don't know very much. Beltram is a famous singer. He stirred up all London. He sang in the very best houses. He is an Italian. How handsome he is ! "

Monsieur Naudié drew his finger along the line of writing below. " And that ? That is his autograph, I suppose."

" Certainly."

" He gave you this picture ? "

" Oh yes."

" With this piece of impertinence under-neath ? "

" That is no impertinence. It is the first line of a famous ballad of Tosti's ; " and she broke out singing to a familiar air, " *Donna, vorrei morir* . . . "

Pastor Naudié's Young Wife

Monsieur Naudié's forehead contracted. His wife again spoke in a dreamy sort of way: "Oh, how beautifully he did sing! You would n't believe I could have been so infatuated with him."

With one movement Monsieur Naudié released the photograph and his wife, murmuring, " Ah, indeed . . . indeed . . . ! "

" Yes, I was seventeen. A singer! An artist! You understand. He came to sing at my relative's house in London, during my Easter holiday. Oh, what a voice! Oh, what eyes ! "

" Don't you think that perhaps you admired him a little too much ? "

Jane did not choose to comprehend the bearing of this delicate insinuation. She went on glibly: " What I mean is that I was completely fascinated by him. Nothing less, my dear. Quite infatuated. I lost sleep, I dreamed only of him, I wished to die. Oh, it was all just like the romances in the novels."

One question pressed forward to Monsieur Naudié's lips. He finally uttered it. " And he . . . did he know this ? "

"There, there! How jealous you are!" retorted Jane, in place of answering his question. " Don't you know that it was only a young girl, my dear? Why do they send us girls to boarding-schools, from fifteen to our marriage, if it is not for us to dream and gossip about love? Well, Beltram lasted about six months. Before that, there was a vicar . . . Oh don't open your eyes so wide, I beg. He was a very old vicar, with a great white beard. Afterward there was a painter, a very celebrated one, of whom I never saw anything except the portrait. And then there were others, whose names I don't at this moment recall. They have passed away like the reflections in a running stream. And then, then you came, — yes, you."

Monsieur Naudié grew darker and darker, as he listened; but he dared not say anything, for fear of being ridiculous. "I think, though," he ventured, "that you have not put me in quite the same category with them."

"Oh no, no!" said Jane, reflectively. "Now, they have all gone by; but you — you are still here."

She was searching among the photographs in the drawer. "Hold!" said she. "Here is the vicar's picture."

Monsieur Naudié gave one glance at the face, — that of a grand dignified old man, much like his own father,—and then tossed the picture back among the others.

"Now," said Jane, "you know all my secrets."

"All?" he asked quietly.

"I wish to tell you everything that I recollect."

"There is, however, one . . . one, which I do not know."

"Oh, what?"

Standing directly in front of her, he took both her hands, looked straight into her eyes, and spoke in a voice which trembled with passion. "There is . . . there," and he kissed her forehead, "there, behind that impenetrable wall, there in that heart, in that soul which belongs to me and yet has escaped me . . . your secret thoughts, those which you have never told me, those which I have not been able to read in your eyes . . . If you really love me . . . or, rather, if there is anything separating us which I do not know about . . . if you have given yourself to me only to tear yourself away again . . . Oh, why do you play with me, and cause me such pain! That—that is what I wish to know."

He groaned with an agony which had been too long pent up, which now for the first time burst forth. Jane disengaged her hands, and said in a calm voice: " I have never seen you like this, my dear. Is it because of Beltram, who . . . ? "

" Ah, it is because," exclaimed he, "because you do not know . . . "

Without speaking, she leaned again over the drawer, took out another picture, and handed it to her husband. " There," said she, "look at that ! This time you won't be so jealous."

It was the photograph of a young girl, of delicate features, somewhat monotonous, with hair arranged in the Greek style; a classic Anglo-Saxon type, such as is often seen in the magazines. " A boarding-school friend," said Jane ; " but what a friend ! She never left me ; she thought only about me. She would not allow me to even speak to the others. And such jealous scenes ! and such fits of despair when the holidays came ! Oh, how it bored me ! "

She tossed the picture back into the drawer, and closed it with a bang ; remarking, as if in a soliloquy, " You never love a person who loves you too much."

CHAPTER III

AS Monsieur Naudié came out of Jane's boudoir after this interview, which caused him much uneasiness, he encountered Madame Defos. Every day, during several months past, Madame Defos had been accustomed, either just before breakfast or immediately after, to present herself at her niece's house, in the rôle of a tender mother, over-anxious, borne along by her maternal solicitude.

Monsieur Naudié, who was always of a trustful nature, believed at the outset in her friendship, and judged her, not by her personal appearance and arrogant manner, but by her general reputation. She was commonly understood to be " a good woman, kindly disposed despite her apparent severity, reliable, of superior intelligence, but very retiring, even a little shy; saying little, and somewhat over-shadowed by the luminous presence of her husband, to whom she always conceded the superior position."

Possibly she deserved this reputation; possibly, also, she never indulged in follies, because she had no leaning that way, and no favorable occasion offered itself.

However her real nature might have revealed itself, those favoring conditions were wanting, in her little circle, which prepare the way for the logic of events; and she was the first to see that, with all the clairvoyance of bitterness. Since the day when her husband went out to the Indies, before the time, even, when her niece came to La Rochelle, Madame Defos had decided that the young girl's dowry must not go out of the family, and that it ought to come into the hands of Henry, her favorite son. This simple idea, whose realization seemed an easy matter, germinated under her low flat brow, spread out to her temples, as if to include all that they contained, and at once became a fixed idea. Monsieur Defos's suggestion regarding the young girl's marriage astonished her as soon as she heard it. She could not appreciate his scruples, honest though ambitious man that he was; but he was capable of giving up all gain, rather than stand in opposition to law or to custom, or even to his own ideals of propriety. She opposed these scruples with all her power, without anybody ever having a suspicion of the anger it aroused in her. If she yielded, it was only because she was afraid that Jane might carry her fortune even farther away, and lay it at the feet of some Beltram. But she conceded the point only because she must, and she held her reservations, and was filled with enmity toward the man who had snatched away from her this coveted wealth. During the earlier days of the marriage, she believed that all was smooth contentment in the new family, and she could not rise above her resentment, but sulked and waited. Later she revived a little, for she detected in this rosy heaven one black spot. Monsieur Naudié, as her cold indifference passed away, rejoiced over her return, even as they rejoice in heaven over the conversion of a sinner, and never questioned for a moment her entire sincerity; his frank eyes could not read the secrets of complex souls; and, in Madame Defos's soul, hatred engraved indecipherable characters on her loyalty.

When she saw him come forth, in a disturbed state of mind, from Jane's boudoir, Madame Defos hastened to meet him, her face wearing a maternal smile which called out his trustfulness.

"You are so pale!" she said. "Are you in any pain?"

"No, no, thank you! I am well, very well indeed."

Insinuating and soothing, she ventured tenderly, "Some little difference with your wife?"

Monsieur Naudié wished to deny this, but she would not listen to him. "Oh, I understand all that!" she said; "even between people who agree perfectly well in general, little misunderstandings will sometimes arise, — mere nothings! — especially during the earlier days of married life. However, it is best to be through with them as soon as possible. Tell me, now, what the trouble is; I will try to arrange matters a little."

Monsieur Naudié perceived neither the wicked delight which gleamed in her eyes, nor the enmity which was expressed by her thin, drawn lips. Trustful and sad, he replied: "It is only a little thing, and I think I must be in the wrong about it. We have been talking, Jane and I, and she has been telling me about some of her earlier love-affairs; the recital caused me some pain, and I did not know enough to conceal it. There! that is all."

"Ah, Beltram!" exclaimed Madame Defos, at once.

"How did you know . . . ?"

"Oh, indeed I did. He gave us a great deal

of uneasiness, that insipid fop. I never understood exactly how he gained such an influence over poor Jane, but there was a time when we feared greatly. Between ourselves, I feel persuaded that if she had not been under age, this robber would have carried her away. Luckily the law is very severe on such deeds as that; but the poor child was certainly much infatuated."

"I did not suppose," stammered Monsieur Naudié, "that the affair went as far as that . . ."

"Has she not told you all, then?"

"All?"

"Oh, calm yourself! There was nothing very serious, no, no! But you must remember that she was a spoiled child, and very wilful. She has changed very much since then. In those days her little fancies went flying and flying. . . . Ah, she might have been led, . . . heaven knows where. Oh, she has had only those childish caprices; at least, I am almost sure about that. They have not troubled us, —us who have had charge of her. But you must not think any more about such things. Don't be jealous! I honestly believe you have no cause to be. Besides, it all went by, six years ago. Beltram is far removed from her thoughts, far! She scarcely ever hums that song of his."

She left him, carrying away a recollection which to her was delightful; it was the sight of Monsieur Naudié, standing as if rooted to the ground, as he stared back at the mysterious past, which made the present, already perplexing enough, seem more perplexing still. And the future . . .

By the time that Madame Defos had knocked at the door of Jane's boudoir, she had matured her plan. With an excited manner and with staring eyes, she advanced toward her niece, crying out, — and glancing swiftly around her, as if guarding against an eavesdropper, — "Oh, my dear child, what have you done? I have just met your husband, there in the hall; he is angry, beside himself. You have said what you ought not. You must have told him things . . . things . . . Oh, Jane, it is necessary to be very careful. With a man such as he is, I repeat, it is necessary to be especially careful."

Jane still retained a vivid impression of her husband's sad and patient manner. He had seemed to suffer, without daring to protest; perhaps, indeed, she was touched by his patient sweetness, and reproached herself for her needless cruelty. Madame Defos went on talking glibly. She said that she had feared for some time that there was trouble in the family. Her own reason, she said, for opposing this marriage had been that she saw beforehand that Monsieur Naudié was a man of suspicious, unjust nature. Such feelings as his, easily understood in the case of a young man, somewhat excusable because of youthful passion, became unpardonable in the case of a mature man like him, cold, calculating . . .

" What did he say ? " demanded Jane.

" Oh, he told me all his woes. He finds you vain and frivolous. He asked me about Beltram, evidently dwelling upon what you had told him. Why did you unfold that little narrative to him ? Be more cautious in the future ! I warn you."

Judging that she had made an impression, Madame Defos prepared to go. " I only ran in a moment, my dear, as I was passing," said she, " to tell you that Henry will not be with us this evening. How I do long to see him again ! And I am rather anxious about him."

" What is the matter with him ? "

" I don't know ; but he is such a stormy nature. A great many things pass through his mind which he says nothing about. His

Pastor Naudié's Young Wife

father never notices anything out of the way; but I notice, I surmise, I have my fears."

Her manner changed greatly as she spoke about her son; her features became more relaxed, and her hard eyes grew more tender. Thus every soul takes on different colors, according to the star which shines upon it.

When Jane was finally left to herself, she fell into a kind of reverie; presently she approached the window, which was half-open; the children were scattered about the garden waiting for the bell to call them to breakfast. Under the old cedar, whose dense widespreading branches cast a deep shadow, sat Esther, with Zelia beside her, explaining to the child some difficult passage in one of her school-books. Abraham, stormy and boisterous, with his cap tipped over one ear, and with his pockets stuffed with all sorts of things, was talking with Bertha, who was standing at the edge of the little pond, and was looking very charming in her white gown. For a moment Jane's gaze wandered over the two groups of children; it expressed only indifference and antipathy. She had dreamed of bringing great happiness into their lives; but between them and herself no affection had grown up. Indeed the reverse had happened; she had been repulsed by their first shyness and distrust, and had lacked that patience which alone could gain their hearts after they had been so naturally offended by this strange invasion of their family circle. The privileges which Zelia enjoyed seemed to arouse jealousy in this young wife; and her will clashed often with Bertha's, which was quite as stubborn as her own, and even more sensitive. Then, too, she saw in Abraham only a volatile, indolent boy, badly brought up; an inferior kind of animal, whom she despaired of ever taming. With Esther, alone of all the family, her relations were unconstrained and pleasant; for the wise, serious young daughter, seeing the peace and order of the family threatened, tried her best by discretion and tact to prevent confusion and chaos. As Jane's glance followed these young people, so near to her and yet so far from her, she said to herself, " What am I doing here among these strangers?"

But she put the question to herself without much sadness, and in a moment made the reply, " I have made a mistake." Then she shrugged her shoulders with a vigorous decisive gesture, which doubtless was a reply to certain vague reflections dimly outlined on her heart; obscure germ-ideas, which the fortunes of the future might bring to fruition.

Monsieur Naudié now reappeared at the door of the room. He had been greatly disturbed by Madame Defos's words, disquieted by suspicions which he could not allay; and, unable to bear the unrest which the unhappy reminiscences had brought to his heart, he came now to seek some sort of explanation, or some reassuring word, or to ask pardon if he had in any way offended. So he entered with timid steps, and with that almost abject tenderness which always vexed Jane, instead of arousing her affection. Although she heard him enter, she pretended not to have noticed him, and went on looking out of the window.

He stopped a few paces away from her, and said, " Jane ? "

She turned sharply around toward him, and keeping her angry gaze fixed upon him, exclaimed, " Why did you complain to my aunt ? "

" Do you . . . mean me ? " stammered he, in amazement.

She would not give him time to explain. " Leave me. Don't deny it ! You went and complained to her about me; I know it. You have been asking my aunt questions about my past, without stopping to think whether such conduct would offend or displease me."

He began again, " But . . ."

Again she interrupted, " No ! no ! you can't say anything to clear yourself."   And she left the room, and he dared not follow; but he crossed over to the window, where Jane had been standing.   The children were still in the garden, seeming to him very well dressed, but not so happy and free as in other days.   Then they had been a consolation to him in his troubles ; but now there had come in between them a fixed distrust full of silent reproaches.

He descended the stairway, and went out to join them ; but at his approach Abraham took to flight, and Bertha sulkily walked away.   He went up to the settee, where Esther was reading with Zelia.   " Well, what are you doing ? " he inquired pleasantly.

Esther answered, " I am explaining a problem."

Monsieur Naudié pressed his hand over Zelia's beautiful hair, and she raised her eyes to his in some surprise; for she had gotten quite out of the habit of expecting attentions from him ; he always seemed to overlook her. The father understood in a moment the meaning of her surprise.

Pastor Naudié's Young Wife

We are all inclined to be tender toward those who are in affliction ; and this father, suddenly filled with pity for the pain which, through his own fault, pressed upon this little heart, raised the child to his knees, embraced her, and comforted her with all kinds of tender but confused expressions. After a trifling resistance she gave herself up to him, pressed her little head trustfully against his breast, and said, " Papa, are you going to love me again ? "

That question brought a chill to the father's heart. " How is that, my dear ? " he inquired. " Do you suppose that I have not loved you ? "

The little girl replied seriously, expressing with difficulty the thought which was dimly outlined in her heart, " Oh, papa ! Of course I know you love me ; but . . . but it is n't quite the way it used to be ; you are not quite as you were when . . . when . . ."

She stopped short, and thought for a moment. " Not quite as you were before this . . . stranger came," was what she wished to say ; but she did not dare ; and she finished, " Not quite as you were when I was small. You don't take me up in your arms ; you don't tell me any more pretty stories ; you don't embrace me so often."

Pastor Naudié's Young Wife

Monsieur Naudié held her against his breast, and the image of her dead mother flashed across his mind. Poor dear woman! so sweet and good and devoted, borne down by a task too heavy for her, gone away without knowing any other joys than those of affection and sacrifice! Then he mused, " If she saw us . . . if she saw us . . ." And he recalled the argument which he had used with his conscience, as heart and conscience had struggled desperately : " They also will be happier; the children will also be happier . . ."

At that instant he felt an emotion in his heart such as he had not known for a year, — a strange sentiment, new and powerful ; and he exclaimed : " Oh, my dear little one, I will certainly embrace you as much as you wish, and I will tell you all the pretty stories that I know. What one will you have now? The one about Joseph being sold by his brothers ? "

He had placed her on the ground, and was leaning over her, and holding her hand ; the two now walked slowly away from the settee where Esther was sitting, surprised and puzzled, trying to understand this new development.

" Do ! " said Zelia. " Do tell me the story of Joseph. I like that very much."

Pastor Naudié's Young Wife

Monsieur Naudié began. "Joseph was a little boy who was so good and wise that his father could not help loving him more than he did the other sons, eleven in number; for Jacob had a large family. So the other brothers were very jealous; they were both jealous and wicked, and they said among themselves, 'If only we could get rid of this Joseph . . .'"

Just then a window was noisily opened on the first floor, — in Jane's room, — and Monsieur Naudié stopped. Eager as he was to be loved, and greatly fearing to displease his wife, he acted the coward again. "I will finish the story at another time," he said softly; "I can't tell you any more of it now."

A beautiful great doll, so magnificent that Zelia hardly dared touch her, was seated near them in an armchair of wicker-work, like any live person. This served as a means of diversion for Monsieur Naudié, who at once said: "How weary she is there, the poor doll, all alone so long! Go, Zelia, and keep her company a little while! Take charge of her a few moments, because she is all yours!"

Then he turned and re-entered the house, while Esther came over and comforted her little sister.

Pastor Naudié's Young Wife

At the time of the Reformation, a certain wise man in Holland summed up the entire program of his life, in the following lines:

> Sol vitæ : Sapientia.
> Sal vitæ : Amicitia.
> Panis vitæ : Temperantia.
> Antydotum vitæ : Patientia.
> Vita vitæ : Conscientia.

There is one formula lacking in this category, namely, Love. And for poets, and plain people, and heroes, this has been, all in one, sun, and salt, and bread, and solace, and life of life. However, this sage was marking out his own program alone. Many people, with a code of morals much like his, have imitated him ; with a moderation of nature similar to his, they can conceive of love only as a thin diluted emotion. They hail it, accordingly, as the soothing sentiment which holds families together, which enlivens and dignifies the hearth, — an emotion slightly more fervent than friendship, indeed, the *salt of life*. But as it presents itself in more fervid forms, they hasten to repudiate it, foreseeing its destructive power. Some there are, however, who are capable of knowing it and of conquering it ; heroes these, of hidden struggles, whose history is a martyrdom. Others may be seen drawn by a secret power whose insatiable demands cannot be estimated beforehand, and these try desperately to bind more closely the loosening chain, delaying as long as possible the hour of defeat. There are those, also, who surrender to it, because they are too trustful or too weak, held fast by their hearts, through sufferings which become soon the very law of their existence. Monsieur Naudié was, perforce, one of these. How could he despise or distrust a sentiment which had entered into his life under the guise of kindliness and well being? Surely not in those earliest days, when momentary scruples reproached him with being all too happy, and of renouncing too readily all self-control ; days when he felt that he was fascinated, and was young again, and was once more a man. By the time he understood what a chain encircled him, it was already too strong for him to break, and in tossing and shaking it during his revolts of conscience, he only succeeded in making its links bite more deeply into his flesh.

CHAPTER IV

THE return of their second son was likely to open for the Defos family an era of unexpected events. When Henry went away, the previous autumn, to college, his father supposed that he was bringing to a close his course of studies, inasmuch as he was now twenty-eight years old. Some chance words dropped by Henry, expressing doubt, aroused a momentary suspicion. Still, Monsieur Defos attached little importance to them. He fancied that his son might become, at the worst, a little "liberal." Rigidly orthodox as he himself was, — and the stricter the beliefs, the more efficient, practically, — he however admitted that the views of theologians must be somewhat different from those of the laity; for the laity need beliefs of a simple character, without quibblings, adapted to the needs of even the coal-heaver; whereas the theologians must be trained to more subtle reasonings, enabling them to argue fine points with philosophers. His elder son, David, he wished to have grounded in simple clear doctrines, such as would fit him for the life of business;

whereas he was willing to have Henry skilful in criticising all dogmas, and able to disport himself with " the infinite," which was properly his domain. That would not prevent his following a profession which, although not remunerative, was one to bring a certain measure of glory. Thus, in his plans, his older son should devote himself to business, and maintain the family prosperity; while his younger son should reflect credit upon the family in other ways. It was the realization of his ancestral motto, *Omnia bene Deo juvante.*

The crisis which Henry was now close upon, which his watchful mother already suspected, from various symptoms, was likely to dash these plans to the ground. A crisis like this of Henry's is not at all infrequent among young men who are over-strained by dialectical exercises; who are turned loose into a science which debates endlessly about the infinite and the unknowable; who are directed in these labyrinthine studies by philosophic minds acknowledging no barriers to their free thought, except subjective barriers. Many of these persons come into their work by a " call;" they obey the voice of the Most High, which readily lends itself to the dreams and visions of youthful hearts. They are set apart, their souls filled with God, their lives pledged to him, their hearts contemptuous of the prizes of the world, and their ears deaf to the words of sceptics or atheists.

They are at first kept within bounds by their masters, then by their wills; but their reason — restless little creature — begins his work, and will not be silenced. Often he accomplishes his work without their mistrusting it; as the white ants accomplish theirs, while the household is asleep. When they discover the damage that has been done, they try to ignore it, or they seek in prayer a release from temptation. Sometimes grace saves them. The spirit bloweth whither it listeth. Sometimes, however, one last blast of the storm drives forth, upon the ocean of doubt, the shattered bark of their faith. Some remain at the helm, holding with trembling hand the broken tiller, while the tempest tears to ribbons their disordered sails. Thus they sail on, half under water. Others of them succeed in saving a few planks from their wrecked craft; these, however, they fasten together. The stronger, the nobler, the bolder of them, rely solely on their own powers; launching their raft, they head for some other port.

Henry Defos was one of these. His faith

being wrecked, he knew not how, out of the wreckage, to shape any sort of a profession. He then made up his mind to give up the ministerial profession. But, before he could carry out this resolution, he must needs consult the wishes of his father.

But his father sprang up, in revolt, at his first advances.

This was after the family-dinner. There was no guest, that day. They sipped their coffee in the parlor, under the tender gaze of Bouguereau's " Saint Jean."

Madame Defos urged upon Henry a glass of old brandy. "You must let me take care of you," she said, with all that tenderness which her second son alone could draw from her. "You have become thin; you are very pale."

In truth, the hard winter, with its mental tumults, hesitations, battles of conscience, all these had really changed the young man. Emaciated as he was, with lack-lustre eyes, sallow skin, hair dishevelled and dropping over his forehead, only to be tossed back at once with a quick, nervous gesture, the young fellow seemed like a convalescent, who had barely escaped the grasp of death. His mother looked at him while he slowly emp-

tied his glass with little sips, not enjoying it.
"I am sure," said she, "that you have been
working too hard."

"Pooh!" blurted out Monsieur Defos, who
was stirring the sugar in his glass. "Anybody
knows how young people fatigue themselves.
A fortnight of rest and he will be all right.
The work goes on well, I trust? How is it
with 'The Prophet Amos'?"

'The Prophet Amos.' That was an essay
to which Henry had given a great deal of time
for several years. It was a subject which had
cost him immense investigation, which opened
up more and more, and now would never be
completed; and in the crumbling and ruin
going on in his heart this cherished plan also
was crumbling, and he was deeply regretful; it
was like the loss of a rare piece of furniture, or
a choice edition of a book, a souvenir, in the
conflagration which was destroying his house.

Monsieur Defos's inquiry led inevitably to
a conversation which must be entered upon.
Henry gathered himself up, tried to quiet his
too expressive countenance, and replied rather
brokenly, "'The Prophet Amos,' father; I am
not thinking about that any more."

Monsieur Defos frowned, slightly puzzled,
and even irritated, as he often had been, by

what he called his younger son's whims and caprices.

"What is that you say?" he exclaimed. "You are not going to give up that plan, I hope, on some slight pretext. Absurd! A person ought to finish whatever he undertakes; that is an excellent principle."

The word "principle," upon his lips, took on great significance; he used it only on important occasions, and never employed it lightly. When he used it he rolled it out with emotion, with all the weight of a prophet uttering divine commands. Coming, as it did, at the very outset of the conversation, this word increased Henry's nervousness; and the young man lowered his gaze, pulled restlessly at his beard, and began in a trembling voice, as if he had been a culprit confessing a crime: " I am afraid I shall cause you all a great deal of pain, but I have hesitated long about speaking, and now must no longer conceal the decision which I have reached, — after careful consideration, I assure you; now I see my duty clear before me; my conscience is my only guide."

Conscience — the *vita vitæ*, as the old Dutch Huguenot called it — was, for Henry, what "principles" were for his father. There was something deep, noble, free, in the word, which put firmness into his voice. He was done now with disguises and delays; and he said very seriously, " I feel compelled to give up the profession which I intended to enter. I cannot become a minister."

Madame Defos gave vent to a startled groan. David, who was about replacing his coffee-cup on its saucer, paused, as if hypnotized, in a half-stupefied way. As for Monsieur Defos, he questioned himself for a quarter of a minute as to whether or not he had heard distinctly, and then exclaimed, " Ah! Indeed! Now hear him!"

That was all. They waited for an explanation. It came slowly and with much difficulty. " And what else would you have me do? What other decision is possible for me? You can well understand that if I stop short in my plans, it is not done with a very light heart. For I have loved this profession to which I pledged my youth, and to which I wished to consecrate my life. But it is best for me to give it up. My religious faith is gone. I no longer believe anything."

Monsieur Defos strode up and down the room with long steps, followed in his movements by the anxious eyes of his wife.

" You no longer believe anything? You no

longer believe anything?" he repeated, stopping in front of Henry. "What is this you tell me? You no longer believe anything? Why, that is only because you are passing through the inevitable crisis of doubt, which comes to all young people; I passed through it myself, just as others have. Your belief will come back again, my dear, — it will come back again."

He spoke more and more reassuringly, judging the situation less seriously, the longer he looked at it; in a good-natured way he asked, "First, now, what is it that you don't believe?"

Henry had that kind of courage which, through its contempt for compromises, is apt to set forth in the clearest light the most repellent sides of truth. Influenced, also, by a wish to state his position frankly, he replied tersely, "Nothing."

The consternation which had been a little softened by Monsieur Defos's conciliatory good-nature, again took possession of all. The father of the family himself uttered an exclamation of wrath. He checked himself, and then he repeated his exclamation, evidently trying hard to control himself. "Nothing, young man? That is decidedly too little.

Nothing? Is that what you really mean? Why, you at least believe in God and in the immortality of the soul?"

As Henry made no reply, his mother advanced toward him, holding out her hands entreatingly, as if she were trying to hold him back from denying everything, and she said eagerly, " Henry, Henry, you surely will not go and become an atheist?"

Her husband quieted her. " A person does n't become an atheist in this way, from one day to another, without some reason. Why is it, Henry? What is the reason that you do not believe more? Come, now, explain to me!"

How to explain to these conventional, comfortable beings, who were as confident of the beyond as of their little snug corner in this life, as sure of eternity as of their rents! — How to explain to them the complex experience of an overturned conscience; how to make clear to them the slow, steady growth of doubt, encouraged by the diminishing resistance of the will, taking possession of the intelligence and the reason so completely that all the facts furnished by practical life seem to corroborate the doubts, — how to explain all that! However, Henry attempted the task.

Pastor Naudié's Young Wife

"One after another," said he, " I saw inspiration, dogma, and miracle crumble away.
Much disturbed, I thought that back of these
ruins the loftiest ideals would be found. In
harmony with the views of some of the most
eminent teachers, I renounced all thought of
an objective external God, as formerly held,
and gave attention to the subjective, interior
God, who is truer and purer, whose message
is higher than the old formulas, whose word
is, indeed, creative. I hoped, by thus breaking away from that superstitious past which
always inheres in religion, to raise myself to
a higher level of piety. God is swallowed
up, for me, in empty yearnings, vague hopes,
in an illusive non-Being. Religious meditation is only a sigh of the soul after an ideal,
which is beyond reach by reason of its im-
material nature. God is scattered . . . God is
hidden in a cloud. I have, however, retained
as strongly as ever my love of truth and goodness. "Whatsoever things are true," — that
is enough for me; and I look to my conscience to guide me, from day to day, amid
the obscurities of a road where my conscience
alone is left to me. I cannot deceive myself
any longer as to taking orders; my conscience
tells me that I would make a poor minister

of a God whose voice I no longer hear. It forbids me to take service in the church. My consecration and my whole life would be a continued deceit."

Monsieur Defos listened, as did also his wife and his older son; but they did not half understand. Does God exist in our hearts, or in heaven? They had never asked any such question; but the mother saw that her son suffered, and she suffered with him. As for the father, scenting peril for his family, he tried to ward it off, and as soon as possible.

"I see what the trouble is," he said, after a moment's reflection. "You have been reading Darwin, Spencer, Renan, and the other naturalists and philosophers. As if science had the final word! Moreover, there have been scientific men who were believers. Newton, and many others. And Taine! Did not he request a Protestant service at his burial? So you see the wisest and best of them could remain Christians. That is perfectly clear, is n't it? And now you come to me, and you say, 'I no longer believe anything.' You fancy that such a statement will be enough to change all the plans which I have made for your future. But it will not. No, sir! it will not. Your imagination has often played you this same kind of trick. You may make ready, now, to go in bridle. It was your own wish to study theology. I did n't force you into this profession. You freely chose it. Well, now you shall continue in it. You do not believe? Then try to believe! Give one quarter of the time to retracing your steps that you have given to advancing into this position of unbelief! That old promise has not lost its meaning, 'Seek, and ye shall find!'"

"Ah," said Henry, quietly, "how that expression has been abused!"

And then, speaking more abruptly, thinking to clear up matters by a plainer statement, he asked, "Just look at the thing candidly, father. How can I consecrate myself to a God in whom I no longer believe, a God who does not exist?"

Never, in that comfortable parlor of the olden time, never had such a speech broken upon the quiet air. David made a gesture which signified, "My brother is evidently insane." Madame Defos buried her head in her hands. Monsieur Defos stood, erect and stern and terrible, in front of his chair, and repeated the blasphemous words, "A God who does not exist! I tell you that he does exist. Listen to me! To me, your father!

I have proved his existence twenty times, a hundred times, yes, a thousand times. He does exist. He is the God of our fathers, for whom they fought; the righteous God, the mighty God, who punishes all who are unfaithful. Beware of his anger, unhappy boy, for he hears you. He is here, in this house which has kept the faith these two centuries, here where I have called upon him — I who now speak to you — in all the trying hours of my life, and often has he deigned to hear me and help me."

A little of the spirit of the old Huguenots, of those magistrates of the old heroic days, those warriors of the times of siege, when even women fought for the faith, those persecuted ones in Reformation times, who remained faithful unto death, — a little of their fervor of soul entered into the voice of this man, and gave solemnity to his position, and lent an unusual fire to his speech; for thus, often, the past still lives, deep down in hearts that have changed outwardly, and taken on the color of their age and generation.

Henry trembled. He was shaken, to the very roots of his being. Was he not also the descendant of those same heroes, of those same pastors? Was not this the faith in which he had been cradled? Was it not the faith that lived still in his blood, despite the supremacy of his reason? And at this moment it awakened within him; it uttered, in his heart, its dying lay. He tried to reply, but he could not. Overcome by his feelings, he could not restrain the sobs which rose in his throat; and, after speaking like a sage, he began now to weep like a child.

"Ah, you weep!" said Monsieur Defos. "It is well; but everything is lost. Reflect upon my words! Lift your hands toward the God whom you have denied! He will not reject you." Then he went out, to take advantage of the impression he had made upon his son.

Madame Defos came forward to her son, with lingering traces of fear, took him to her arms, with the same tenderness which she had shown him when he was a child; and he murmured, growing each moment calmer: "Oh, I am so unhappy, mother. But I cannot, cannot deceive my own conscience."

CHAPTER V

TROUBLOUS times were coming to the Defos family. Again and again the discussion, thus broken off, was brought up in some form; and from day to day the irritated feelings grew more irritable. Sometimes the exchange of a remark or two between Henry and his father served to show that each held to his position; or at other times they entered upon endless discussions, which seemed only to increase the misunderstanding. Monsieur Defos, after the heat of his first attack, had sunk back to his normal level. He argued, without much choice of arguments; and was tenacious and rigid, especially where he felt any obstacle to his will. Henry remained firm and respectful, though almost insulted, intellectually, by the weakness of his father's reasoning. For a time nothing was known in the outside world of this fissure which had yawned in the old substantial household. "Henry's doubts" were concealed from the sight of strangers, as families often conceal those maladies in their midst which move on to a fatal termination. If Monsieur Lanthelme

Pastor Naudié's Young Wife

or Monsieur Dehodecq made inquiries about the young man's studies, or about his consecration, or about "The Prophet Amos," they were put off with some deliberate falsehood, and were given to understand that everything was going well. Henry, for his part, became more taciturn than ever, more shut up within himself; and if similar inquiries were made of him, he either evaded them, or, out of regard for his family, forced himself to answer about as the others did. However, their vigilance in time relaxed. Madame Defos, who was more concerned for Henry's body than for his soul, could not refrain from confiding her anxieties to her niece. Jane at once took a lively interest in the affair; it furnished unexpected food for her fancy, which had been suffering from enforced idleness. She at once wished to know all about it, seeming to understand; and she gave him great sympathy, while she also sought to probe the affair to the bottom.

On the other hand, Monsieur Defos confided in Monsieur Naudié, whom he counted on as an ally; but he counted on him in vain. While the pastor had not the strong intellectual gifts of his father, yet he had considerable breadth of mind and, above all else, a clear conscience. He defended the right of each individual to the control of his own soul; he inveighed against the " professionalism " to which Monsieur Defos bowed blindly; he urged that there should be no invasion of the personal faith of the heart. " For a man to regulate his acts by a code of feeling which he does not really hold is nothing short of Jesuitism," he said. " It is a man's duty to act in accord with the voice of conscience, without vitiating its commands by external considerations of self-interest or expediency. For, as the apostle said, everything which is not done in agreement with a person's convictions is a sin."

The suggestion that he could possibly resemble, in any degree, the sly disciples of Monsieur Reynard, alarmed Monsieur Defos, but it did not lead him to give up his plans.

Henry never once suspected the help that was given his cause by Monsieur Naudié; he mistrusted him, and did not feel inclined to confide in him. His plan was to wait, to avoid all discussion with strangers, and to maintain toward all outsiders a reserve regarding his own affairs and those of his family. One day, however, a mere chance drew from his over-full heart its pain and anguish, so that all could see and know.

Pastor Naudié's Young Wife

It was a Sunday, at one of those dinners which the two families often held together; the dinner was at Monsieur Naudié's house. William, who had come up for the day, was present. He was in his most cynical mood; for he had escorted his sister-in-law and his nieces to church that afternoon, and had listened to one of his brother's sermons. The discourse had been a trifle abstract, revolving about that somewhat disturbing text from the first epistle to the Corinthians, "What has caused thee to differ from another? And what hast thou, that thou hast not received?" It was a sermon full of dogmatic discussion, involving the problem of free-will.

At Monsieur Naudié's house they had the custom of serving the soup before grace was said, but of leaving it untasted until that brief formula had been recited by Zelia. William had forgotten about this custom, and had begun at once to taste some of the bits of toast in his consommé.

His brother immediately called out, "Zelia!" and he stopped. All heads were bowed reverently over the steaming plates; the waiter himself, who was about to serve the Madeira, drew back and waited. The timid little voice lisped:

Pastor Naudié's Young Wife

" We thank thee, Lord, for the blessings which thou hast given us.   Amen ! "

For a few moments only the sound of spoons was heard.   William's forgetfulness, emphasizing, as it did, this little act of customary piety, threw a feeling of unusual constraint over the party.   In order to break this oppressive silence, Monsieur Defos said to Monsieur Naudié, " You gave us to-day an excellent sermon.   I especially enjoyed your reply to those who deny the freedom of the will.   You were correct in speaking as you did.   It is time to make an end of those specious theories whose consequences are hateful."

William never neglected an opportunity to " toss a stone," as he said, "into the theological garden."   Moreover, the discourse which had stirred him up, and his little blunder of a moment before, and Monsieur Defos's calm assurance, all these led him to sharply contradict. " You think it is all so simple," he remarked ; " you seem to believe that one of my good brother's sermons suffices to end the whole matter."

With a spoonful of soup in his hand, Monsieur Defos replied : " One good sermon counts for more than many evil paradoxes."

" Oh," said Monsieur Naudié, " we do not

deceive ourselves as to the value of our words. We simply speak that which we believe to be right and true. That is the seed, which falls on the various kinds of soil."

"You shake up your little bottle of truth," said William, "and you scatter it around like rain. But the liquid is changed, according to the times, according to circumstances, and you are not aware of it. The bottle is the same, with its label. As to its contents, they vary; they become spoiled, they evaporate. Never mind! You distribute it with entire confidence. Again, take this question of free-will. You settled it, Simeon, in ten minutes. Now, you are too good a student to believe that so complicated a problem can be disposed of in that brief time. To-day you defended · free-will against the attacks of the Determinists ; but yesterday did n't you argue against it ? "

"Explain !" called out Monsieur Defos.

"Certainly !" assented William. He experienced a wicked delight in teasing theologians with a display of the learning which he had gathered while attending some lectures on Chance. And he went on, in a tone of good-natured raillery : "Here, in this very city, was approved in the year 1571 the Confession of Faith, prepared a dozen years before, by the synod of Paris. Is n't that so?"

Monsieur Defos, very strong in local history, assented.

"Well, then! You can read in that document — I think it is article twenty-one — the following: 'We believe that we are enlightened in the faith by the secret grace of the Holy Spirit in such a way that it is a free and peculiar gift, which God imparts to those to whom it pleases him to give it, . . . Now, is that so?"

Monsieur Naudié, who was well acquainted with the polemical temper of his brother, was not eager to enter into a discussion which would probably be endless. Monsieur Defos knew that he had not the equipment to plunge into a debate which abounded in terms unfamiliar to him; so he preserved a discreet silence; and it was Henry's voice that broke in. He said: "This problem of free-will is the most vital of all problems, because often our other beliefs rest upon the decision which we reach in this matter. And how can it be decided in the affirmative? We are caught between the rigid texts which establish the theory of Grace, and the inexorable conclusions of Science, which teach us the inflexible chain of cause and effect, making us what we are."

Pastor Naudié's Young Wife

"Oh! Science!" interrupted Monsieur Defos.

"Science and religion," replied Henry warmly, "here find themselves in harmony; for what is this Determinism, but the scientific statement of the doctrine of predestination?"

"Good!" said William. "What is this doctrine of predestination, but the first formula, entirely instinctive, of a truth which it belongs to time to establish! And when this position is conceded, what, then, remains of the scaffolding of the other doctrines? It is a ring which falls out of the chain, and the chain is then useless; it falls at the feet of the prisoner."

"What!" cried Monsieur Defos. "Do you mean to say that we are not masters of our own actions, that I cannot do the thing which I will to do, that I cannot go out this evening, if I am inclined to, or to-morrow, if I prefer?"

"You have no power over the motives which determine your decision," said William.

With the exception of the children, who could scarcely understand, everybody listened eagerly. Jane especially noticed, with interest and sympathy, the peculiar and increasing zeal which Henry brought to the discussion. He trembled with excitement, as if each of his

words had for him personally a direct vivid
meaning, beyond its general bearing. His
slender frame vibrated with an intensity of
passion which gave to it something almost
beautiful. In the midst of this ordinary group,
among these commonplace beings, he seemed
suddenly transformed, and to furnish an illus-
tration of that higher humanity whose struggles
bring about revolutions.

He continued: " You reason correctly.
You can only arrive at the causes which bind us
to unavoidable slavery; ' my actions depend
upon my will,' you say. But your will? Some
people hold to material links of a locked chain,
which they scrutinize unceasingly. Others, if
they refer everything back to God, are simply
compelled to put into his hand the key of
their chains ; since it is he alone who awards
the gifts of the Holy Spirit, he alone who can
loose them. I hate " — here a splendid light
flashed from his eyes — " the cowards, the poltroons, the hypocrites, who discover somewhere
in space, I know not where, a sheltered spot of
exemption, where these truths do not enter.
They retreat before the pressure of evidence.
They draw back before the conclusions of their
thought. I know no greater cowardice."

With the exception of Abraham, whose fork

was in constant use, nobody went on eating, and nobody replied. William said nothing, because he saw that his own cold cynicism had been outstripped by the burning ardor of this young thinker; it had been annihilated by his passionate reasoning. Monsieur Defos was silent, because he desired that the conversation should cease before it reached such a pitch of intensity as to make itself heard throughout the town.

Monsieur Naudié, however, could not concede to such ideas as these any position of supremacy, at his table. "You have called it 'cowardice' unsoundly," he said with gentleness. "No! no! It is trust and confidence in God. There are some problems which we cannot solve; or, rather, which we must be content to solve in a practical way, in our own lives, in accordance with the dictates of our conscience. To harmonize free-will and grace? It is not my work to do it. Yet my heart is at peace. I know that I am responsible for my acts, and that I can guide my conduct and my thoughts. That is enough for me. I believe that it ought to be enough for everybody."

"I am sure it ought," remarked Monsieur Defos.

Henry now seemed inclined to retreat a little.   Perhaps he regretted having spoken so very boldly, and having disturbed the serenity of these other hearts. The dinner went on. Conversation continued, but it went lamely. Henry, who was following out silently the thread of his own reflections, scarcely heard some of the replies, whose crudity never discourages anybody, —

" . . . Then there will no longer be any criminals."

" . . . Such doctrines as those go a long way."

William, however, began to find the discussion irksome; after having demoralized the larger part of the dinner, it now seemed likely to spoil the dessert. He desired to end it. "The fact is," said he, "we are apt to believe a good deal as we wish to. Indeed, the belief of that great man our father has furnished me proof of this. Do you suppose that it has passed through all possible gradations, even through those of superstition? Let me tell you an anecdote. It will be better for us than our dogmatic discussion, and still it bears upon the subject in hand. I was very small when our father passed through one of his crises of intense mysticism ; the one which gave value to that old treatise of his on the

Pastor Naudié's Young Wife

' Miracles of the Apostles,' one which he does not much care to have read to-day. There was at that time at Montauban a good woman who healed by the laying on of hands. Now, I happened to be stung by a wasp just under the eye, and I made as much outcry as though I had been flayed alive."

Here little Zelia broke out into a laugh. Poor child! She was half perishing with desire for some kind of amusement.

" My father seized me and led me quickly away to this old healer's house. I can see her now, the old witch; with her nose like a crow's beak, her gray hair, and a little tuft of hair, like a goat's, under her chin. She took my small hands in both her own, raised her bleary eyes toward heaven, and muttered some prayers. I cried incessantly. Indeed I believe that her hypocritical ways made me cry all the more. Suddenly she announced that she was through, that I was no longer in pain, and that if I continued to cry, it was out of perversity only, and a good whipping would remedy that. Well, I howled in fine style, for I really felt pain. My father became very angry; he spoke to me in an indignant voice. I swallowed my tears as best I could, though I was suffering all the time. ' You can see that he is cured,' said the old sorceress. Cured! Oh yes! I had enough belief in miracles then and there to last me the remainder of my life. But my father seemed to accept it all."

The children were greatly amused ; and Monsieur Defos began, " But the miracle, that is another question."

However, the dinner was now finished, and all arose from the table.

Jane, whose range of interests was limited, had followed this discussion only because of her growing regard for the passionate eloquence of her cousin. Until very recently she had looked upon Henry with entire indifference, and even with a little of that hostility which she now felt toward all church affairs. The confidential talks with Madame Defos had made an impression upon her. This calm interest was now changing into a romantic curiosity, for she felt drawn by those secret sentiments of soul which had so stirred him. The coffee was served in the garden, under the wide-spreading branches of the old cedar ; and, as she sat there, she could still seem to hear the vibrant tones of his warm, earnest voice, and those strong, bold words which had taken such hold upon her. When the cups were distributed she drew near

to Henry, who sat alone and thoughtful. Soon
she adroitly managed to draw him away for a
walk in the other part of the garden. The
sound of the conversation which was going on
under the old cedar now became only a remote
murmur, broken now and then by loud laughs
at William Naudié's jokes. They exchanged
a few remarks about the beauty of the evening, and about the shadows which were deep-
ening on every side ; then they walked on in
silence among the flower-beds. The fine gravel
crackled under their feet ; the roses, before going to bed, seemed to send out their sweetest
odors upon the soft air. Presently Jane said
tenderly, " You surely are unhappy, cousin ? "

Her voice was very compassionate. And this
was the first time that Henry, in his hard trial,
had had any sympathy shown him. At Paris
his chum had left him as though he had been
a criminal ; his favorite professor had not been
able to understand him ; here his father condemned him, his brother avoided him, and
even his mother seemed to be afraid of him.
However, his reserve did not at once give way
under this first appeal. He avowed nothing
of the distress which was really in his heart,
but he was a little startled by the directness of
the question ; and he put himself somewhat

on the defensive as he replied, " Unhappy ?
How so ? "

" Oh, I understand you," said Jane. " Back
of your words I could feel the things which
you did not say; and, besides, your mother,
who has talked freely with me, has given me
an idea of matters. I am aware that you wish
to give up your profession, but your father
will not consent to it. Oh, that surely must
be very hard to bear."

Henry did not notice that she brought the
question at once to its most extreme form.
" Yes, it is most unfortunate," said he, not yet
speaking very freely ; " but others have gone
through it as well as I."

" All people have sorrows, but not all people suffer in the same degree."   .

What man, in his hours of unhappiness, can
withstand offers of sympathy from a woman ?
Almost always, sincere pity is a powerful talis-
man ; for, when women hold it out to us in
their little hands, we always take it for love.
Henry was not acquainted with either the
sweetness or the dangers of confidences. He
did not know how to keep his own counsel.
" Ah," said he, " they think that it is treason,
when it really is utter ruin. They reproach me
as if I had committed a crime, and they know

little how dearly it has cost me. Just think of it! A man puts his strength, his courage, his hope, upon a certainty, and behold, it fails him. Everything crumbles at once. Life has no aim. It stretches out before the eye, far away, dull and dreary, and must be followed to the end; but it leads to nothing. As for the busy, earnest youth of this century, this religious crisis often comes to them without their being aware of it; for it is in the very air, it is characteristic of our times. I am sure that nobody can talk any more about the 'terrors of doubt,' and no poet to-day can write the ' Faith in God.' Conscience is concerned with very different matters. But as for us, disillusioned ministers, what laceration of heart! We are like Levites who have forsaken the temple. Everybody mistrusts us and scorns us, and we have great need of help and sympathy."

With a caressing movement, Jane laid her hand on the young man's arm. " Oh," said she, " how all that does touch me and move me! *They* " — here she threw a hasty glance toward the end of the garden, where the others were talking under the old cedar, — " they are all conventional. In everything they have a ' guide-book ' inside them. The lines are straight, and run out to the edge of the paper; but you . . . but *we* . . . Oh, we are white leaves, blank pages, over which glide swift hands, making marks which are profound in their meaning, but are very difficult to decipher. See, now, how well I understand! *They* have no doubts, because they never think. They do not wish to disarrange their straight lines. They put aside, beforehand, whatever is likely to trouble them. And we . . . there are such voices that speak to us! and we listen to them. Oh, I hear them constantly, all around me. They come forth from these old mansions, from the trees, from the sea. Oh, nobody ever knows what they say to me. I believe they are the same voices that have spoken to you."

Then, in a tender and almost supplicatory tone, she added, " Oh, cousin, I wish so much to know how these voices have taken from you your early beliefs."

They walked slowly along the same path, which led up to a clump of bare lilac-bushes, hiding the wall.

" How can I explain that? " said Henry. " Certain Christians claim that faith is a gift of grace. That ought to be true. Well, grace is departed from me. My spirit has been tested; I have succumbed."

Jane repeated, "Your spirit has been tested? But when, for the first time?"

Henry searched in his memory. How could he find — so far back in the past it was — the first sign of the "Spirit that denies"? How could he trace back the long chain of reasoning, conscious or unconscious, even to that hour, so critical, so momentous, when the first doubt had entered his soul, like a flash of lightning leaping forth from heaped up masses of distant clouds."

"Truly," said he, "I am not quite sure about my memory in this matter. I do recall, however, that once I was reading Cicero's essay on the 'Nature of the Gods,' and I was struck by this idea, which had often occurred to me in my own thinking: 'If the gods do not exist, then what is the good of the temples?' That struck me as establishing a humiliating relationship between Divinity and the clergy; it seemed to place the former in dependence upon the latter; it seemed to throw a kind of troubled light upon the early human expressions of religious life. But that was a long time ago. I made ready, then, my baccalaureate address. The other idea was transitory, and soon faded out."

He paused a moment, reflecting, and then went on. "Another idea, or impression, was more recent and more lasting. It dates back, I think, five or six years. One evening, in the spring, I was reading the Gospel, in my room . . ."

His speech grew slow and hesitating. There was something connected with the memory of that reading, which he did not care to reveal to his cousin; shadowy recollections of a period when temptations of another sort shook his youthful frame, as it stood expectant before life. That time the spirit had conquered; but what feverish, visionary nights there had been!

" I had then been only a short time at Paris; I suffered much from loneliness. The reading of the Bible, and prayer, comforted me greatly. On that evening my attention was drawn to a little place which had never struck me before; it was the parable of the unfruitful fig-tree. You recall it, cousin! Jesus was coming from Bethany; he came up to a fig-tree which had only leaves on it, ' for it was not the season of figs.' And he cursed the innocent tree. Before this injustice of one who was previously all sweetness and goodness, I saw suddenly open up a long vista of divine injustices, from the beginning of history down. There was God rejecting Cain's offering, and condemning him to become the most hated of men, Abraham driving Hagar and Ishmael into the wilderness of Beer-sheba, Isaac blessed because of his shameless deceits, and so on,— so many, many of them! At that hour, also, light broke through; it has changed the color of heaven. Since then lessons, readings, meditations have seemed only to dethrone in my mind the personal God of my childhood. I tried to free him from all base alloy, such as had attached to him by the superstitions and the visions of the prophets. I tried to worship him in spirit and in truth, as our instructors wished; but a day came when I could not . . . well, I could not any longer . . . find him. I hardly know any better way than that in which to express my idea. He faded from my life. I had given to my reason the right to discuss everything. How could I forbid it going to the very end? Between the criticism of science and that of history, what could faith avail, when grace no longer sustained me?"

Over across, under the old cedar, the remote voices had become faint. The odor of the roses was wafted from dainty chalices, as if to anoint the new-born evening. A gentle breeze, coming from afar, mingled with these delicious odors a breath of the sea. The lights of those strange worlds which are strewn through space illumined all corners of the heavens, as if a mysterious hand had traced once more upon the firmament those indecipherable hieroglyphics which another morn would blot out. No word could banish, from his true realm, the Divine, which filled the heavens,—a surer abode than are human hearts,—riding upon the wings of the wind, murmuring in the storms, glowing in the stars. And, within these two souls, drawing every moment nearer each other, were born faint intimations, sparkling yet uncertain, transient, deceptive emotions. Henry was glad of this solitude, which was now shared with another, and was perhaps also glad because in his pride he had spoken out bold words regarding life and destiny. As for Jane, she much desired to know more, and to follow, as closely as possible, the spectacle of this soul passing through storm and stress.

After a long silence, she said, lowering her voice even more than before, " I would like to read the books which you have read."

" No!" answered Henry. " Forget as quickly as possible what I have been saying to you! Why disturb the peace of your soul? I wish nobody to experience such pain as mine has been."

She repeated, " Tell me in what books these ideas may be found!"

Pastor Naudié's Young Wife

"Ah," exclaimed Henry, "books are only echoes, which bring to us nothing new, nothing but the sound of our own voices, the reinforcement of our own thought. If you really hold to your wish, read some of the works of your father-in-law, Abraham Naudié!"

"His works?" exclaimed Jane. "Why, he is a believer!"

"He is not of that class of believers who neither write nor think, but who suffer and pray. That man is a noble spirit. He has completed the whole voyage, and in his old age he comes again to his point of departure. I admire him. But I am far from being able to sail over the course which he has sailed. In short, I do not at all believe in his faith; it reasons too much; it is an illusion which he himself gives to himself."

At this moment, the gravel on the path behind them crackled; William had come to look them up. "Aha!" he called out facetiously, "what are you doing there? Talking theology?"

With that mobility of nature which women so often show, Jane at once replied gayly, "Oh yes! It is extremely amusing."

Henry did not catch this word "amusing," which fluttered so lightly from the young woman's lips. Even if he had heard it, would it have enlightened him much? He felt, as so many did, the fascination of this beautiful creature; her angelic eyes, her soft low voice, and all that charm which radiated from her presence, which seem to wing its way out into the world from a tender sympathetic heart. At each moment, if her words inclined to dispel the illusion, her actions served to bring it back; and even when one received a direct blow to his feelings, he took it without quite understanding it, or even daring to understand it.

Her dryness of soul, her egotism, her hardness of heart, had long been manifest; it showed plainly in her readiness to be free from the children committed to her care, and especially in the savage animosity with which she pursued little Zelia; a hatred altogether inexplicable was hidden far down in the obscure corners of her heart, where burned evil passions. Monsieur Naudié did not wish to see or understand it. If he had at first given his little ones a place in his dreams of the coming happiness, he now had become drawn into the toils of his own personal passion, and no longer had eyes or ears for anybody but her. The best that he could do was to

Pastor Naudié's Young Wife

conceal as far as possible from intruding eyes
the ravages of his own heart. And, bound
fast in the shameful slavery of his passion, he
never interfered from day to day in the quarrels
which constantly arose between his wife and his
children. The first time that Bertha or Zelia,
flaming with anger, and confident of the justice of their cause, came to him to seek redress,
" Papa, do you think . . .", he interrupted
them admonishingly : " It is best to obey, my
dears. It is best to obey her as if she were your
mother, or as you would obey me. All this
which she tells you is for your good . . . "

They beat a retreat, with wide-open eyes,
which expressed their surprise, their indignation, their despair. Justice vanished, they perceived that they were doubly orphans; they
ran away to weep in Esther's arms, who could
only comfort them in silence, and suffer with
them.

One Friday — the day set apart by Monsieur
Naudié for the preparation of his sermon —
he chose his text from the Epistle to the
Romans : "*I delight in the law of God after the
inward man. But I see another law in my members, warring against the law of my mind, and
bringing me into captivity to the law of sin which
is in my members.*"

Pastor Naudié's Young Wife

A multitude of thoughts crowded confusedly into his agitated heart; not only those which he could proclaim plainly from the pulpit, thoughts which were in harmony with the ideas and customs of the time and the public mind, but others, others more subtle and penetrating, which applied to his own situation. Guided by the inexorable Apostle, he entered into the secret chambers of his own soul, whose closed doors so often refused to open. There, in his soul, he read, instead of such grand abstract reflections as his text ought to have aroused, a poem of despair, much more like the songs of the Sulamite woman's royal lover than like the lessons of Paul of Tarsus; a poem of desire and grief, a poem of love and anguish. Like to the weary hart of the Psalmist, he thirsted for the living God, and no longer found him in his path of life. In hours when his thought ought to have borne him aloft to heaven, it threw him heavily down upon the earth, — upon the earth, where dwelt one only creature, whom he loved to idolatry, loved with a boundless unreasonable passion, with a passion of the flesh and blood. Thus triumphed in him "the law of sin." And his eyes remained fixed upon the block of white paper, placed there to receive edifying thoughts.

Pastor Naudié's Young Wife

Suddenly cries aroused him,—doubtless one of those frequent quarrels which he was careful not to meddle with. He waited. The noise did not diminish. In the confused sounds which reached him he distinguished the excited voice of Esther; his heart was smitten with anguish. How could he overlook this affair, if even she had become involved in it!

He hastened away toward the scene of the strife. One of the maids was listening with some curiosity. She disappeared as he approached. Zelia was sobbing in the arms of Bertha, who stood holding her in a pose worthy of Niobe. Jane and Esther stood facing each other, with hatred in their eyes and threats upon their lips. With a simultaneous movement they turned toward him, and Esther, panting, exclaimed: " Papa, she struck her, she struck Zelia; and with no reason for it, none whatever. She . . .."

Here Jane interrupted, with considerable anger, " Oh, for nothing? "

Then their two voices mingled in a confusion of angry complaints, each reciting a list of accumulated grievances, when open war had been avoided by only the slightest barrier. So far as this present affair was concerned, Monsieur Naudié had not grasped the details of their contradictory statements; for their two lists of grievances seemed to contradict each other.

"Father, you ought to protect us. It is time . . ."

"You will have to do what is right, I warrant."

Then he tried to speak to them gently, with calm voice, hoping to pacify them. "I have not yet understood just what your difference is. I am sure it is not a very serious thing; better than to excite yourselves more by rehearsing it, you would do better to forget it. It takes two to make a quarrel . . ."

A double cry of protest broke in upon his words. "Well, then, she is the one who is most in the wrong, and she does not forgive."

"How do you suppose I can judge between you? All that I care to know is, that you are my life and my blood, and that I love you both, and I would have you love each other also. I know that much, and I would be glad to ignore all the rest."

"Coward!" exclaimed Jane; and, turning again toward Esther, she was about to go on with her quarrel. But Esther had gained control of herself; she turned away, with scorn upon her lips. Jane, who was raging still, turned once more toward her husband. "Ah,

Pastor Naudié's Young Wife

I know well that you are on their side, against me. I thought so. All right, keep there! keep there!" And she rushed away like a whirlwind.

Five minutes later, Monsieur Naudié was begging her pardon, and comforting her with tender words; for, as soon as her anger ceased, she fell to weeping; and, to dry her tears, he promised her that in future he would be stricter with his daughters and would punish them; he promised all, everything that she asked. He belonged to her, soul and body; a great tumult of emotion made him forget all except her.

PART THIRD

CHAPTER I

ON a beautiful October afternoon, clear and balmy, Henry Defos went out, for the first time, into the garden, which was an enclosure much resembling the Naudié garden. It extended from the porch of the house to the wall, covered with its screen of vines; it had its old cedar-tree, its magnolia, and its oleander bushes. It adjoined other similar gardens, which continued the line of the fortifications and that of the houses. All was regular and quiet, much resembling the comfortable habits of the families themselves, who met beneath their shade or gathered their beautiful flowers.

Henry Defos was recovering from a long illness. The fatigue of revolving, for so long a time, within the circle of theological thought, and the excitement of carrying on a struggle against his father's will had exhausted his own more delicate nature; the pressure of all these emotions had drained his vitality, and prepared him for an attack of typhoid fever, which had, however, not been fatal. Coming out again into the balmy air of autumn, with the flowers still blooming, he experienced that tenderness of feeling which always attends convalescence. The faces about him were friendly, and seemed very dear to him, after passing through that period when all of them had expressed coldness or anger. At this time he was walking, with the feeble step of an infant, leaning upon his mother's arm ; and Madame Defos's bulky form lent a very substantial support.

At his other side was another attendant, who gave him many encouraging smiles, such as you often see on the faces of young mothers. It was Jane. She had seized the occasion of Henry's illness to give full play to that faculty of zealous devotion which burned within her ; she had been unwearied in her efforts, ceaseless in her attendance at his bedside, buoyed up by courage and faith that was almost sublime. The one word which all the family used, to express her conduct, was " admirable." This word of commendation circulated freely in the town, attached to her name like a Homeric title. It was repeated by the friends who came to learn the news, and by the gossips, who found in Henry's illness a pleasant theme of conversation. Twenty times a day it was repeated, "Young Madame Naudié is truly admirable."

When Monsieur Fridolin, or Monsieur Dehodecq, or some other person encountered Monsieur Naudié on the street, and inquired about the sick man, he always ended by remarking, "Your wife is admirable."

And Monsieur Naudié responded, "Yes, she is truly admirable." But his own personal love for her was wounded and bleeding, although he dared not complain; and he envied the happiness of the invalid, and reflected sometimes, with a tender sadness, "Ah, if I were in his place . . ."

Monsieur Defos, with an affectionate manner, slowly came across the garden. "There, now! The whole distance! Well done, my boy!"

"Not yet very strong, father!"

"Pooh! at your age you will quickly build up. I had the typhoid fever myself, when I was a young man; and at the end of a month there was no sign of it."

David appeared above them on the porch, and called out, a little facetiously, "They say that you are learning all over again how to walk, Henry."

Pastor Naudié's Young Wife

It was now about time for the two men to be at the office, so they did not linger any longer with the convalescent. Henry was soon fatigued with his effort, and sat down in a large wicker chair. Jane was all attention, and hastened to spread her own shawl over his knees; but he protested, with a quick, kindly gesture. "Be careful, cousin!" said he; "you will take cold yourself."

She shrugged her shoulders. "Cold? On such a day as this?"

He looked at her gratefully, holding the shawl in his thin hand, and shivering slightly. "How good you are to me!" he said. "You have given me your strength, your time, even a part of your life. If I am once more able to enjoy this beautiful autumn sunshine, it is to you I owe it, and to my dear mother. Oh, do not try to contradict me, mamma! I know how ill I have been."

After a brief silence he added, with a half-suppressed sigh of regret, "Now, cousin, you can go and be free again."

"Oh!" exclaimed Jane, "not until you are well. However, perhaps you would like to be rid of me." She smiled the mischievous smile of a pretty woman who knows well that her presence is very acceptable.

Henry did not reply in the protesting way which she perhaps expected. Then Madame Defos said, " Jane is an angel. I never believed that she could be so devoted, especially since she is not very strong. She is small and delicate, much like a bird; but when I, your mother, sank from fatigue, she kept up, as strong after two nights of watching as though she had just gotten up from her bed."

" Ah ! " said Henry, " sickness does some good. For a person is loved more when he is suffering, when he seems to be at the gates of death. Afterward the ordinary life claims its rights. The quarrels and cares which have been broken in upon for a while, commence again. The misunderstandings and enmities have to be taken up anew . . ."

His brow clouded, already troubled by his old reflections, here in the sweet enjoyment of the sunshine, and the garden, and the flowers, with these loving, comforting hearts beside him. But Jane spoke : " Never mind, cousin ! Your father will not annoy you any more. He promised me that, while you were very ill. I suspected the real cause of your sickness; and I took advantage of one of your worst days to obtain from your father his promise to let you do as you wish. He will not change his mind."

Pastor Naudié's Young Wife

The sick man's eyes opened wide. " Is that really so ? " he asked.

" Henry," said Madame Defos, " your father loves you more than you realize ; and if you still retain those ideas of yours, he will not oppose you."

In the common joy which all three shared at that moment, Madame Defos regretted, a little, having allowed her niece to break this cheering news to the invalid. She, however, never would have dared ask her husband to alter a decision which he had once made, nor would she have ventured to hope for such a change. The only power that could have worked the miracle was Jane's hardihood, her quick instinct for seizing the favorable moment, her self-confidence, and that indifference to all obstacles which usually brought her success in her plans.

At this moment Monsieur Naudié came into the garden. He often appeared in this way, partly to take the air, and partly to see his wife ; he longed to get her attention, slight as it always was, and was grateful for a word or a look. But she generally ignored him. For several weeks she had passed the greater part of her time at Monsieur Defos's house, often eating and sleeping there. Sometimes she went back home, in the evening, shut herself in her own room, and in the morning came away to resume her duties at the sick man's bedside. So far as her own home was concerned, she was like a stranger, lodging in a hotel. Her husband had thus far not dared to make any complaint. He tried to hope for some happier change, but, in his heart, knew that no such change would come.

Monsieur Naudié's dark form, descending the steps of the porch, disturbed somewhat this little scene. He was clad in his long black coat, with a narrow white tie, badly adjusted, around his neck. He had a restless manner and a sad expression of countenance; and he came up like some remote relative, uninvited, dropping down into the midst of a family party. Henry extended his hand; which Monsieur Naudié took, and said, in rather a depressing way: " What a pleasure to see you again out in the garden, my dear Henry! You seem to be getting on very well indeed. In a few days you will be quite yourself again."

" You see to whom I owe it all," said the convalescent, glancing from one to the other of his two attendants.

Monsieur Naudié noted that his first glance went toward Jane.

"And I owe you a great deal," he continued. "Yes, I do; because you have been very kind to let Jane come to me so much."

Then he added, and his voice wavered a little, "Now we shall be able to return her to you."

A flash of joy irradiated Monsieur Naudié's face as he said at once: "I have just come to invite her to dinner to-day. It is now as much as a month since we had her sit down to a meal with us. This will be almost like having her back from a distant journey. You will come, Jane, will you not?"

"Oh, certainly! If you wish it." There was so little spontaneity in this reply that all four members of the group looked at one another and remained silent, as if each were stopped by some hidden train of thought.

Henry was the first to regain his composure. "We shall miss Jane very much, this evening," he said, "because we have fallen into the agreeable habit of seeing her with us; but you have been without her a long time, my dear cousin. Each must take his turn."

While he was thus speaking, trying to conceal the regret which was behind his words, his mother looked straight toward Monsieur Naudié, and her glance was black with hatred, much like that of some wild beast ready for attack. "Jane is now a veritable daughter to us," she remarked.

And then, as if to deepen the antagonism which lurked in her remark, she repeated, "She is one of our family, you know; we love her like a daughter."

As she spoke, Madame Defos stood erect, with head thrown back, and seemed to indicate to Monsieur Naudié that Jane belonged to him just as little as possible, and that, after all, she could very easily be taken away from him.

He perceived her meaning, and, with his feelings hurt, turned to her and said: "For that very reason, my dear madame, I shall be deeply grateful to you for allowing her to come to me even one evening, — to me; and I am, you know, only her husband." Then, having shaken hands with them, he departed, leaving Madame Defos somewhat out of countenance, Henry anxious, and Jane annoyed.

Jane kept her word, but made them wait.

With the thoughtlessness of childhood, the children, when they saw less of her, took for granted that they would never again be troubled with her presence. When it was announced to them, as a joyful piece of news, that she was coming back, they learned their error in thinking she would not come again. Esther followed her father's nervous, anxious look, as he walked again and again around the dinner-table, and glanced expectantly at the door. The other three whispered together in a corner, suppressing their voices as if by instinct. Then Zelia's merry laugh burst out like a pistol-shot, — the clear, happy laughter of childhood, the laugh of other days. But she stopped short, the door opened, there stood Jane. "Ah, you are waiting for me!" she said, "you are very kind."

The nervous impatience and annoyance which Monsieur Naudié had shown, as he waited, took instant flight; and, kissing her upon the forehead, he said to her, in a low tone and without any accent of reproach, "Yes, I have waited for you . . . waited a long time."

They sat down at the table. Monsieur Naudié tried to start a conversation. Jane replied only absent-mindedly. Her thoughts seemed to be far away, — so much so, that the children, little by little, began talking among themselves; very much as though this stranger, who was eating at their table, had ceased to be interested in them. The meal seemed long. When it was finally ended, the children scampered away, and Monsieur Naudié and his wife went into the little parlor. With nothing to occupy her, Jane stretched herself out in an armchair. Her husband approached her.

"Are you tired?" he asked.

"Tired? No, not at all!"

"You seemed weary and sad at dinner."

"What an idea!"

She arose and went to a little table, with drawers in it. From one of them she drew out a bit of fancy-work, left there several weeks before. This she brought to the centre-table, spread it out under the light of the lamp, and began to examine it attentively.

Monsieur Naudié took a seat near her; again he tried to draw her into conversation; but she had resolved to keep silence, as if to show how unconcerned she was. Repulsed in these attempts, and nervous but still patient, and resolved to fortify himself against any temptation to be angry, he began cutting open a package of papers which he found near at hand. It was the "Journal of French Missions," and he tried to glance through one or two articles.

"What!" he remarked. "Here is a letter

from Lessanto; that is where my brother Marcel is, but it does n't say anything about him."

"Ah! . . ."

"Poor Marcel! He went back a short time before we were married. I wish that you could have met him. Heaven alone knows when we shall meet again. He especially desired to be with us on that blessed day. Do you ever recall it, Jane?"

"Certainly!"

"What a beautiful address my father gave! Do you remember it?"

"Of course!"

"How wisely he spoke about the mystery of love! Do you remember his words, Jane? 'Love, sanctified by marriage, makes of the two beings whom it unites one being, new and unique. It is a part of eternity disclosed to us. For love satisfies us only as we see that it is capable of outlasting our transient emotions, just as it survives, in passing into youth and beauty.' Those were noble words, Jane. Don't you approve them? They explain to us our ideal."

Jane bent her head over her work, and silence ensued, broken only by the light sound of the silk in the canvas. Monsieur Naudié, by a great effort, restrained the annoyance and anger which were rising in his breast, took down a huge book from a shelf,—a missionary work, by Coillard, "Upon the Upper Zambesi," and, finding his place in it, began skimming along through its pages. He turned the leaves mechanically, glancing at the paragraphs here and there. Presently he chanced upon a striking scene ; the death of Madame Coillard, in one of the remote villages of the black continent, where she had gone with her husband. He read : "She has lived, and worked, and suffered, as have few of the missionaries' wives. The Lord has taken her, and taken her tenderly. For more than thirty years she has identified her life with mine ; and has been, next to my Saviour and my God, my strength and shield. She was the heart and soul of all my plans. In sharing my life, she has heightened my joys, softened my griefs, borne her part in all my labors, through good and ill report, modest and humble, always effacing herself, with an unequalled devotion. In losing her I have lost a true wife, one that I had received at the hands of God. I could always rely upon her judgment and her wisdom. When we were first married, she told me that I would never find her standing between me

Pastor Naudié's Young Wife

and my duty. And she spoke truly. When God called me to this remote end of the world, she came with me joyously, without thinking about her own wishes or comforts."

For a moment he fell into a revery over this beautiful description of a Christian marriage. "That is the way to love," he said to himself. "Sinking one's own will in the will of God, always ready for whatever he asks. But I . . . and . . . she . . ." Here his gaze wandered to his wife; and he saw upon her lips a smile, elusive, fleeting, enigmatical. It occurred to him to read aloud to her this page which had so stirred him; but he shook his head and closed the book; she would not understand it at all. There she sat, before him, pretty, silent, mysterious; a dainty being, full of caprices and changes, whom he was constrained to love for her own sake, and his own, with a boundless love; a being who was angry with him for his timidity and constraint, but one whom he could not bear to lose, having once possessed her.

Why did she scarcely speak to him? Why did she barely glance at him? Why did she avoid him? And why sit there, a few steps away, more remote from him than she would have been had that table been a wide, impassable sea?

Pastor Naudié's Young Wife

Upon the mantel a little Louis XVI. clock, in a voice like tinkling crystals, struck the hour of ten. Jane went steadily on with her work, and, raising her eyes, met her husband's gaze. "Jane," said Monsieur Naudié, moving over toward her, "are you going to shut yourself in your room again to-night?"

She made no verbal answer, but nodded her head in the affirmative. Then he spoke, in a voice of entreaty, "Even to-day?"

"Yes, even to-day."

The harsh way in which she spoke that word "to-day" showed clearly that she was fixed in her resolution. With a manner which was almost threatening, Monsieur Naudié came close to her, and cried, "Jane, what do you mean by this?"

She made no response, but looked straight at him. Then, for the first time, a touch of suspicion and jealousy smote his heart. Instantly and instinctively he braced himself to throw off the evil suggestion, so utterly did he recoil from such odious thoughts. His action had brought him quite close to Jane, who did not draw away from him. With an impulsive movement he drew her to his heart and kissed her lips. She showed no traces of emotion, made no effort to avoid the caress, neither to return it; her passivity was a completer repulse to him than any active protest would have been.

"Jane," he exclaimed, stepping back a few paces, "are you not my wife?"

With entire unconcern she replied, "Oh, yes, I am your wife." Then she walked past him toward the door. "You are a little nervous. Good night!" And she was gone, and Monsieur Naudié sat him down and wept.

CHAPTER II

HENRY DEFOS'S recovery was continuous and beautiful. Around him were tender friends, and their affectionate glances were showered upon him, and, in his sickness and need, their hearts opened lovingly to him. His mother showed a lingering trace of solicitude, and she heaped upon him all the warmth of her nature, which contrasted strongly with the coldness and indifference which she showed toward all the others. His brother took a friendly interest in him. His father, who was not a man to waste himself in vain regrets, accepted the situation, took for granted that his second son was not to become a minister, and planned to make a place for him in his business, whose steady growth demanded, constantly, new methods. But Henry was in no hurry to begin work. Wooed by the balmy days of the beautiful autumn, he gave himself up to the joy of this new awakening life within him, and his soul sought those hidden joys which sleep at the heart of things. Thus it was that, with Jane near him, devoting all her time to him, he experienced exquisite hours of self-abandonment, far from the world, here in this beautiful garden, with its winding paths, and its rustling falling leaves, and its rugged old cedar. When the doctor advised exercise, they went out; and you might have happened upon them on the mall, or met them strolling along the rocky seashore, where the fishermen, in idle hours, dig for shell-fish, after the tide has gone far out beyond the crumbling ruins of the great Cardinal's dyke. Often they ventured to go out together for a ride; and could be seen cantering along the rather dismal country roads, where the strong west wind lays low the harvests, and twists the young saplings, while the gray sea rolls in over the marshes.

Their near relationship, Jane's well-known English training, and Henry's reputation for seriousness of character,—these things tended to silence any gossip which otherwise might have arisen. Nevertheless, as they rode through the old streets, looks of surprise sometimes followed them; and, as they passed, various remarks dropped from the bystanders. "An Amazon! Who is she, now?"

"Pastor Naudié's wife. She is with her cousin, young Defos."

"The one who started to become a minister, and gave it up?"

" Exactly ! "

They usually stopped there. Henry and Jane knew nothing of these comments. With smiles they replied to Monsieur Lanthelme's cynical greeting, or to the elaborate salute offered by Monsieur Fridolin; and they cared little what echoes in unfriendly hearts might be raised by the clatter of their horses' feet on the pavement. They were happy, and they cared for naught else. Although they may have felt now and then a passing doubt, yet the increasing intensity of their growing passion blinded them to their own situation, and to the opinions of the outside world.

In the course of their long rides, their conversation often became serious and confidential; and Henry's earnest methods of thought seemed really to make an impression upon Jane's frivolous little mind. She always gave him to understand that she saw his meaning. At first she had been alarmed by his atheism; but she soon grew used to it, and accepted it, vaguely willing that he should be condemned if she could be condemned with him. Besides, there were other considerations which helped reconcile her to his views : one was the mischievous desire to annoy her husband; another was her vanity over her own daring, in thus overstepping all the old bounds of her thought. She had a vague idea that in accepting his point of view, she was freeing herself from all the old pledges, and was cutting off, at one blow, all the moral restraints of society. This last-named line of thought she worked out quite by herself, according to the law of secrecy which dominated her nature and rarely came out into the light. Henry was really far removed from a nature like hers. He had, essentially, the soul of an apostle; and in giving up his old theological views, he had relinquished not an iota of his high idealism of conduct. The serious words which fell from time to time from his pretty cousin's lips, caused him some uneasiness; with a woman's logic, she under-mined foundations which Henry never thought of touching. At a certain point he always stopped, forcing himself to give up his destruc-tive processes, and attempting to make repairs. He talked about "a fixed mysterious power," which pushes humanity on toward a higher and higher ideal; he recognized the weight of usage and the authority of the already estab-lished code of morality; he took account of those accumulated traditions which are closely intertwined with the conditions of present prog-ress. Thus, while he gave up his old dogmatic system of theology, he preserved the scaffolding which had surrounded it; but Jane, finding it difficult to understand, threw it bodily away.

Meanwhile, Monsieur Naudié suffered in silence, now that his wife had gone out of his life. He did not see the exact state of affairs; he knew only that each day she seemed to draw farther away from him, each day become more indifferent to his presence. He could not divine what was going on in her heart; the chief point, to him, was that she was neglecting her duty, was disregarding all the obligations which her marriage had laid upon her. There were her duties toward the children, her duties as wife of a minister, and her duties as the possessor of a large fortune. Now, in the life of a conscientious Protestant, duty takes precedence of everything else; it is the motive power and the regulative power. That a person should disregard the voice of duty, and be careless about all obligations, small or great, — this indicates, always, a serious disturbance of mental and moral health. Jane's cool disdain simply threw a cloud over the timid bursts of passion which Monsieur Naudié exhibited at times; but when he reflected upon her neglect of duty, he felt that he must take some positive action; and he ventured to remonstrate with her. His manner of addressing her showed clearly the chaos of his affectionate, wounded heart; he spoke to her merely about certain concrete duties, — as, for instance, her attendance at public worship, or her visitations of the poor and sick, or her care of the house. And all these Jane put at once away from her, without giving them a moment's thought.

"Jane, are you going out to walk? Have you, then, forgotten that this afternoon there is a meeting of the Charitable Society?"

"I am aware of it; but I am not going."

"Why not?"

"It's too fine a day."

Or, again, it would be like this: "Jane, aren't you going with me to see that poor widow whose husband was lost at sea?"

"Not to-day. I can't to-day."

Or, at still another time, "I have just been talking with the master of the academy, and he is full of complaints about Abraham. How much that child needs careful, affectionate oversight!"

"It seems to me that you or Esther would better attend to that."

In reality, these were not the things which

most tormented Monsieur Naudié. Under these mild complaints lurked far stormier thoughts. He struggled to control them; but the slightest incident might suffice to turn them loose.

On a certain Sunday, when heavy dense clouds hung over the sky, he had come back from preaching at Marcilly. He had made the journey on foot, as in the olden time. The long walk across the country, where the wind cut into his face, had not much served to quiet his feelings; he took up again the burden of his home cares about where he had laid it down on his departure. As he strode along, with bowed head, through the Place d'Armes, he met Monsieur Merlin, who stopped him.

Monsieur Merlin, for some little time past, had been declaring himself the advocate of complete rest on Sunday. He argued for man's moral and physical needs, in various pamphlets which he carried stuffed into his overcoat pockets. He now drew out one of these packages, to offer it to his minister. In addition, he opened one of them, and was indicating, with his finger, a certain important sentence, when a noise drew his attention. He turned, and saw Henry and Jane out for a walk, and just passing; keeping step with each other as they walked briskly along.

Monsieur Naudié raised his eyes and greeted them, trying also to smile. Monsieur Merlin raised his hat and made them an expansive salutation. For a moment the two men stood and followed the young couple with their eyes, as they turned at the corner of the Place d'Armes, and passed along — keeping very closely together — in front of the massive classic façade of the cathedral. Monsieur Naudié repressed a sigh. Then, as he glanced at his companion, he saw that the notary's countenance was agitated; and, behind those bluish glasses which concealed his eyes, Monsieur Naudié felt sure that his secret was discovered; he felt sure that Monsieur Merlin had divined what tormenting suspicions he held deep in his heart; and as he stood there he grew pale and trembled.

Monsieur Merlin closed his book. They both turned at the same moment, and the notary remarked, "Young Defos is about well again?" And his sharp eyes seemed to pierce the blue tint of his spectacles.

"Oh, yes; thank Heaven!" replied Monsieur Naudié.

"I am told that he has given up his studies."

" Yes, he has."

" Doubtless, to remain at La Rochelle ? "

Monsieur Naudié replied, with a rather weak voice, " Yes, I believe so. He is going into business with his father."

" Ah ! . . ."

With this exclamation, more suggestive than all the immoral literature so familiar to Monsieur Merlin, the two men separated. But Monsieur Naudié, instead of returning to his house, walked out to saunter near the harbor. The boats were putting in, driven by the threatening sky. Many of them were already quietly moored within the calm basin, crowded closely together, their bare masts looking like a leafless forest. They had been warned by signals from the shore, had hurried in before the wind, and now rocked idly upon the water ; while outside, the open sea began to toss and lash itself into a fury. Their crews were lounging around the public house, playing at " bottles," drinking up the little silver for which they had risked their lives. Several women, near, seemed restless because of some craft which had not yet put in ; and, at one moment, anxiously questioned the sailors, or, at another, strained their gaze out over the rising sea, whose waves seemed clamorous for prey. Monsieur Naudié wandered about among the groups, with bitter care gnawing at his heart, with his spirit tossing on as wild a storm as the one which was perhaps now swallowing up husbands and brothers on the great deep. Much as these poor women strained their eyes, seeking to penetrate the thick obscurity that hung over the sea, so did his own gaze search through the clouded depths of his own breast; and the wayward flight of his own wild thoughts was like that of the flocks of birds which came sweeping wildly in, driven before the fury of the tempest. He passed, without noticing him, his son Abraham, who was playing with some ragamuffins. He returned home, finally, he hardly knew by what streets. And he had the strength, still, to keep his own counsels, and to reply pleasantly to his daughters as they greeted him. He was able, also, to let his glance fall quietly on the beautiful face of his wife, crowding back into the depths of his heart, as a master might bolt and bar some slave into a dungeon, the wild suggestions which had been aroused by Monsieur Merlin's evil words.

The next morning, however, the first cry of anguish burst from him.

At the hour of the daily ride with Henry, Jane was ready and waiting. She was evidently impatient to be off, and her horse was pawing restlessly in the courtyard. With one hand she held the skirt of her dress, and with the other she cracked her whip, not caring whether or not she revealed her impatience to her husband, who stood, unnoticed, near. The hour came and passed. Her whip cracked more restlessly. Monsieur Naudié remarked, without betraying his feelings in his voice, "Your friend is keeping you waiting to-day?"

The restless whip cracked once or twice against the innocent air. "A little, that is so."

"You have been waiting since half-past three; there is four o'clock striking now. Perhaps he will not come."

Jane's eyes gave her only reply. Monsieur Naudié understood their silent answer. She was quivering with tender vexation against Henry, and with hate for him, her husband. With a touch of cruelty he remarked unconcernedly, "Doubtless he had some engagement, at the last moment."

Jane looked at him a second time, and her glance expressed a hatred even greater than before. "He will be here," she said, "I am sure."

She paused a moment directly before her husband, then resumed her restless walk. Her spurs jingled on the flagstones. In an altered voice Monsieur Naudié said, "Jane!"

"Yes."

"Don't go out! Don't go out, I beg you."

Again she stopped, in front of him. "Why not?"

He could only repeat his entreaty: "Give up this ride! For to-day, at least. To please me."

Although his tone was more one of entreaty than of threatening, Jane grew uneasy for the first time. With that rapidity of adaptation which women often show, she became at once apparently calm, and replied in a tranquil, innocent way, "To please you, my friend? Why, I don't understand you."

Monsieur Naudié had now lifted away the weight which was crushing him into silence. Behind the first sentence, which was too difficult of utterance, others rose into view, like the waves behind the line of foam which dies out upon the beach.

"Oh, there! You . . . you do surely understand. I know that you must. Don't force me to explain! You can read my thought. I hardly dare utter it. Oh, I am sure that we understand each other; that we are going to understand each other better, in the future. I don't doubt that; I cannot doubt it. But . . . but why do you thus withdraw from me, after . . . after you have given . . . Oh, don't you see how I suffer, even unto death, at seeing you avoid me so, and always seeking the society of another?"

Did Jane feel pity, for an instant, as she saw his anguish, or was she simply artful? She seemed to wait with interest and even sympathy. "My poor friend," she said, glancing at him tenderly, "what foolish fancies do fill your head! How strange they seem to me, coming from such a serious, sensible man as you are! Just see how simple the whole matter is! I need a little variety, a little exercise; Henry does also. There! We ride out together. You are not able to go with us, is n't that so? Think of it! A clergyman on a horse! What would people say?"

She reasoned in such a serious way, with such convincing words and tones, that Monsieur Naudié lost countenance. He began to feel that perhaps, after all, his suspicions were ill-founded and absurd. He reflected a moment, and then replied, with some hope and yet with hesitancy: "I have asked nothing of you heretofore, Jane. I have never been able to tell you how much I love you, and you have not realized it. Now, I beg you, make this one little sacrifice for my sake! Give up this ride to-day! Just to-day! Just this once! It is only a little thing, but it will help to restore my confidence; and I shall be very, very grateful to you."

All his youthfulness, all his simple honesty of heart, could be felt in this pathetic entreaty.

Quickly, very quickly, with her instinct for intrigue aroused within her at any sign of danger, Jane reflected upon the great gain she would make for herself by this slight concession, and the harm which might result to her plans if she refused; moreover, time was passing, and Henry, perhaps, would not come. She forced a smile into her face. " There, there, my good friend!" she said. " Since you make such a serious matter . . ."

The sound of a horse, trotting rapidly, interrupted her, and Henry came riding into the courtyard. She went out, with Monsieur Naudié, to meet him. He excused himself. She felt that he would be greatly disappointed, and, perhaps, he would think she had been offended at his delay; whereas she had already pardoned him, in her heart. The trifling annoyance of the man whom she loved seemed to her, at that moment, a thousand-fold more important than did the anguish of her husband; and her one wish was to relieve Henry of his uneasiness. She turned toward her husband. "You see, he has come," she said, and she made an attempt to conceal her joy. "How can I send him away! And I am all ready, too. It is impossible, is n't it? Some other day, to-morrow . . ."

And she leaped lightly into her saddle, smiled upon poor Monsieur Naudié, waved him a farewell, and the two rode away.

CHAPTER III

WHEN Jane waved a farewell to her husband with her riding-whip and smiled upon him, she had also promised — was it out of prudence or pity? — that on the morrow she would make the slight sacrifice which he asked. But the ride was delightful, and had to-day a spice of daring in it; there was, also, a suggestion of romance and melancholy in this closing season of the year. During the night a squall had stripped the elms, on the mall, of their remaining leaves. Along the highway the slender trees raised their bare dry branches imploringly toward the sky. The heavens frowned, and a sharp chill in the air portended the near approach of winter. Nature seemed to reflect the sadness which was in these two hearts; the end was approaching.

Henry spoke, without looking at Jane. "We must give up these pleasant excursions before long; winter is almost here. Besides, I am about well again; and my father expects me to set about my work."

He sighed. Jane made no response. Perhaps she thought he was too easily resigned to such a change. But any such annoyance passed quickly away; for, when he said, on leaving her, after the ride, " To-morrow ! " she answered, without any thought of her promise to her husband, " To-morrow ! "

If she had dreaded a scene with Monsieur Naudié, her fears were quickly set at rest; he never mentioned her half-promise. In a soul like his, temporary explosions tended to postpone the supreme crisis. The severe training which his heart had undergone, in his youth, still kept him back from violent expressions of emotion. His theory of life, simple, consistent, stable, optimistic, served to reinforce his patience; he said softly to himself, again and again, " Youth . . . caprices . . . She will see her danger . . . she will recognize her mistake . . . God will hold her back from any serious error." These reflections allayed, in a measure, his anxiety. Then some tempest of passion would sweep over him; and he shuddered at the abysses which were revealed by these flashes of illumination. He struggled to control himself. He summoned his most considerate and charitable interpretations of her nature and actions. Thus he waited a long time, and said nothing. All that he dared attempt was to recall Jane, now and then, to her formal duties; for she disregarded these so openly that he could not affect to be ignorant of the neglect. She always tried to avoid contradicting him; explanations were soon over.

If he asked, "How was Monsieur Fridolin's sermon, to-day?" she answered, —

"I was not at church."

"Ah! you were not at church last Sunday, either, I think?"

"You think? Well, I will go next Sunday."

One day, a violent wind prevented the usual ride. However, no sooner was breakfast over than Jane made ready to go out. The conversation failed to interest her.

"Are you going out on such a day?"

"I'm not going far."

"To your aunt's, doubtless?"

"Certainly! Besides, there is a meeting of the charitable society this afternoon. I would like to be there. My aunt can go with me."

"Yes, yes! At what hour is the meeting?"

"Four o'clock."

"And until then!"

"Oh, the time will pass somehow."

Monsieur Naudié himself went out a few

minutes after her. At about a quarter of four he saw Madame Defos walking along near the Aufredi Hospital; naturally he inferred, "*They are alone together.*" And he at once hastened toward the Rue Reaumur. Even now his hopefulness did not quite desert him, but kept whispering, "Jane is about to follow on, after her aunt; something has delayed her; she will surely follow soon."

He quickened his steps, as he drew near the house. The black grating, made of iron, bearing its coat-of-arms, barred his passage, as if guarding a fortress. For a moment Monsieur Naudié gazed at this iron gate, as if he expected it at any instant to open and allow Jane to come forth. But it did not open, and the gilded motto at the top struck him with a sense of irony: "*Omnia bene, Deo juvante.*"

Despite the sharp wind, he walked back and forth on the sidewalk, fully expecting Jane, at any moment, to come hurrying out after her aunt. A quiet, dignified street it was, lined with its silent old mansions; along the sidewalks a few human forms might now and then be seen rapidly gliding, with faces half hid, and bodies closely wrapt. With a half-unconscious gesture, Monsieur Naudié partly opened his overcoat, to glance at his watch. Every second that flew by diminished the probability of his seeing Jane come forth. The great bell struck the half-hour. He still tried to invent reasons : "The cold weather has kept her in ; the wind . . . " But two words, which inevitably joined themselves to these, to complete the sentence, were too much for even his self-restraint : "Has kept her in . . . *with him.*" And he retraced his steps until he stood before the gateway, and then he rang. He was admitted, and was shown into the parlor.

There he found Jane and Henry, alone together. They were on opposite sides of a card-table. A lamp was burning, throwing its light upon them, and leaving the other parts of the room in shadow. She was half-reclining in an armchair; he was seated upon a small sofa, reading aloud. He stopped reading as Monsieur Naudié entered, arose, and laid aside his book.

"You are alone?" asked Monsieur Naudié, unconsciously disclosing his thought.

"Oh yes!" replied Henry. "My mother has gone out; my father and brother have gone to the office. Won't you be seated?"

He drew an armchair forward; and Monsieur Naudié sat down. As he did so, his glance fell on the closed book which Henry had laid upon the table; and he read its title, " L'Abbesse de Jouarre."

"You have been reading from Renan," he said with an effort. "He is a great author. What a pity that such marvellous talent as his should serve so perverted a nature!"

Henry and Jane, who had not stirred, exchanged a glance, and almost a smile. "Oh, Renan is not the man he is often made out to be," said Henry. "Nobody ever spoke more profoundly of the Infinite, or defended more soundly the rights of the soul."

"Yes, I know," responded Monsieur Naudié. " I am aware that he simulates a certain idealism; but I believe that this idealism is only a veil which he throws over a sensualism which he dares not openly avow."

These "isms" fell heavily upon the air in the dim room, already charged with the vibrations of languishing passion; quite as some gloomy night-bird might settle himself upon a branch where a nightingale was still warbling his delicious melody. Jane thought the suggestions absurd, and saw that she was being humiliated. How could such as she understand that underneath Monsieur Naudié's commonplace words burned a passionate devotion, which deserved to be expressed in words of gold or in winged metaphors!

Henry replied, defending his author, and maintaining those theses which seem always new and true, because they are so close to our primal instincts.

Monsieur Naudié did not keep up the discussion. "I have not read Renan's latest writings," he said. "I know, merely, that my father held them in very moderate esteem." Then he arose to leave. "Shall I escort you?" he asked, looking toward his wife.

Underneath the forced calmness of his words she did not perceive the hidden tumult of his heart. Because he was, at this moment, disturbing with his disagreeable words the smooth current of her pleasant dream, she thought of her husband as a contemptible fool. She was unable to see that he had any other purpose than to humiliate and threaten her.

"No, thanks!" she replied, "I will remain a little while;" and added, "I will dine here."

He had the courage to respond, as always, "Very well, very well!" And he went out, with head bowed, like one who had been defeated.

Monsieur Naudié's instincts, lashed by his sufferings, were slowly awakening; feelings of rage and hatred, which had been fomented by the wounds his heart had received, were rising slowly but surely to the surface. Moreover, their voices, which were to him new voices, found themselves in close accord with still another voice, namely, the voice of wisdom, to which he always gave heed. Like the others, this monitor urged him now to shake off his passive submission ; he felt it his *duty* to protect his wife ; the same malign influence which was drawing her away from him, was drawing her also into dark and devious paths. Was he not, in large measure, responsible for this ? " Husband, know you not that you may save your wife ? "

Several slight incidents, which followed one another through the day, impressed more and more clearly upon him the perils into which, through his excessive patience, he had drawn several people. Esther being weighed down with her anxiety, the household was at sixes and sevens. Abraham did not come home to dinner. Zelia coughed all the forenoon without anybody's concerning himself about her. Bertha had a violent dispute with the chambermaid. Ah, surely these children were more truly orphans than in the former days, when their father devoted himself to them. After dinner, Bertha and Zelia went up into Esther's room. Monsieur Naudié followed, a few moments later. As he entered, they looked at him as coldly as if he had been a stranger. Esther was the only one who gave him any welcome whatever; she tried to smile as she held out her feverish hand. After he had asked a few formal questions, he perceived that he had little or nothing to say to them. They chattered away among themselves, and he went over and sat in a corner, upon an English sofa, his head in his hands, chewing the cud of bitter reflections. Presently a little hand slipped softly into his. Zelia was standing before him, as he looked up, gazing upon him with an expression of pity. Then she spoke, "Papa!" and climbed upon his knees, and embraced him, as in the old time, when she was his favorite.

As she did so, Monsieur Naudié intercepted a glance which the little one sent across to Esther, — a glance which asked, " Is this it ? Did I understand you ? Did you mean for me to embrace him ? "

But the father did not linger over such a discovery; he gave his entire attention to the dear caresses which were bestowed upon him. He pressed against his poor storm-tossed heart the little innocent head, and murmured, " Dear child ! my own dear child ! " only that. He was too much overcome with memories and fears.

The sick daughter looked on at this little silent drama, doubtless comprehending its hidden significance; for she said softly to Bertha, who was leaning over her shoulder, " Be good to our papa ! He is very unhappy."

After he emerged from Esther's room, Monsieur Naudié waited a long time in his study. He reflected, " I must go and speak to *him*; " and he said it aloud, in an audible voice, as if his wife had been within hearing.

Jane returned late, her heart vibrating with that mysterious birth of love which had come to her, which she tasted again and again at her leisure,— an experience which was unfolding slowly within her, like a slowly blossoming flower not yet fully blown. She wished to reach her room with steps unperceived, there to continue her blissful reverie, — a reverie, a dream, which sleep alone interrupted, which began anew with each new day, which she took up each morning where she had laid it down the evening before.

Her husband's voice made her tremble. " Jane ! "

Pastor Naudié's Young Wife

She turned, surprised at the authority with which he spoke. " What is it ? "

" Come in here, please ! I have something to say to you."

" But it is late."

" Never mind ! "

She went in. A heavy cloak was wrapped about her, nearly covering her lace ; her splendid eyes, made brilliant by her passion, looked forth at him. She said again, " What is it now ? "

" Oh, several things ! " replied Monsieur Naudié.

She knew well that she was approaching a crisis. Boldly she laid aside her cloak ; and she stood forth, ready for battle, like a soldier who, in an excess of audacity, lays aside his helmet. " Ah, well, go on, then ! "

Monsieur Naudié intended to speak calmly, soberly, as one of his character ought, without giving rein to his passion. His great effort to maintain control of himself so utterly absorbed him that he did not notice the challenging attitude which his wife had taken. " In the first place," said he, " you read rather bad books."

Jane's lips curled with scorn, because this indirect attack corresponded so poorly with his aggressive manner.

"And you are yielding all too much to a dangerous temptation."

At this second sentence she was reminded of the game which children play, and she said to herself, "He is burning now." But she waited in silence; and Monsieur Naudié continued, in a gentle tone of reproof, which was almost paternal: "Surely, Jane, you ought to reflect a little more carefully upon who you are, upon who we are. You keep yourself far from me, you separate your duties from mine. I will say nothing about the children, to whom you promised to be a mother; inasmuch as you have no love for them, it is perhaps quite as well that you leave them entirely to the care of their older sister. She is capable of taking your place. But, most important of all, you are a minister's wife, Jane. You are not, and you cannot be, a woman of the world. You have something better to do than to busy yourself with these rides and visits and elaborate toilets. You have thrown off wholly your . . . your *duties*." The word came to his lips often; it seemed to him to comprise everything. "You do not go to church any more."

"Ah, indeed!" interrupted Jane, quietly. "I shall go less and less."

Pastor Naudié's Young Wife

The curtness of her remark, and the indifferent tone in which it was muttered, almost disconcerted her husband. "How is that?" he cried. "What do you mean?"

She was seated in front of the hearth, where an autumn fire was dying out; she held out toward the flame a small foot, which was shod, despite the cold weather, with a delicate shoe that did not cover her ankles. And she began, without looking at her husband, who stood erect near her: "You always talk about duty, my dear friend. But duty is not equally binding on everybody; things that are duties for those who believe, are not at all duties for those who do not believe."

Her dainty foot moved restlessly in front of the embers. As her husband did not at once reply, she raised her eyes to his face. "Those who do not believe?" he repeated slowly after her, as if he were weighing each of the heavy words which had come bubbling so lightly from her pretty lips. "Is it best for you to talk in this way, Jane? Is it you who does not believe? And you tell me this?"

The little foot remained poised before the fire, wilful, capricious; while the head, a little disordered by the cloak, nodded in affirmation.

"Jane," said Monsieur Naudié, "you speak

with astonishing levity regarding extremely serious matters; you sit there, in that chair, and your words pierce me, even to the bottom of my heart. What then! These talks with an atheist, and these readings from pernicious books, could not fail to sap the foundations of your faith, and perhaps even of your morality."

His voice trembled as he spoke these last words, but she did not offer any comment; and he continued: "What does man's reason avail, as against the commands of conscience, or as against the affirmations of the heart? All the discussions of the philosophers in all past times, Jane, have not established as much truth, regarding these problems, as have the simplest prayers of the humblest hearts. How they have debated and written! However, this one thing is sure: we see God all about us; when we stretch our hands in entreaty out toward the Infinite One, they are never repulsed. I have myself verified that, in my own troubled experience."

He seemed to grow larger, while he spoke, as does any man who speaks out of deep conviction. But his voice trembled, when, coming down from the heights of abstract thought, he began to speak of his own concrete, poignant grief, saying: "It is when the great crises of life come — just as one has come . . . to you, Jane — that we ought to call upon God. You remember, do you not, those words of the Psalmist, ' God is my rock ' ? "

She was ensconced in her easy-chair, her head was lowered, her gaze was fixed, and her foot had ceased its by-play and was withdrawn under her gown. Presently she spoke : " These things, doubtless, are all true for you, my friend ; for me they have ceased to be so. What can I do ? I thought I had some religion, as you have ; perhaps I did have some. However, now that is all over."

" There is no vacillating, Jane, within the circle of the divine order, as there is in human affairs. God never mocks us. He is sure. He never takes back from us that which he has once given us. He only asks us to supplement his power with our weak efforts. When he leaves us, it is simply that we leave him. But I know well, Jane, that in what you have been saying, it is not you who have spoken, but another has spoken through you."

His voice quivered, and he seemed to gasp for breath ; then he regained his voice, and it vibrated with emotion. " It is another, a stronger, whose words and thoughts you but echo. He has robbed you of your rightful mind; he has drawn you away from duty, and beguiled you from your true path of life. It is he whom I cannot bear to have near you; I protest against the influence which he exerts over you."

Soon the inevitable point was reached in their interview, where the real question at stake was brought plainly forward; and they discussed it, laying aside the theological side issues, and Jane defended herself with all the daring of her nature; her passion of love nerved her, and she spoke plainly, disdaining all disguises and subterfuges.

"Yes, you are right," said she. "It is Henry who has opened my eyes. I was a closed book to myself; he has given me the key which enables me to understand myself. I will conceal nothing. It is his lofty thought which guides me, it is the light of his soul which illumines my path. Why should I deny it? It is the living truth, and you know it."

As she spoke, she stood up and confronted him. He stood before her, towering above her with his superior height, and his wrathful countenance was filled with threatening.

"Go on!" he exclaimed. "Tell it all! Let me hear everything!"

" I have told you all."

" No ! "

" What more do you wish ? "

" The most important thing of all; that which you keep guard over in the depths of your frail little heart. Oh, I begin to know you, Jane. There is more which you have not told me."

Jane entrenched herself within her impregnable silence, and Monsieur Naudié went on impetuously: " It is not alone your reason which he has gained possession of; I know well that I find behind your actions, behind your words and reasonings . . . Oh, you need not reply to me. I can read in you at this moment . . ."

For an instant he paused, awaiting some response; but it came not, and he continued: " Do you suppose that I am blind to these secrets ? No ! Not as much as you might think. Have you not complained that I watched you, and followed you, and spied upon you ? Not one of your emotions has gone unobserved by me. It has been some little time, Jane, since I have known, *since I have known* . . . Perhaps I have waited too long. Perhaps it is now too late. But no ! you are mine. I wish to protect you. I can save you."

Pastor Naudié's Young Wife

He had a greater shrinking from threats of violence than had she, and his tone changed to one of entreaty. "Oh, Jane, have you not an atom of pity for me? You loved me when you first came to me? We have had happy days together. Oh, the memory of those blessed days, Jane! do they not awaken some kindly feeling in your heart? As for me, they recur to me without ceasing. You would have me blot them out; but I cannot, I cannot. I cannot live with this pain gnawing always at my heart; I cannot. You know not how I love you."

She drew back a step, and her instinctive act of repulsion smote him. "I desire that you should know," he cried. "After all, my wife, you are mine. I have rights over you; I alone have rights over you. I will not let you go, I will not."

She drew back even more; and, as a wrestler profits by his antagonist's retreat to move forward to a better position, Monsieur Naudié followed her, feeling that she was weakening. For the first time in his life he lost all control of himself; he became a creature of instinct; his blind wrath maddened him. And Jane, so frail, so feeble, before his masculine strength, perceived that only the greatest coolness and self-control could avail to save her from his vengeance. She rested her left hand on the mantel, and said sweetly, as if she were dealing with a fact long established, "You have known only too well, my friend, all this which separates us . . ."

He broke in, "Ah, take care!"

With a calm voice she asked, "Of what?"

Her husband saw the full force of her simple question, and his wrath flickered like a flame half quenched by water. She perceived her advantage, and at once took the offensive. "Yes, of what?" she repeated, in a tone of scorn and sarcasm. "And have you, in your turn, forgotten who you are? Ah! my friend, you are a minister. Do you think now that such an outburst as this is very becoming in you?"

Monsieur Naudié changed countenance as these words struck his ear. It was like the triumphal return of a train of exiles, silencing all sedition. They recalled him to reason, reflection, discretion.

Jane perceived her advantage, and her sarcasm grew keener. "Whither do you think this rage will lead you? Tell me that! You know well that there must not be a scene, a public spectacle. There are many things, my friend, absolutely impossible for a man in your position. I fancy myself reading in the daily papers, 'A dreadful affair has taken place at La Rochelle. Monsieur Naudié, a minister,' etc., etc. . . . Remember that you stand on a very slippery place, my friend! How would you like such a scandal as that? What do you say to it?"

Then she continued, in a calm, serious way, as if giving wise counsel: "What you must do is to remain faithful to your position, your profession, yourself. There, now!" And with these words, she quietly passed out, leaving him stupefied.

CHAPTER IV

JANE'S plain, hard words put to flight the last of Monsieur Naudié's illusions. Their cruel frankness tore away all his hopefulness. He saw his own heart clearly, and saw his fate. He recognized his error. He saw that he was now given over to the worst of certainties, betrayed and forsaken; and the man who faced this certainty, whose heart bled at the horrible thought, was not at all a calm, wise father of a family, careful of proprieties, bound down by the cords of his profession, which would make a public scandal seem more a disgrace than a misfortune; no, it was a man of flesh and blood, who existed underneath the exterior gloss of professional customs, and, of himself, was able to rise up and throw off all these calamities. But a swift review of the situation soon brought him to face the real facts; and he saw that he could hope for little aid outside himself. How could he make a stand against the daring spirit of his wife? He could go away? He could leave La Rochelle? Alas! She certainly would not follow him. How could he keep her away from Henry Defos? Could he resort to force? That would only hasten the dreaded outcome. Besides, he knew that his vengeful hand would drop harmless, at the least sign of tenderness from her. Infatuated through and through, he was weak, as always those are weak who love and are not loved in return. Once more the old story of Samson found a new application; the champion of Israel fell under the eyes of Delilah: "*And she tormented him day after day by her words, so that his soul was afflicted even unto death.*"

So close was the resemblance, that he ventured to refer to the old story, one Sunday, as he was preaching upon that text from Proverbs: "*A virtuous woman is the crown of her husband; but she who brings him to shame is as rottenness in his bones.*" In a monotonous, weary voice, with mechanical gestures, he urged the lessons of good order and propriety. He spoke of the beauty of family life, and of the nobility of that affection which grows purer and purer as the years pass, as wine grows sweeter with age; he spoke of the sanctity of conjugal duties, shared equally, and softened by mutual consideration. And, underneath this idyllic, conventional picture of life, sketched thus by him in gray outlines, moaned and groaned the pent-up storm of sorrow in his own heart.

Pastor Naudié's Young Wife

Several of his observant parishioners, whose sharp eyes had detected trouble in his household, thought they could perceive many personal allusions, in the sermon. Worthy Madame Dehodecq, simple soul, who always took words in their plainest bearings, said, as she was coming out of church, "Since Monsieur Naudié has become so happy, his sermons do me a lot more good."

There were others, however, who smiled maliciously. "What a pretty picture he gave us of a good Christian wife!" said Monsieur Lanthelme to Monsieur Merlin. "He has had a good model to draw from."

The two walked along the arcade of the Rue Minage. Presently Monsieur Lanthelme stopped his companion, and, raising his eyes toward a placard which was covered with lettering, he remarked, "Can you make out what is written there?"

"No!" replied the notary.

"Ah, well, this is what it says:

> *Mieux vaut avoir sagesse*
> *Que posséder richesse.*

A good idea, that! Good for everybody; isn't it! Indeed, for a minister it is four times as good. Ours is in a fair way to gain some experience."

Pastor Naudié's Young Wife

Thus the words and reflections of people grew sharper and sharper.

Monsieur Naudié, however, was casting about desperately for some means of resistance. At one moment he entertained the idea of asking Henry Defos for a frank personal explanation, but the violence of his own jealousy blinded him to the real character of his rival. Should he speak to Monsieur Defos? That would be to lay bare his wound before a hard dry man, who doubtless would simply shrug his shoulders and hold him up to scorn. His own evil genius then led him to decide upon the worst possible plan. He resolved to confide in ˉMadame Defos; he fancied that her maternal tenderness might be shocked, but certainly she would give him good counsel.

Ah, if on that day when, with his forehead wet with the sweat of anguish, he went to ask of his "aunt" a confidential interview, if only he could have seen inside that heavy stolid figure who listened to him, he would have drawn back in horror, stupefied, astounded, at the inky gloom which gathers sometimes at the bottom of such proper conventional souls, when envy and avarice have entered there.

But Madame Defos's little colorless eyes and her low flat forehead kept well their secrets. Monsieur Naudié, like most people, held her to be "an excellent woman." He was naturally trustful. When he had once broken the ice, he poured out, without reservation, his anxieties and sorrows, barely repressing the one most poignant of all, — his betrayed love, his real anguish. He explained that a serious problem had arisen in their household. Doubtless neither her husband, nor her other son, nor she herself had suspected it. They had no idea of people's malignity in putting the worst interpretation on everything. Perhaps Henry himself had too high an opinion of his own powers. Perhaps he forgot that there is more wisdom and courage in resisting outright a temptation, than in dallying with it.

After this fashion Monsieur Naudié tried to keep his problem under cover of ordinary conventionalities, and within the bounds of the minor morals. Madame Defos listened, without helping him by a word or a gesture; she heard his cry of pain, and the sound filled her with an evil joy. She felt less and less sympathy for him, after he had defeated her plans, now that this new affection between Jane and Henry had justified her shrewdness in forecasting it. To her, this man was only a robber who had stolen from her; he was an obstacle in the path of her son's happiness. Others, in her position, might have been satisfied; but she was not. Without looking for any means of repairing the breach, without even considering the possibility of finding any, she rejoiced to see her evil scheme maturing, and she found a fiendish pleasure in turning the knife in the wound.

"Why don't you tell all these things to Jane?" she asked. "Without any doubt the dear child will understand."

The question made it necessary for him to confess his futile efforts in this direction; and he recounted his fruitless entreaties, renewed day after day, his repeated failures, after which, he had come to her, as his last resource. "I have said everything to her that could be said, everything which would be at all likely to influence her; and now, madame, I have no other hope but you."

This despairing appeal made not the slightest impression upon Madame Defos. "My son is above all suspicion," she said coldly, after a few moments' reflection.

"Doubtless," assented Monsieur Naudié. "But for this once, don't you see how dangerous this intimacy is?"

Pastor Naudié's Young Wife

Madame Defos knew that even a slight word of encouragement from her would be enough to reawaken the hopefulness of a trustful soul like this man's, so she was very careful about speaking it. "However irreproachable a young man and young woman may be," she said, "yet an intimacy, carried very far, always holds elements of danger."

She distilled her words carefully, to make them give out their full venomous effect.

"Here, of course, the danger is just so much the greater in proportion as their natural sympathies are keen; greater according to their natural fitness, the one for the other. Certainly their ideas are much in harmony. Besides, Henry realizes how much he is indebted to your dear wife; he realizes that she has saved his life by her devotion and affection. And what a field for gratitude such a situation offers! But these young people, my dear friend, are well-bred and regardful of proprieties; remember that! Oh, I think you may be quite easy in your mind!"

Each of these sentences lacerated his wounds, so that, as he listened, he grew pale and ghastly. Then he said, "Nevertheless, madame, do you not see that despite the high esteem in which I hold your son, and despite the confidence which I have in my wife, I cannot, cannot allow them to go on thus? Oh, I will take my oath that I do not suspect either of them of anything really evil. It is simply this: that I see her agreeing with him in his ideas, sympathizing with everything he does, preferring to be with him rather than with me. I and my children and my home have no interest for her. She is as a stranger in our midst. It is that which I wish to lay before you, my dear madame, because it is you alone, so far as I can see, who can have any power over her. She has no mother. To whom shall I go, if not to you, for counsel and help?"

Like those self-respecting poor people who perish of hunger while asking for work, Monsieur Naudié forced himself to conceal his deepest distress. But his sad voice, his drawn features, his attitude of utter humiliation, these betrayed his real anxiety. And Madame Defos saw it all clearly, and rolled it as a sweet morsel under her tongue, this joy of torturing a defenceless wounded foe.

"Advice, my dear sir," said she, reservedly, "is very difficult to give in such delicate affairs as these. Each person must act according to his own ideas and feelings. As for any help that I can give you, I really do not see what it could be.   What can I do?"

"You might . . . might speak to . . . your son," said Monsieur Naudié, with much hesitation.   "Or . . . or to . . . your husband . . . perhaps."

"Oh, to my husband!   These matters are not in his line."

Then she appeared to hesitate.   "Henry . . . well, I might if. . . if you expressly desire it, my dear friend?"

"Do whatever you think is best!" said Monsieur Naudié, after a short pause.   And he went out, with one more arrow in his already bleeding heart.

CHAPTER V

SLACKENING the speed of their horses to a walk, Henry and Jane turned to the right and took the broad open road which stretched away from La Pallice. They chose this rather than the smaller, more picturesque road which led along the shore; for, under the dark canopy of the cloudy sky, the sea seemed to exhale a sadness which depressed them. There was a gloomy leaden tint upon the water, and light mists hung over its surface, breaking the black line of the old dyke and tower, where hung the bell which warned the sailors. In the eyes of these two the sinister calm seemed more threatening than an open storm.

Henry, who was very sensitive to the influences of physical nature, avoided this route, although the ocean-view, even to-day, was not without beauty. So they took the broad travelled highway; which was less beautiful to the eye, but, with its many houses, on the one side and the other, afforded a corrective to the gloomy thoughts which would have been deepened by the wide open spaces along the shore.

Pastor Naudié's Young Wife

From the moment when they set out, Henry had something he wished to say, but the words halted upon his lips. However, after they had left the town behind them, and the road stretched far away in front, he gathered up his courage and said: "Our ride is not particularly joyous; we have had better ones. This is perhaps the last one, too; at least for a long time."

With an involuntary movement of surprise, Jane pulled up her horse, exclaiming, "The last? Why so?"

With his gaze fixed upon the long gray line of the highway before them, Henry said: "My father wishes me to begin work at once, and I have no sufficient reason for delaying longer. This reading and sauntering and chatting is all very well for an invalid, but I am now well. Active life asserts its claims over me."

"But," said Jane, "you are surely not going to enter the office simply as a salaried clerk?"

"My father expects a great deal of work from me."

"Oh, I hoped you were not going to tie yourself down as your brother does. In his case, of course, it is all very well; he is cut out for that sort of thing; but you . . ."

The word " you " thrilled with admiration. Henry answered sadly, " As for me, I must adapt myself to my new duties."

She replied immediately, " I hope this will not affect our relations ? "

He did not echo these friendly, hopeful words. The thing which he wished to say was more than ever difficult. After a few moments' silence, during which he leaned over and scanned the feet of the horses, as they pattered upon the hard dry road, he continued, without lifting his eyes : " I have not told you all, cousin. My father — you know him, you know how strict and exacting he is — my father fears that our friendship, if it goes on, will lead to public talk. Doubtless some unkind words have already come to his ears. You know that we live here in a small town; and, with your free English habits of life, you have no idea how rigid and conventional our customs are."

Jane's forehead began to wrinkle with vexation. Could she then never have a little affair with anybody except weaklings and poltroons?

" And you think, then," she exclaimed, with a charming gesture of defiance, " that we ought to pay attention to the tittle-tattle of these stupid people ? "

"Ah, but what if we give them grounds for it?"

"What is it to them?"

"But they are not the only ones who threaten to break off our friendship, Jane. Your husband himself has taken alarm. He has conferred with my mother, who has reported his words to me."

"He! the idea!" And Jane's eyes burned fiercely with hatred. Then she repeated, "He! he! Why, you know well what he is to me."

Henry replied gravely, "He is your husband, Jane, and you are his wife."

A carriage, which now came up at a rapid pace, proved to be the equipage of Monsieur Dehodecq; and he and Madame Dehodecq occupied it. There was only time for a hasty greeting, and the vehicle was gone; but not before Henry noted the quick scrutiny of watchful eyes, and fancied some such words as these between the two persons in the carriage: "Together again! They are relatives. All right! Monsieur Naudié is very patient."

This meeting had broken off the thread of Henry's remarks. But he began again, a little farther on, as if no break had occurred: "Doubtless the speeches of evil-minded people have little weight; but one must remember what pain they sometimes cause. I never let myself be stopped in any right path by outside barriers; but there are barriers more formidable, those which are within. You have saved my life, Jane; so they tell me; and I have found such sweet pleasure in your society. Oh how swiftly these weeks of convalescence have sped away! Each day has brought us into closer sympathy. My strength, as it has come back to me, has only made me feel more keenly the joy of your presence, the joy of seeing you again after you have left me. Something strange and wonderful is unfolding within me. You know my situation well enough to understand how entirely alone I am in the world. Even my mother, who loves me dearly, is very different from me. Yet, up to the time of my sickness, I had hardly realized how great her love was. In that old house, where I was born, I never knew the joy of reading, in another's heart, the thoughts which deeply stirred my own; rather, I should say, never did I know that joy until I met you. Oh, Jane, I have given myself up to this joy all too freely; I have been unmindful of the voices of calumny, which should have warned me. They are cruel, but I am glad I have heard them; these evil-minded people have had some reason for their talk, too much reason, and it seems to me best to give up our dear, delightful interviews."

Then, speaking in a lower tone, he added, " Perhaps I even ought to go away for a long time."

Jane at once broke out: " Go away? You? I will not have it so."

He understood perfectly the meaning of her imperious exclamation; and he quivered, intoxicated, in spite of himself, with the bliss and the unwonted pride of being loved. Around them gathered the fog, and they rode forward into a dense vapor which shut out the objects around them; they seemed to each other like ghosts moving on through the mist.

" As for me," continued Jane, " I also am lonely and sad. You will do me the justice of admitting that I have never complained. Now listen to me! I am a stranger at that fireside, which I foolishly sought, with all the wilful heedlessness of my twenty years. Oh, Henry, is it my fault? I don't know. But they don't love me, they hate me. Yes, even the children hate me. Why? Never mind! They hate me; that is enough. And I suffer. I have only you; and now you wish to leave me."

Very seriously and carefully he replied, after a considerable pause: "I wish it now, Jane, more than ever. After what I have said to you, and after this response which you have made, do you not see that a separation is necessary for us? I need you very much, Jane, and you, perhaps, need me; the parting will demand all our courage. It will cost us much pain, and it will seem very grievous to us to-day; but on the morrow . . ."

She did not at once reply. Her small soul could not climb so high; Henry's words clashed and resounded in her heart, and they wounded her self-love. Finally she said: "The morrow? I don't know anything about the morrow. I know only that I shall be sorrowful without you. Is n't that enough to keep you from going away?"

All that Jane had been saying had been translated by Henry into terms of his own illusions. "Oh, dear pure heart that you are!" exclaimed he. "As for me, during these happy days I have explored the depths of my heart; I have seen what it sought, and sought with eagerness and even with madness. And then, I took note of the path upon which we were entering; I have found there the little real life I have ever known.

In this way I have come to understand how much I love you."

She trembled, as he spoke. The avowal had come. Then Henry went on: "It is in this way that I have been led to believe that our parting must be. Only thus can I pay to you the debt I owe; for I love you so much that I wish not even a breath of suspicion to rest upon you. I wish you to be surrounded by the same purity of atmosphere which already exists in your soul."

As she listened to him, Jane found him weak and cowardly. She was one who could say boldly, "I do whatever I wish to do." But he was so tender, withal, so genuinely over-whelmed with his passion, that she felt like forgiving him for deceiving himself with regard to her.

"A Christian?" she calmly remarked.

"Perhaps so!" he replied quickly. "Perhaps a Christian who holds no longer to the faith, but cherishes the same ideal. I do not believe any longer in Christ, as you know. I do believe, however, in the lofty character of his teachings, and in the light which shot from him across the world. I believe, too, in the supreme value of self-sacrifice; this faith is in my very blood; it is inherited from my ancestors. It is your faith also; for it belongs to all souls who maintain in their lives purity and nobility. It is because I do not wish to bruise or deface it, that I say this to you. You and I cannot break the tie which unites our hearts. So let us strive, with sincerity and courage . . ."

They turned about. Lights began to appear, dimly visible through the fog. Red gleams shone forth from the windows of the first houses. Without being able to distinguish the dripping outlines of the park and fortifications, they found themselves re-entering the town. Enveloped as they were in mist, they avoided the gaze of any scrutinizing eyes. But surely there were some attentive ears listening for the familiar sound of their horses' hoofs. A vague sense of mystery kept them silent. Each fancied that he could hear the heart-beats of the other, because each could hear his own. Although the voices of their souls were really more inharmonious, the one with the other, than the violins of a discordant orchestra, yet Henry obstinately cherished the delusion that they were in closest sympathy. They rode by the inscription which was over the Defos gateway, dim in the fog of the evening, "*Omnia bene, Deo juvante*." Then they stopped, a few doors farther along. A porter opened the gate.

Pastor Naudié's Young Wife

Now had come the moment of parting. And Jane said: "We have not yet said all that should be said. I must see you again. Don't go away! Come to-morrow!"

He replied, "I shall go."

And she reflected, "He loves me; he will not go."

CHAPTER VI

A S soon as the bell announced Jane's return, Monsieur Naudié appeared on the porch. She took no notice of the fact that his eyes were filled with tears. She passed by him, giving him merely a formal greeting. He followed her to her room. She was in a state of irritation, and was about to upbraid him for his visit to Madame Defos, for his jealousy, and for his suspicions. But before she could begin, he handed her an open letter, saying, " My father is very ill; he may possibly die. Read what my sister has written me ! "

She took the paper, which was in Angelica's handwriting, and glanced through it. There were four pages regarding the old man's illness, which had now lasted several days, and was increasing. There were in it various devout phrases about the goodness of God, and the trust which must be placed in him, even though he sent heavy trials to his children. The brothers and sisters had all been notified. Those who could come, would doubtless do so. They counted especially upon Simeon, who, with William, was close to the father's heart.

Pastor Naudié's Young Wife

Even from afar the sight of Death and his inexorable work softens our animosities. Jane was affected by the news; and she could recall two interviews which she had had with the patriarch, and she remembered his grand presence, his imperial manner, his thoughtful brow, and the dignity of his long, eventful, honorable life. "You will go?" she asked.

"Certainly. Will you not go with me?"

This simple question dissipated Jane's tenderer feelings. For, with her selfish nature, she had at once begun to balance the danger of missing Henry against the exigencies of this new duty. "It seems to me," said she, "that you would do better to take the children along, especially the older ones. As for me, neither your father nor your sister is really much acquainted with me. I cannot believe that my presence there would be of much account. At such times one desires to see about him only the most familiar faces."

She spoke sweetly, as one instinctively speaks to those in sorrow. Her voice even took on an accent of pity, which mitigated somewhat the harshness of her refusal. Overcome, as he was, by his grief, Monsieur Naudié did not feel like urging his request.

"Just as you wish," he replied. "I will go,

then, to-morrow morning; and I will take Esther and Bertha with me." But, scarcely was he again alone, when the real sense of Jane's refusal, sweetly as it had been expressed, came over him. "After all," he repeated, " how can she have for me more than the most commonplace pity! She has never expressed one word of affection for my father, who, on the day of our marriage, seemed to renew his youth in his admiration for her. Instead of mourning with me, she very likely is glad at my departure, knowing that it will free her for a time from my surveillance. After I have gone, there will be no barrier whatever to restrain them. They will be wholly without restraint. That is what she desires."

Such were the reflections which came to him, with his heart aching. During the dinner, which came a little later, he scanned Jane's countenance, looking for some sign of favorable compassionate feeling. He was as sad as though already the days of mourning for his father had begun; but on her face he could see no sign of tenderness. How could he expect to read the thoughts which were hidden behind that beautiful impassive face, or in those marvellous eyes, which could, on occasion, shut out inquiry like closed windows. In this respect she much resembled Esther. They both remained silent; the few words they spoke had almost the same accent. In order to break the silence, something was said about dying. Esther recalled her last visit to her grandfather; Jane murmured a few words on the same subject. Then Monsieur Naudié said: "If God takes him from us, it may well be said that he fought a good fight, like a brave soldier. Only last month the 'Christian Review' published an article of his, 'Some Reflections upon the Real Apology.' There were pages in that article full of the noblest spirit. It was a powerful statement, adjusting the defence of Christianity to the real demands of conscience. Monsieur Fridolin said to me, 'Your father writes like a young man.' Oh, my poor dear father!"

A tear rolled slowly down his cheek into his beard. He looked around him, at his children, bound together with himself into a little circle of sorrow. Then his gaze fell, in particular, upon Zelia, with her eyes full of sympathy, and yet, in all her wealth of naïve compassion, so ignorant of real grief. Greatly moved, he ventured to call her to him, and took her upon his knees. As he caressed her soft hair, he cast a furtive glance at Jane, who always had taken offence if he showed any attentions to his little girl; but now she made no sign, and sat in entire indifference. "She does not love me even enough to be jealous of these caresses," said he to himself. "She must go away from me, far away from here."

The children now left the dining-room. As Jane followed them, Monsieur Naudié called her back. "I have thought it all over," he said, "and it seems to me best that you go with us. My father loved you; and do you not recall the friendliness which my sister has shown toward you? My poor sister! Your absence would lead to misunderstandings."

Jane had been making all sorts of plans, in her own mind. "I am inclined to think that my presence, rather than my absence, is what leads to misunderstandings," she said coolly.

"But at such times as this, there is need of everybody's affection and sympathy."

The young woman seemed to hesitate, either from fear of showing too little concern in the matter, or because she was really touched, despite her selfishness, by the grief of the family. Sometimes, in crises of misfortune, even the hardest and dryest souls seem to soften; but her hesitation was brief; her selfishness swept her away. "Perhaps his sickness is not as serious as you think," she urged. "Your sister would have telegraphed. You see she only sent a letter. There is no pressing danger."

"Do you mean that there is no need of my going?"

"I did not say that."

"Then why do you urge me to wait?"

"I mean, simply, that the case is not serious enough to warrant you all in going to Montauban, thus running a risk of frightening the sick man. You could go, and then I could join you later if it is best to do so."

Then she added, having in mind no remoter point of time than the following day, "I will make ready for the journey, if you advise it."

Monsieur Naudié was pacified once more by this half-concession. But in the night all his anxiety burst out anew. He went over again the events of the past few weeks. The facts took on a new meaning, the wrong seemed more serious than ever, and the danger seemed more pressing. At the same time, these latest suggestions of Jane, although he could divine their real source, agreed closely with his own theory. Still following his evil genius, he said to himself that very probably his father was not as ill as reported; and he soon quite persuaded himself of this; while through all his reflections ran the keen prescience of this other very different peril, menacing him in his own home. Once before, he remembered, a letter from Angelica had called him to Montauban; and after he had hurried anxiously to see his father, he had found him in the garden trimming his rose-bushes. Perhaps this would be a similar case. Moreover, if he went away from Jane, what might she not do, — she whom he felt it his duty to protect, even against herself?

So he did not go. In the morning, when Jane met him, she exclaimed, "How now! You are still here?"

"I am in some pain," he explained. "During the night I was feverish. I am going, now, to send a telegram and ask for the latest news."

"You must be careful! Your father has reached an age when sometimes . . ."

He quickly interrupted: "But it is you who assured me that I was over-anxious, and now you seem eager to hasten my going."

"Have it as you will! Each must act according to his own feelings."

Monsieur Naudié delayed starting. Jane, after thus allaying somewhat her husband's anxiety, did not dare leave the house. She ventured, however, to send a note to Madame Defos, to inform her about the condition of affairs. Toward the end of the afternoon Henry came over to learn if there were any later news. While he waited a telegram came. Three words only, vague, indefinite, leaving the field open for the worst possible fears. "Condition the same."

"You will decide to go, I suppose," said Henry to Monsieur Naudié.

Monsieur Naudié took this as an artful suggestion on the young man's part; and, out of the anger and hate which burned in his heart, he answered sharply: "No! Not to-night! To-morrow we will see about it."

"At least," suggested Jane, "you will telegraph again?"

"Perhaps so! Presently!"

He did not go out until after Henry had departed. Then he went to send off another despatch: "Impossible to come just now. Send particulars!"

A letter came, the next morning, but gave no new details. Angelica wrote about the symptoms of the disease: "frequent coughing, fever, cold perspiration, gradual weakening of the body." She also quoted the latest opinion of the physicians: "His condition is unquestionably very serious; but, owing to his excellent general health, there is still hope." After having added these words, vague and confused, like most human science, she wrote the following: "William has been here since morning; Paul sends word that he will soon arrive. The others have not yet been heard from. But you are the one, dear brother, whom I most wish to see; you know how much our father has thought of you; he often speaks about you, and recalls your goodness. In his delirium he often speaks your name and your dear wife's. For my own part, I long to have you near me, because you always understand me so well. Come, then, as soon as you can! I will tell you frankly that I put very little confidence in the hopes held out by the physicians. Something tells me that our dear father is fast approaching his end, and I often weep over it. However, it is all for the best; it is right for him to go; like the good servant, he has finished his work. The Master will have no reason to reprove him. But what a loss to us and to the church! As for me, I have lived under his protection like a weak little plant dwelling at the foot of a mighty tree. What emptiness of life I foresee for myself, when he who has filled it so full shall have gone away! What will become of me when I can no longer hear his voice! Ah, how hard it will be for me to feel resigned! I shall need all your help to enable me to say ' The Lord hath given, and the Lord hath taken away. Blessed be the name of the Lord!' Alas, the greater the gifts which he gives us, the harder it is to have them taken away. Still, it will be a sad yet tender consolation for us to remember how noble and grand a man was our beloved father."

Monsieur Naudié read this letter, in a clear voice. The children ranged themselves about him, affected, according to their ages and temperaments, by the suggestions of mortality which rang through the pages, silenced by the shadow of death which they felt to be hovering over their grandfather, — that grandfather whom they heard mentioned as a sort of prophet, and whom they recalled, in their minds, as very grand and smiling and beautiful. Jane was more repressed; she sat alone, with bowed head, leaning her chin upon her hand, and with her eyes closed, as if to conceal any unsympathetic thoughts. She opened her eyes again, when she heard her husband's voice break, over that last phrase; and, as he glanced at her, he believed that he read in her face words like these: " Now, surely, he will go."

This seemed to open afresh the wounds in his heart, and to make them bleed anew. He recognized that here, in his own household, was a more terrible sorrow than the grief of a son for his dying father. The envenomed dagger seemed to pierce his heart deeper than ever.

Esther, always undemonstrative, wept in silence. Presently she said, " I think we would best go this evening."

Monsieur Naudié knew that he could not go, but he hardly cared to admit it. He replied, " In any case, we will hold ourselves ready."

Meanwhile, the news of Abraham Naudié's illness spread through the town. Every person in this Protestant community was much concerned about it. He was known to them not only because of his fame as a Father of the Church, and as a powerful thinker, before whom all antagonists bowed ; but as well they thought of him as a legendary and heroic figure, such as they associated with the historic points in their own town, reminding them of the old days of war and glory, before these modern days of ease and indifference had come in. Many of them who had never read his voluminous works were yet acquainted with their general character; and some persons could repeat a few pregnant phrases, which summed up his principal theories: "The Christian spirit consists in finding joy in giving one's self in sacrifice." Or this: "The first point is, to make people understand that the moral law is rigorously obligatory." Most people saw, more or less clearly, that with the death of this man, who had won such victories for the faith, an epoch was drawing to a close; and that a successor would be hard to find, one who could lift on high the banner after it fell from his hand.

Thus there was a steady stream of visitors flowing into the Rue Reaumur; among others, Monsieur Dehodecq, Monsieur Merlin, Monsieur Fridolin, and even Monsieur Lanthelme, who clung to that remnant of his ancestral faith which really existed underneath his ostentatious parade of atheism. As these men were going out, he said to Monsieur Merlin, with one of those expressive shrugs which usually accompanied his humorous fancies: "The Creator doesn't realize what he is going to lose in Abraham Naudié. Now he will have left, to defend him, only those who do not believe in him."

Pastor Naudié's Young Wife

All the visitors to the house drew the same inference, namely, that inasmuch as the pastor had not set forth at once to go to his father, there could not be imminent danger. Monsieur Naudié himself rather encouraged this view; despite the voice within him, which contradicted him, he replied to inquiries, "Yes, my sister's letters give us room for much hope." Then he added, "But we are quite ready, and can start at a moment's notice."

Every time that the door-bell rang, Monsieur Naudié trembled; for he knew that he was partially deceiving these callers, in order to deceive himself. Sometimes, as he was uttering his reassuring remarks, he heard the housemaid's steps in the hall, and with a shudder he reflected, "Perhaps it is the telegram, *the* telegram;" and his anxiety almost stifled him.

His children were a greater care to him than were these outside people. Their senses were quickened by the excitement about them, and they observed, and reflected, and formed opinions. Esther, more serious than ever, seemed to him a living reproach. There she was, full of compassion for a sorrow which she perceived without being able to understand; she was reasoning continually about the matter, and had almost reached the point where she would say,

Pastor Naudié's Young Wife

" My father has a plain duty, and he is putting it aside."

The others were following in much the same line of reflection, though not, perhaps, as consciously as she. Indeed, Monsieur Naudié overheard, between his son Abraham and Bertha, this fragment of a colloquy: " Oh, yes! He's going to die, you know," remarked Abraham, with an air of utter nonchalance. " Sure! he's so old."

Bertha's forehead grew furrowed, as she replied, " You think so? Then why does n't papa go? "

Abraham, with the grimace and gesture of a street Arab, explained, " It's because of *her*; that's why."

Monsieur Naudié was but little like his former self. Calm, self-composed man that he had been, walking serenely among the shocks and perplexities of life, he now betrayed the unsettled state of his heart by his nervous tones and actions. Seeing him in this state, Jane softened a little in her manner toward him, fearful of what he might be goaded into. And truly there was cause for fear concerning this man, who was being undermined by a double current of griefs ; who, for perhaps the first time in his life, was standing out against his conscience, while an insistent voice of affection in his heart was condemning him for his negligence and cowardice.

Two long days passed in this way. There was nothing really new. Angelica's telegrams contained nothing definite. "Condition the same," she reported, using exactly the same words. But Monsieur Naudié had seen similar cases, and knew well that, in the case of so old a man, death would very like come in this way, by slow, sure steps.

One or another of the Defos family came over frequently. Sometimes Jane went over there, under pretext of carrying them the news, and without daring to remain long. Her husband made no effort to prevent her going. Neither to her nor to any one had he spoken frankly about the source of his greatest anxiety. On the fourth day, in the evening, when her absence was longer than usual, he, in his turn, went out, — not to follow her, or to spy upon her, but, rather, to avoid the pain of meeting her as she returned. Instead of ascending the street toward the Defos mansion, he went down toward the shore. He walked rapidly, with his hands plunged into his overcoat pockets, without having any especial goal in view. In a short time he found himself upon the path

Pastor Naudié's Young Wife

near the beach, back of the row of trees that bordered the mall. The tide had gone out, and the sea moaned slightly in the distance. The place was like a desert, flooded by the moonlight, which illumined the sand on the beach and glimmered on the pools left by the ebbing tide. Here and there, scattered about, lay mounds of mud, like oases in this desert, showing black and gloomy, despite the bright moonlight. Dimly outlined, the distant wharves closed in the scene, and were merged, above, in the shadowy gray tones of the sky. The outline of the Richelieu tower seemed to waver, like a flame flickering to its close; and, at intervals, the lighthouses on the island of Ré shot out their gleams like flashes of lightning. Standing erect upon this path, Monsieur Naudié filled his eyes with the shadowy scene where darkness and light were strangely mingled, and drew into his lungs the heavy salt air coming in from the broad expanse of the ocean. Suddenly he saw a couple advance into the moonlight, gliding noiselessly along like phantoms. They drew nearer, until they were directly in front of him, when they stopped short.

Monsieur Naudié recognized them, and moved toward them.

Pastor Naudié's Young Wife

"Ah, it is you!" he exclaimed.

Jane immediately answered, "I was in need of a little exercise, and I asked my cousin to walk with me."

Innocent as he was, Henry perceived that he had put himself under grave suspicion; and his heart became a prey to confused emotions. In the presence of this man, her husband, a man who stood for propriety and law and established customs, he saw in advance that he was in the position of a detected criminal; and he bowed his head, without daring to defy him, and without the power to deceive him.

"Well, then," said Monsieur Naudié, "I think you may as well finish your walk with me. Come!"

He spoke with such authority that Jane dropped Henry's arm at once, in order to take her husband's. For the first time she was afraid of him. Hers was a physical fear in the presence of superior force, and the fear of a culprit standing before a judge. Her hand trembled as he held it firmly beneath his arm.

They went back to the house, nothing being said. Henry followed. Monsieur Naudié set a rapid pace, for he was greatly agitated, and he was revolving in his mind what he would say when they were alone, in that house already full of mourning. There would be entreaties again. There would be the plain, hard speech of a master. How the sharp reproofs and commands would burst forth, when once they had crossed that threshold!

The three reached the gateway, which opened to them. Monsieur Naudié thrust Jane in before him. She had barely time to cast one look of distress at Henry, who stood motionless, powerless, despairing, outside the closed gate. At the sound of the gate, violently closed, Esther appeared on the porch. She held a telegram in her hand. "Father," said she, "the news is much worse."

Like a helpless waif which a powerful wave seizes as a weaker wave gives it up, Monsieur Naudié felt his strength forsake him, and his anger vanish away. "Dead?" he asked, with a cry of touching distress.

"No! Listen! 'Father has asked for you. Come!'"

"We have time enough to catch the midnight express," he exclaimed. "Let us go!"

He gave no further attention to Jane, who at once disappeared. He had only one idea now. He could think only of the father who had called him, who might die without see-

ing that son at his bedside, that father forsaken by him in his supreme hour of need,
that father against whom he might perhaps
be committing, by his neglect, the most irrep-
arable of sins, since the victim could never, in
this world, speak words of forgiveness.

PART FOURTH

CHAPTER I

MONSIEUR NAUDIÉ and his eldest daughter were seated in the night-express; they were opposite each other, and remained a long time without speaking. Whenever his eyes encountered hers, he saw in them pity mingled with reproaches. He averted his gaze, but in vain. The words of reproof which he sought to avoid seemed to come to him out of his own heart. Gradually, however, he grew calmer. Certain recollections of his childhood rose before him, and served to divert his thoughts; yet even these memories revolved about the grand figure of his noble father. He recalled his smiles, gestures, words, — those words, so eloquent and trenchant, which the old professor could use with such skill and effect. Sometimes those remarks fell from him, as he sat in his professorial chair, and they bewildered the young heads about him; or, again, they were uttered in the bosom of his family, and then they were always tempered by a charming tenderness. Oh, what gay times there had been at the great table, when the mother was there to keep order! And how observant she always was of her illustrious husband, himself a child of genius! At dessert, if the occasion was at all favorable, he often scattered around him a handful of rhymes,—good old verses, taken, perhaps, from Béranger, with a refrain at the end of each stanza. Sometimes he interspersed snatches of drinking-songs; for Abraham Naudié dearly loved the good red wines of his native land, "which," said he, "are generous, aromatic, and sparkling, and help bring joy and gladness."

> "*Le vin de France, amis, a l'âme bonne,*
> *Le vin de France est un homme de bien.*"

As he recalled these lines, Monsieur Naudié remembered also some of his father's bright sayings, and he could not resist the inclination to lean over and speak of them to Esther. "Nobody ever saw a man as good and genuine as he was. Those who never met him pictured him as an unsympathetic, self-absorbed thinker and pedant. How mistaken was such a notion! He loved everything that was good or beautiful, with all his soul. Do you know what he said to me, the last time I saw him? He said, 'I would like, before I die, to write a little treatise on wine-making; and it shall not be, by any means, my poorest piece of work, for I have never tasted a glass of good wine that I have not remembered it with pleasure.' There you have him! The plain, honest, kindly man. So *human!*"

The young girl did not clearly comprehend her father's meaning; and she said simply, "I have greatly longed to see him, and to know him better."

"Such is life. People fritter away hours and days over trifles, and the hours and days pass, and can never be recalled."

Again there was silence; the fast train made few and brief stops. Esther grew drowsy. Monsieur Naudié became more and more restless and excited. Certain prayers welled up from his soul. He murmured them in a low, soft voice, and they were lost in the night. "O God, I pray thee, grant that I see my dear father once more, and that he recognize me! I know well that in my blindness I have neglected the most sacred of duties, my duty toward him, in his old age. Oh, grant that he may forgive me! Afterward, I will be patient and resigned, and will bear whatever trials thou shalt send me; and I will suppress the complaints of my wounded heart, the cries of my tortured soul. I will put away from me all that is base and mean. With thy aid, O God, I will become again thy faithful, humble servant. I will consecrate all my powers to thee alone. I will love thee, as I ought, more than all else. . . ."

As he said these words, he recalled the photograph of the Italian singer, which he had once seen in Jane's hands, and the quotation written under it, *Vorrei poteri dar quel pò che resta.*

With a shudder he exclaimed, "The little that remains! the little that remains!" He felt that he was offering to his God only the few fragments of affection which still remained in his empty heart.

Presently, however, this mood passed, and a more exalted mood took its place; and he went on with his prayer, where it had been interrupted by that hateful memory of the past. "O God, give me back all my strength, and set my feet in the right path, and help me to walk in it! Whatever sacrifices thou mayest ask of me, oh, I will make them readily. Even my father, even he whom thou art calling up to thy better kingdom, even he departed sometimes from thy ways. He has had his trials of the spirit, even as I have my trials of the heart. But it is in thee that he will sink to sleep, having finished his work, like a faithful servant. Oh, may thy presence strengthen my will, as it has often strengthened his! Oh, may I never forget, even in, my sorest trials, that I am thine, as he did not forget his duty to thee, amid his highest flights of thought! O God, may I find peace in thee for my troubled heart! Give me this! Give me a pure heart! Give me poverty, and the simple duties and cares which were once mine, which did not draw me from thee, which did not embitter my soul! Give me that calm which was mine, ere this storm broke over me, — that calm spirit which is promised to thy faithful servants!"

As they drew near their journey's end, in the early morning, Esther noticed tears in her father's eyes. She seated herself beside him, in the carriage, and drew him toward her with that instinct of maternal feeling which so often had comforted her little sisters. " Poor papa!" she murmured, with accents of sympathy.

" Esther, dear," said he, " do you think I shall see him once more?"

" I hope so."

This kindly, trustful word raised his spirits again, until he felt in key with the calm of the beautiful new day; and the glorious light which bathed the hills and plains, seemed to bathe also his soul. But when the dim outlines of Montauban came into view, his fear returned to him; and this fear grew upon him, minute by minute, as the train slackened speed. Indeed, he felt almost stifled, as he descended from the compartment of the train, and, afar off, saw William's tall figure upon the platform.

"How is he?" was his first question.

"He is alive."

"Thank God-for that!"

"But I don't feel sure that he will be able to recognize you."

"There is, then, but little hope?"

"The physicians think that he will hardly live through to-night."

"But he was so strong."

"The disease has accomplished its work. Why did n't you come sooner?"

Monsieur Naudié could only look at his brother, and murmur, "I could not, I could not."

The little group hastened at once on the short journey to Villebourbon. As they walked along, William said that Louise had arrived; much changed, grown older, little like the pretty sister of whom they had once been so proud. Angelica, he said, was keeping watch at her father's bedside. The dying man did not wish anybody else. Paul had surprised them by his lack of interest. "He can talk only of his work," said William. " I really believe that he begrudges the time which his father takes in dying."

" And the others?" asked Simeon.

" They have all written or telegraphed, except Marcel, who is too far away. But father will not see any of them." A moment later William added: " What a vacancy he will leave! We did not see much of him, to be sure, but we knew he was there, alive, — old oak that he seemed; and we hardly more than weak saplings, which have grown up around him. Now the end has come; the oak is ready to fall. And we children are not the only losers; the whole world will lose by his death."

As they entered the old mansion, they paused a moment at the foot of the great staircase, and, with one thought in common, glanced at one another's faces. It was indeed a house of mourning; the cold breath of the

Infinite seemed present in the very air. The silence was funereal. They seemed to feel, at their side, as they climbed upward, the pale phantom, who was there, awaiting his hour. They entered the sick-room. The odor of drugs was very strong; a door opened noiselessly, and some careful footfalls met their ear; then Angelica stood before them.

"God be praised, Simeon!" she said, in low tones. "He has just opened his eyes again. He has taken two spoonfuls of champagne. The physician does not allow him the red wine, which you know he was so fond of. I have told him of your arrival, and I think he understood. Just at this time he ought to rest in quiet."

She broke off her hurried narration, to embrace her brother and niece, and then led the way into the library, where Paul and Louise were seated, reading. They exchanged a few words of greeting quietly, as if they had parted only the day before; but Simeon could not help feeling that his sister, with her gray hair and worn wrinkled face, was almost like a stranger to him.

"You probably need something to eat and drink," said Angelica to the new-comers.

"Yes . . . yes . . ." replied Simeon, "but

Pastor Naudié's Young Wife

I would so much like to see . . . to see *him* first."

" Well, then, come with me," she answered; and Esther, trembling, followed behind them.

The sick room was kept dim, and the old carved furniture was scarcely discernible. There was an old-fashioned clothes-press, with one or two busts of famous men upon it; there were also family portraits of men, looking very stiff in their doublets, or gazing gloomily down out of black pastoral gowns, with one white band at the neck. The most striking object of all was the great high-posted bed, which had been occupied, in both life and death, for two hundred years, by members of the Naudié family. Upon this historic bed Abraham Naudié was half reclining, propped up by pillows, and apparently asleep, with long beard flowing down over his breast, and with head crowned by his thick white locks. His features were drawn, his nose thin, and his mouth half open, showing clearly the ravages of disease; but despite all, he preserved still the beauty and dignity of the grand old king, in the legend. Presently his eyes opened slowly, heavily, and, after wandering a moment over the room, fixed themselves upon the group standing beside his pillow.

Pastor Naudié's Young Wife

" Father, father," whispered Simeon, " do you know me ? "

There was no response. The old man's body trembled slightly. His eyes closed again, then re-opened; but the gaze wandered vacantly around, without seeing anything. Esther was frightened, and half turned away.

" Merciful Heaven ! " cried Monsieur Naudié, wringing his hands, " he does not know me ! He will never recognize me again."

He looked helplessly at Angelica, who said nothing; and, divining what was in her mind, he murmured, " Ah, my dear sister, if only you knew ! "

Touched with his grief and regret, Angelica said, " Was somebody ill in your family ? "

" No ! They are well, but . . ." Then he stopped. This was not the time and place to speak of his own private troubles.

" I will explain to you later," he said.

Sad, silent hours passed. Among the long-separated brothers and sisters, whom life had scattered as the wind scatters wheat-grains which have grown upon one stalk, the old-time intimacy was reviving again ; they quickly found, however, that they had very little in common, and fell to asking questions about one another's children and their doings. Louise told about her five children, of whom one was feeble in body, but quick and intelligent in mind; her eyes grew bright and her manner became animated, as she spoke of this little one, on whom she evidently lavished an abundance of attention and affection. Simeon spoke briefly and carefully of his young wife, whom William declared " charming," and regretted not having seen, for a long time. As for Paul, he recounted incidents of his religious work, referring to persecutions, and appeals to the civil authorities, and miraculous conversions. His committee had thought of displacing him, because of some public talk which had arisen; and this had filled him with bitterness. He quoted from Scripture, "' I came, not to bring peace, but a sword.' But his followers are cowardly; even the best of them think only of keeping along in a comfortable path of life, and are incapable of sacrificing themselves in his cause."

" That shows," remarked William, dryly, " that some advance has been made in the direction of tolerance."

Paul replied, " Our father often told us that tolerance was only a mediocre virtue."

" But he practised it most consistently," retorted William. " Has not his whole life been a testimony to this generous quality? Intellectually he kept in touch with all systems of thought, he examined all kinds of doctrines. The faith to which he personally adhered was broad, tolerant, and yet modest and humble. I recently opened one of his books; this is what I read there."

William took down from the mantel an old yellow-covered volume, and read slowly and respectfully: "If our faith is not great enough to remove mountains, if we are drawn toward God without clearly apprehending him, if our belief is weak, and if duty alone seems left to us, we can at least preserve carefully the little we have; and that will be a starting-point for our efforts, — the effort of our thought toward truth, the effort of our conduct toward higher ideals; and that is the lesson which may be disentangled from the web of all systems of morality, the lesson which lies deep down underneath all beliefs. When we understand the moral impulse, and use it humbly yet confidently, it teaches us to respect other men's consciences; for the conscience is the true temple of the true God."

"There! that is what father thought," said William. "His words will live after him. They have the freshness of youth, the vigor of sincerity, and yet the hand that wrote them has not now strength enough to turn the leaves whereon they are inscribed."

Paul bit his thin lips, and said nothing.

Toward evening the old man showed signs of uneasiness. Probably his breathing was difficult; for he leaned forward, and his breast heaved; moans and inarticulate sounds issued from his lips. The attendant suggested administering an opiate; but Paul opposed anything of the sort. "You can see that he is in pain," said Angelica. "Why not do something to quiet him?" And the evangelist consented, though with that air of disapproval which seemed almost stamped upon his features.

Little by little, Abraham Naudié sank again into a comatose state. The children, who had been summoned during this crisis, now returned to the library, where, in his books, their father seemed more truly to live than in the upper room, where his poor body was stretched out in pain.

Simeon alone remained at the bedside, awaiting any possible return of consciousness, hoping for some slight return of animation to those vacant eyes, or for some brief word from those lips which soon would lapse into eternal silence. But in vain. Some few movements of the muscles testified to the fact that death had not yet come. The quiet of the room was broken only by the ticking of the clock, or the troubled breathing of the dying man. The silence was heavy, fateful, like that of the eternity which seemed so near; and out of it rose the prayers of Simeon's troubled soul toward the Infinite One.

About midnight, Monsieur Naudié noticed that his father's breathing was becoming slower. He aroused the attendant, who was dozing. "Listen!" said he.

The woman leaned over the motionless body, and put her ear down to his breast.

The sound of the breathing became lighter and lighter. It was as if some sea-going craft were floating gently out on the swell of the ocean; and with a gentle voice she said, "I believe that this time it is really the end."

Simeon repeated, "The end! the end!"

Then it seemed best to call the others.

"Yes, yes!" exclaimed he. "Call them! Call them all quickly!"

They entered, in silence. Angelica held Esther to her breast, and the child trembled, and dared not come very near. The aged man's eyes opened once more, glassy and expressionless, touched already by the shadows which were enveloping him. His glance wandered aimlessly about. Again he closed them, and again they opened. His breathing became slower still. His head half lifted from the pillow, thrown forward by two or three spasms in the throat; and, after that, all was silence and peace.

Said the attendant, " It is over." And at the same time, accustomed to such scenes, she closed the lids over the eyes which would never see again, and, ready to perform her last duties, raised in her strong arms the inert body and the noble head whence had issued so many grand thoughts.

Standing near the bed, Simeon wept, in the arms of his sister and his daughter. A step or two behind him, Louise and William stood, hand in hand, waiting. And Paul's dry, hard voice, rising above the sound of the weeping, recited verses from the Psalms: " Thou turnest man to destruction, and sayest, Return, ye children of men ! Thou carriest them away, as with a flood ; they are as a sleep. In the morning they are like grass which groweth up. . . . For we are consumed by thine anger, and by thy wrath are we troubled."

CHAPTER II

ON the morning following Abraham Naudié's death, Henry Defos went down to his father's office. He crossed the dingy dusty ship-yard, littered with heaps of coal and wood, where great windlasses creaked, and strong men bent under their burdens. It was not of his choice that he entered this world of noise and activity, in which he must now become one of the wheels. He had never had a liking for business affairs. But, in examining himself, in his conscientious refusal to go on with his chosen profession, he did not find that he had quite the courage and hope to begin in some other one, and thus attain full freedom. Besides, there were other factors which entered into his present condition of mind ; he was worn out with his recent struggles, he was bruised and wounded by the victory which he had achieved during the night. He was exhausted by the transition to a higher purpose which his soul had achieved, a purpose which he was now hastening to put into practice ; and he was obeying the voice of duty, but he took no interest in his work or in his future.

Pastor Naudié's Young Wife

Monsieur Defos was very glad to see his second son' coming thus into the office. It was a rather sombre place, with windows opening upon the coal-yard ; but it was the scene of his own output of tireless energy, and from it he ruled a little world. Since Henry's illness, his father had felt toward him a certain timidity, such as men of affairs often feel toward more sensitive men of books and letters. He fancied that he might find the young man rather indolent, and slow to learn ; but he resolved to be patient, and not reprove him.

"Ah !" said he. "So you have decided to come and try the air here in the office. That is good. I am glad to see you here. Would you like to go to work? To-day? Or to-morrow?"

Henry sat down, opposite his father, who laid down his pen, pushed back his papers, and swung around on the light revolving desk-chair, which cracked under his weight. "As soon as possible !" said Henry.

Monsieur Defos's face brightened.

"Only, one thing, father ! I would like to begin by taking a journey."

Monsieur Defos was roused at once, and was ready to blame the young man. "A journey? What journey? Some pleasure tour, doubtless! In Italy, of course !"

" No, some useful journey, I mean. Some journey, for the good of the business ; if such a one is possible."

" Well, now! That is more like it! That pleases me. At this very moment, we have a contract in Norway, which needs immediate attention. I will explain it to you; and if it suits you . . . "

" North or South, it is all the same to me. I wish, simply, to get away as soon as possible."

" Why ? "

A protracted silence was the only reply to this question. Monsieur Defos repeated his inquiry. Henry bowed his head.

" Ah ! what is it now ? " asked Monsieur Defos, knitting his brows. " Don't you understand that I ought to know ? " And vague suspicions and fears crossed his mind. This strange son was constantly bringing him surprises.

" Don't ask me, father ! The reasons which urge me to go away are not from any fault of mine. They have existence only in my own heart and mind. You need not fear that I shall do anything to cause you anxiety. On the contrary, I am not sure but that my stay here might be a source of complications. I have asked much of you lately, and now I ask only this one thing more; that is, to go away. I will return when I can. You will then have in me an obedient son, who will try to compensate you, by his faithfulness, for your many kindnesses."

Dull as he was to all that pertained to the romance of life, Monsieur Defos now partially understood. But he had very little sympathy with the idea that any such journey would be necessary. He believed that any and all the caprices of the heart could be easily conquered by reason and determination. Moreover, he was a little fearful of some accident to his second son, if he went far away, in his present state of mind and body.

" Go away? " he exclaimed. " Do you think it would be best for you to go away? Let me tell you my opinion, which is, that this journey is not at all necessary for you. To take it, as an important necessary step, is not according to the ways of our family. In our household we have never indulged in romances. We take life seriously. We accept whatever comes, without indulging in any foolish opposition. But then, you are made of a different stuff. I have come to see that. I have been much pleased to see that you have still kept alive your sense of duty. Doubtless there are cases where heroism is best shown by taking one's self away. So, then, play the hero after your own fashion, my boy!"

Henry hardly cared to go any further into the details of his humiliating condition. He accepted thankfully the position reached by his practical, prosaic, impassive father. "Well, then," said he, "let us arrange about this journey, since you consent to it! And now will you do me the favor, this evening at dinner, in the presence of my mother and my brother, of asking me and even ordering me to go away?"

Monsieur Defos consented to this also. Then he began upon a minute explanation of the transaction which would warrant this sudden departure.

Henry did not see Jane again. She, however, passed a dreary afternoon with her aunt, foreseeing clearly the deep impression which the scene of the evening before must make upon the young man.

That evening, at dinner, the little drama which had been arranged between father and son was carried out. They were a little ashamed of the parts they were playing; but when one has entered, be it never so slightly, upon a course of deception, it is often necessary to practise still more deception, in order to carry out the original plan. Thus it was that Henry, in order to make his ruse a success, was compelled to speak and act boldly.

Monsieur Defos, according to his custom, returned thanks, after the dinner ; then, rather clumsily, in the confusion of leaving the table, he remarked : "By the bye, Henry, I have something to propose to you. What say you to taking a journey? A long one, too, to assist in carrying out one of the business transactions of our office?"

With his face somewhat red, the young man replied, "I am at your command, father."

Madame Defos listened, with eagerness and surprise.

Monsieur Defos continued : "Very good! It shall be soon. You will need to set about it directly."

"Just as you say !"

"Well, then, let it be to-morrow! Perhaps to-morrow morning rather than to-morrow night."

Madame Defos, stupefied, now protested. Her son's health, she said, still needed great care. But Henry interrupted her, cheerfully, "Oh, never mind about my health, mother ! I am remarkably well."

"But the preparations! A man can't set off on a long journey with merely a cane and an overcoat. There must be some supplies. Trunks must be packed."

"A valise will be enough," said Henry, "quite enough. I can buy what I need, on the way."

"I've done that many a time," remarked David.

"Surely you won't hurry away in such a fashion," stammered Madame Defos, "without taking leave of anybody, as if you were running away?"

"The idea!" protested Monsieur Defos, stoutly. "Why, he goes away just as any active man would, when business compels it. David and I have often done it."

"You may make ready whatever you like, mother dear," said Henry, touched by her deep interest, "and then I will thank you and give you a kiss. Now that I have entered upon business life, I must be ready to meet its demands."

"Very well," she replied reluctantly, "I will do the best I can."

Her features, which had become for a few moments alert and expressive, now sank into their habitual immobility. But, behind her impassive countenance, a great anxiety and disquietude was taking root. This unexpected departure was a new contingency, which she now longed to meet and overcome. There were her other plans, which she had expected would bring about certain results. She had struggled and schemed to bring to her favorite son what she believed rightfully belonged to him.

Monsieur Defos now remarked, casually : "I have myself been only once in Norway. I found the journey, however, rather interesting and instructive. I hope Henry will profit by it." And he began upon a long dissertation regarding the northern countries.

With all that careful attention to details characteristic of good housekeepers, Madame Defos spent a long evening between the closets and bureaus and two trunks, which she slowly filled. She had come to look upon the proposed journey as natural and necessary, but she was much disturbed in heart, and her thoughts were restless and active. Toward midnight the trunks were full, and she went up to Henry's room, to say good-night to him for the last time. She found him seated at his desk, writing. He arose to welcome her, made her sit down, and took both her hands in his.

"Poor, dear mother," he said tenderly, " you

have been sitting up on my account. You must be very tired."

She glanced at the letter, which he had begun, and then at him. He noted the silent inquiry of her look, and replied: "Yes, I have been writing . . . to Jane. You will give her the letter yourself to-morrow, so that she may learn from you of my departure. I have not yet told her about it."

He spoke with that calm which strong natures show, when they are carrying out some difficult but fully arranged plan. It was plain that he had counted the cost.

"Why have you not seen her, to tell her yourself? What prevented your going this evening?"

"I assure you, mother, that this is the better way."

How could he expect to deceive his mother regarding his real motives? She loved him too dearly to be very blind to what was passing; she had known, for a long time, his secret, and she had been very indulgent to him in his temptations and trials. Knowing, therefore, as he did, that she read his heart, he felt now a measureless need of her kind words and consolation. "Yes, it is better this way," he repeated. Then he continued, slowly: "Ties and bonds

soon form, before one realizes how strong they
are becoming.   We easily fall into easy, pleasant relationships.   Affections build themselves
about us, and we know it not, until they have
taken firm hold of us; and then a day comes
when we open our eyes, and see what paths
we have travelled.   Mother, my eyes are open
now.   What do you think I ought to do?"

He waited for her reply, expecting about the
same words to which he had listened, as they
came from his father's lips that morning; for
his mother, according to the idea which he had
of her, was, despite her obvious affection for
him, a woman of strict honor and clear sense.
However, she contented herself with murmuring, "Ah, if Jane had only listened to me, she
would never have married that man."

This plaintive regret, this vain protest,
touched him deeply; but he did not weaken.
"Yes," he replied, "if . . . if; but she is now
his wife; and how can I play the part of some
thief, prowling about his house!   How can I
bring harm to his household and his heart!
And then, up to what point can one struggle
against circumstances?   Indeed, I think too
highly of her to bring harm to her.   I love her
for herself.   Her honor is dearer to me than
my happiness.   I cannot tempt her out into the

paths of deception. I wish her to be a good woman, who may, indeed, suffer in her feelings, but whose conscience is unsullied. And, for that, I must go away. I will write to her sometimes, and I will come back when we have both become strong enough to be able to meet. It shall be a beautiful friendship that shall unite us, sincere and honorable, for which we shall have no occasion to blush, either before others or before our own souls."

Madame Defos followed, astonished, this plain language of the poor young lover. All that she comprehended, or desired to comprehend, was that her son was in suffering, and was renouncing a happiness which she was by no means willing he should renounce. Such was the high influence, over her, of his nobility of nature, that she could not reveal to him her own dark plans. How could she speak plainly to such a young heart, seriously bent on honorable self-sacrifice, concerning purposes which she had revolved in her mind for many months! How could she remind him that marriage is by no means an indissoluble bond, and that the Code even allows the taking of a neighbor's wife!

"Oh! this man Naudié!" she exclaimed, with animosity.

"He is not to blame," said Henry; "and he is in great trouble about it all, himself. There, there! It is my duty to go on this journey, I am in the way here."

He seemed upborne on a wave of exaltation, triumphing over his selfish instincts; while his mother, altering her tone, gave her approval, compassionated him, comforted him, and ended by expressing, with tears in her eyes, her great distress at his sad conditions. "Come back! Come back soon!" she cried. "I am so accustomed to having you with me. It seems, now, that I must consent to your going, but it is all too cruel. I need you more than ever, after having so nearly lost you. Oh, how I hate those who are the means of sending you away!"

When Henry was left alone, he finished his letter. He had begun it in a calm, reasonable way, unfolding the reasons why he ought to go away. But the longer he wrote, there in the solitude of the night, the more heated he became. The violence of his passion and the mighty struggle through which he was passing, found vent in eloquent words, and page after page was covered with writing. Without weighing his words or his fancies, without holding firmly to his resolution, his pen revolved about the one thought, "I love you, I love you, and now I must go away." It is a never-ending theme, whose bitterness only they learn who experience it; a theme through which vibrates something which is the noblest in the soul of man,—the power of love and the power of sacrifice; a theme which lovers, famous or obscure, in all ages, have chanted or wailed, each in his own sad heart, as each has felt the wounds of separation, and the weight of duty. When the letter was finished, Henry paused, with an aching heart. What would she think, as she read this? Perhaps . . . intolerable thought . . . that he no longer loved her.

The day broke. He opened his window. Through the rosy mist of dawn, he could distinguish the great cedar in Monsieur Naudié's garden, rising dark and dignified. Then, after a moment, as if he were reflecting upon the distance which in a few hours must separate him from her, he groaned, "Oh if I could stay! If I could only stay!" But he was one of those whose very weaknesses challenge them to embrace the dreaded suffering, rather than to flee from it.

CHAPTER III

JANE was ending a quarrel with Bertha, when Henry's letter was brought to her. Madame Defos was not especially desirous of softening the blow for her niece; its very violence might help her own plans. So she did not bring the letter over herself. Jane, in her closed room, gave way to a storm of rage, sorrow, humiliation, ending in sobs which did not cease for an hour. Then the storm abated, the young woman's elastic nature rebounded, and she rose above her feelings. She had doubts as to whether he had really gone. She revolved a thousand projects for bringing him back, or for keeping him from going. There was some uncertainty regarding his plans. He had said little about the journey, and much about his feeling for her. Surely it was best to make sure; and she drew a cloak around her morning-gown, wrapped a shawl about her head, and hastened over to her aunt, on whose assistance she felt that she could count.

Exhausted by the unusual emotions of the previous night, Madame Defos was wandering about in the vacant house, surprised still, and hardly realizing the great change which had come. She seemed old and feeble, and more shapeless in figure than ever; and her impassive face seemed fixed and rigid, lined and creased with heavy care. But Jane knew well that under this outer mask of lethargy could be found a restless, vigorous spirit, as often it had been found before. She was instinctively certain that she would have, in this mother, an eager, powerful, and perhaps triumphant ally. Moreover, while she had never taken her aunt wholly into her confidence, she had not at all concealed from her her feelings. Accordingly, as the two met, Jane asked, in the tone which one involuntarily uses in a house where death has come, " Is it true ? "

" Yes, it is true."

" How so ? Why ? Where ? "

Madame Defos made her niece seat herself, and slowly explained. . . . Norway . . . important business . . . the interests of the firm. In a very calm and collected voice she dwelt upon the practical, business side of the affair.

Then Jane gasped: " Business ! Gone on business ! "

Madame Defos looked at her a moment, then took her hand, and said steadily : " Business is the pretext, my child. As to the real cause, you know better than anybody else. I am sure that he must have written all that in his letter."

She was casting about for exactly the right words, words which would convey more hidden meaning than they might outwardly carry ; while Jane, with face clouded, still held her hand.

" Gone ! Gone ! " exclaimed the young woman. "And in this way ! It is cowardly."

" No, don't say that ! If you could have seen him last night, you would never say that. I saw him ; I saw his grief and his tears ; I saw his despair ; I saw his resolution. He has by no means gone, out of cowardice, I assure you ; he has gone because of duty."

This word "duty" awoke very slight response in the young woman's wilful, hungry soul. "Duty !" she exclaimed scornfully. "Always duty ! You have a great deal to say about it, all of you. You think when you have said it that you have said the final word. They try to tell us, do some of these people, that duty is the one supreme arbiter of life ; but I think . . . " Here her voice became low and vibrant. " Well, duty ! Do you suppose one thinks of that when he loves ? "

" Henry is one of those who never forget."

" Because they do not know how to love."

"Or because they love too much."   Madame Defos made a show of correcting herself.   " It is well that you tell me these things.   My duty, — the word is habitual with me, you see, — my duty will not suffice to make me conceal from you what I know, for the sake of helping you to forget him.   I cannot bring myself to it.   How can I live without him, after I have seen him brought back almost from death's door, and now that I was expecting to have him always near me !   Besides, I have always had his happiness and welfare close at heart.   In order to make him happy, mark you, I would overturn the world, if I were able. But how can you expect him to choose happiness, if evil must be linked with it !   You do not know my son.   His heart is eloquent with feeling ; but he has the self-control to repress it.   My son never could love anybody, except as his wife, Jane ; and you, Jane, alas, can never be that to him."

Jane sat thoughtfully, knitting her brow, with little of her old animation evident. " And I cannot be that to him," she repeated mechanically.

After a few moments more of silence, she

spoke again. " I am only twenty-five years old. I am just beginning life. Why should I carry, all my days, the burden of my mistake? For undoubtedly I have made a mistake. And just there is the pity of it. My error did not come from God or the devil; but arose simply from my own inexperience, from my youth and impressionability, — from a silly dream. And because I have been deceived once, because my foolish school-girl fancy led me on a false scent, and I was allowed . . . "

Madame Defos interrupted : " Oh, I warned you."

" Well, warned or not, what difference does it make? I made a mistake; there is the plain fact. And, because of it, I must needs take in tow this man and his family, whom I cannot make happy, and who make me most miserable. And I have only one life to live. Now look at it all! Is it fair? Is it as it should be?"

Madame Defos sighed. " It is marriage, my child; it is the law."

" Oh, yes! Law, duty, conscience! All those words from your dictionary! I don't understand them, I don't wish to understand them. They seem to me false and meaning-less."

Pastor Naudié's Young Wife

At these violent expressions, given with much feeling, Madame Defos replied, with great show of resignation : " I was once young, like you, Jane. I think I may add that I was pretty, also. I too had my dreams, as most young girls have. And then I was married to Monsieur Defos. You are acquainted with his nature. Need I say to you that he does not closely resemble the hero of my girlish dreams? So, for a time, I thought myself very unhappy; and, perhaps, I was. However, life has gone on."

" But I do not wish to have it go on in any such way for me. I will not have it so. I must have my life beautiful, and free, and filled with love. I am suffocated with these bonds and burdens which are heaped upon me. Why should I not burst through them? I have courage enough, I am not afraid. Law! You forget that while there is a law which binds, there is also one which sets free. Yes, yes! There are laws that liberate. Why don't you say something about them?"

" Here, my child, in this house, in this city, within the bounds of our faith . . . well, one must yield in silent submission."

" But I am not one of you. I am in rebellion against your ways, your faith, your city, your traditions . . . I am ready to defy them all. I will walk over them, head in air. And you — surely you will not oppose me?"

"Ah," said Madame Defos, "if I believed that separation would heal my boy's heart, I would indeed oppose you; but I know that he loves you too deeply to forget you."

One brief sentence, in a letter from Bertha to Esther, apprised Monsieur Naudié of Henry's sudden departure; the news came to him on the morning of the day of his father's burial, and found him already too much overwhelmed with grief to be greatly affected by it. For four days, all thoughts of Henry and Jane had been well-nigh effaced, by the pangs of remorse which had taken hold upon him. He felt that he had neglected his duty. His thoughts reverted to his father, dying without a last good-bye, more than to his wife and his rival; and when he did think of them, it was without the bitter feelings of wounded love or irritated jealousy. His passion had crumbled, in the general misfortune which had come to him; and he now had only the desire to protect and preserve, as a man should, the respectability and honor of his hearth and home. So that, when Esther read him Bertha's letter, he only said to himself that this departure had come too late, all too late. And he straightway gave himself up again to the current of memories and regrets, which swept him along, — memories and regrets which were kept constantly in his mind by the scenes around him.

The death of Abraham Naudié, coming, as it did, only eighteen months after his jubilee, brought back to Montauban many of the long gowns and snow-crowned heads from the universities. Professors there were; and pastors; and philosophers, with their calm, serene souls, subdued by reason and reflection; now they found themselves a part of the funeral cortège, behind the hearse, which was loaded with wreaths, and was bearing away, to its last resting-place, the now empty body of this noble old man. The solemnity of the occasion greatly moved Simeon. He walked with the others, and felt that all were in harmony. He listened to their words, as they stood around the tomb. Long speeches, many of them, eulogizing the great work of the deceased, and some of them uttered with more zeal than discretion. The words which fall at such times upon a bier, much resemble the empty, fruitless funeral trappings themselves; the one whose body

was then and there consigned to earth transcended all their power of expression.   But
what of it?   Words so often fall ineffective,
inadequate, and the wind sweeps them away ;
while, far away, in the remote corners of the
world, within the hearts and minds of growing
youth, bending over their books, — *his* books,
— good seed was germinating, sown by the
hand of the aged husbandman.

After the official ceremonies had taken place,
and the delegates had gone, family questions
came to the front.   Plans, rearrangements,
settlements needed to be discussed.   All felt
pity for Angelica, that tender vine, torn off
and cast upon the ground by the woodsman,
who came to cut down the mighty oak about
which she had twined.   So many years of
sweet, willing slavery had accustomed her to
sacrifice.   What would become of her, alone,
in the future, with no being to work for, obliged
to concern herself with herself only, and
hardly knowing how to do that?   So great
was her disruption of life and lack of definite
plans, that one might very aptly have applied
to her these words from the " Dialogues of
To-day " : " Sacrifice expects no recompense.
Its sole joy is in going forward to new work ; for
if it stops, it leaves a greater vacancy than do

the warmest affections. And this is, perhaps, because it would be hopeless, had not Christ — that supreme master of human hearts, knowing how to touch them so as to ennoble them — given it the loftiest place among the virtues, and made it the foundation of morality, and built upon it all our other faiths and beliefs." Poor Angelica! Like a swallow, left behind in the hour of migration, she wandered about through the empty rooms, and said, again and again, to one and another of her brothers, " Certainly I ought to be able to do something for you."

Alas, she could not. Their affairs were all arranged. What could she do in the strange, unaccustomed, irregular life of William ? Or, as well, with Paul, whose intolerable fanaticism was very different from her standards of goodness. Or with Simeon, who belonged to his young wife ? Thus, at the close of many years of self-abnegation, she found solitude weighing upon her. Already she began to reflect that it might be necessary for her to give up such spacious quarters, and go away from the dear old home, where no Naudié, save herself, was left ; and perhaps to depart from the town itself, so familiar to her and so full of memories. These anxieties, mingled with her sorrow for her father's death, gave a very practical turn to her ideas. Still, she was, and must always be, an unpractical creature. She ventured to confide her anxieties to Simeon, when she found him in the library,—that room where she had turned over the leaves of so many books for her father.

"How lonely I feel in these days!" she exclaimed; and her eyes, as she spoke, fell upon the armchair, where, fifteen days before, Abraham Naudié had sat, comfortably smoking his pipe of Marseilles clay, with its long reed stem.

"My dear sister, do you fancy that we can ever forget your goodness to him?"

"But you all have your lives, your duties, your ties. I know that perfectly well."

"At first," said Simeon, "my plan is to take you home with me, to give you a chance to rest, and think over your plans, and reach some decision."

She murmured timidly: "I fear that I shall burden you. Your wife is young, and I shall be rather gloomy. And then, she has her ways of doing things . . ."

Simeon almost groaned aloud at the words. "I will see to it," said he, grimly, "that my wife does not neglect her duties toward you."

Pastor Naudié's Young Wife

Far from reassuring Angelica, the threat which lay half hidden in his words frightened her all the more. But she said nothing; she was content to fix upon her brother her tender, grateful eyes. At the question which he read in this mute appeal, Simeon said more gently: "Yes, my good girl, you can come to me without any hesitation or fear, for there is in our house a great deal that needs looking after. My home is by no means a happy one. You will have there a good field for the exercise of your sweetness and goodness. And when I have more trouble than I can bear alone . . . well, I shall come and weep over it with you."

Angelica, however, did not go away with Simeon and Esther. She remained, last of all, in the old home, which the saddened children left, one after another. Paul departed first; his evangelistic work needed him. Then William went, reaching Rocheport at about the same time that the others reached La Rochelle. Louise remained a week later, picking up again the thread of the old child-life, which her near departure would break off, probably for the remainder of her days. Then silence reigned in the old rooms, and solitude spread itself through the whole house, like a deep shadow, and Angelica glided aimlessly about among the old furniture and the old books.

Monsieur Naudié's return was followed by an interval of calm and quiescence. No explanation was offered, between husband and wife, no reference was made to the storm of rage and jealousy in which they had separated. No questions were asked concerning Henry. In his depression of spirit, the pastor accepted this half-reconciliation gladly; with such peaceable natures as his, points of strife which are not raised openly, seem no longer to exist. He fancied that Jane's heart was in much the same softened conciliatory condition as his own. Once outside that fiery circle of suspicion and jealousy and anger, where he had come into sharp antagonism with her interests, he loved to believe that she too had come outside it with him, and was trying to forget it. The silence, and Henry's absence, and the readjustment of the old habits would suffice, he thought, to blot out the unpleasant past, and scatter its dark shadows. More than this, he even dreamed of a full and frank reconciliation, and of a return of that tranquillity of heart which had been his during the early days of his marriage with her. Upon his hearth, free from all taint of dishonor, the good man thought he could see a clear flame of peace and joy again shedding light around. In this mood, as if under the protecting care of that father who had been such a blessing in the home of his childhood, Monsieur Naudié passed several happy days. Entire peace reigned in the household, where he and his dwelt, finding joy in one another's society. In the evenings, after Zelia had been put in bed, Esther and Bertha busied themselves with some fancy-work. Both said very little; Bertha seemed silent and reserved, Esther appeared sweet and serene. Abraham, one evening, arose, after reading one of his books of travel, and said, as he closed the volume, "There! there's where I would like to go."

A remark which brought upon him this response, "It is best to remain where one was born, and it is best to obey one's father."

Even Jane herself, whether she read or worked, or sat idly dreaming, with her little shapely feet on the fender of the fireplace, seemed very tranquil, and had the innocent expression of a little child. Monsieur Naudié lived over and over again the details of his sad visit to Montauban,—the sickness, the funeral rites, the eulogies; and discussed, one after another, the plans of the family.

"We have made over," said he, "to Angelica

the trifling rentals which our father left, and also the authorship rights of his books."

Then he glanced at Jane, and added, "I think we are all in agreement upon these matters."

Jane nodded her head, without showing any especial interest; and he continued: " Paul was the only one who claimed any part of the property; and not for his own use, but for carrying on his work. He finds that God has more need, than has my poor sister, of these small amounts."

At these words Esther laid down her work. " Poor aunt Angelica ! " said she.

This was the favorable moment, which Monsieur Naudié chose, for announcing the coming of Angelica into their little family circle. "You have doubtless heard," said he, "that she has promised to come to us. I hope she will be able to do so."

Jane at once showed more interest. " And she will really come ? " she asked.

" Doubtless."

" Soon ? "

" As soon as she can."

" Ah ! "

Evidently Jane approved; and Monsieur Naudié, thinking he understood her, said to himself: " How easy everything becomes, when violent passion has passed away! How often it happens that some sign from God, some call to duty, suffices to set our feet in the right path!"

So it was almost with gayety that he informed his wife, one morning, that Angelica would certainly come. "It will be on Tuesday of next week," he said, holding in his hand a letter which he had just received. "She names Tuesday, but she may perhaps be a little later than that. She is not much used to travelling."

"At least," said Jane, "if it is not Tuesday, it will be Wednesday or Thursday? She will remain here some little time, I hope."

"I hope so."

"Very good, then! I have been awaiting the news of the exact date of her arrival, my friend, to convey to you a decision which I reached some· time ago. I have put off speaking to you about it, out of regard for your state of mourning. Now that your sister is really coming, I do not see why I should wait any longer."

She spoke calmly, in a steady reflective tone, like a person who is very clear as to what she is about to do.

"A decision?" inquired Monsieur Naudié.

Looking him straight in the eyes, Jane

replied, " Yes, my friend ; my decision to leave this house."

The shock to Monsieur Naudié was very great. He could only stammer, " Have I heard aright ? Do I understand you ? "

" I think so. Certainly it is very clear. I wish to go away. I desire my freedom. We have never understood each other, my friend ; and we never will. So, then, let us separate, without any hard feelings ! You have tried to reform me ; I am aware of that. But I made a mistake. And I have not been a source of joy to you or yours ; neither have you brought me any happiness ; then, why keep on in our mistaken course ? "

She hardly raised her voice above the calmest level. Her apparent tranquillity gave a strange effect to her surprising words. She was laying aside the most sacred bonds, like a child tossing away precious gems which he has used for playthings.

" But you forget," exclaimed Monsieur Naudié, " that we are married."

" By no means ! But I don't consider marriage an indissoluble bond."

" It is, if looked at in the right way, nothing less than a sacrament."

" I certainly do not see it in that way."

"But I do."

"Oh no, your church allows divorce."

"It may allow it," protested the astonished man, "but deplores the scandal of it. And I, as a minister of the gospel, how can I consent to such a thing! How can I consent . . . to give you up . . . at the very moment when . . . when I thought I had found you once more! You surely cannot understand how sweet it is for me to have you near me. You cannot realize that, however you may have wounded my heart, however you may have trampled underfoot my love, it still lives and beats for you, and, at any cost, would seek to save you from yourself. Moreover, we are . . . we are pledged to each other for life. And your true place is here—here. Give but a sign of your wishes, and you shall have all possible attentions. Here, too, are your duties, duties which dignify human life. Ah, poor dear heart, when you speak thus lightly of breaking the bonds which unite us, you must have forgotten the solemn words of the service which made us one; you have forgotten the holy troth which you plighted in church."

Jane, who was listening to his excited words impatiently, here interrupted: "You are preaching me a sermon?"

Pastor Naudié's Young Wife

" No," exclaimed Monsieur Naudié ; " it is, rather, a prayer.   It is the prayer of a despairing man, who addresses it to your reason, to your heart, to your conscience."

" Shorten it, then, I beg !   I find it a little tedious."

Up to this point Monsieur Naudié had spoken in a tone of entreaty.   Now, as if lashed by her heartless words, he drew himself up to his full height, and his handsome face wore an expression of wounded pride.

" Ah, take care ! " he cried.   " If you will not listen to my prayerful supplications, I will change my form of address.   You are unworthy of the words which I have used.   Are you, then, lost to all appeals of reason ?   Have you no sense of goodness, no moral sense ?   Then I will remind you that I too have something plain to say upon this matter.   A wife has no right to leave her home, in obedience to some slight caprice.   And I here state to you that I will not give you the freedom which you demand."

" But if I claim it, how can you hinder me ? "

" By legal steps."

" Will you go and bring in the constable ? "

" I will forbid and prevent you from going."

Pastor Naudié's Young Wife

"An injunction, then! You will put an injunction upon me; if that is what they call it? But, my dear, think a moment! Listen to what I tell you! I am determined to have my liberty again. I will gain it by any means possible, legal or otherwise."

She paused a moment, to give full effect to her hard, relentless words; then went on:

"Besides, I expected this resistance from you. It is perfectly natural; not because you love me — I know all about that — neither because you are, as you say, a minister of the gospel; but because . . . you are poor . . . and I . . . am rich."

"Jane!" cried Monsieur Naudié.

"Yes, when I am gone, is it not poverty and distress for you and your children? It is not I that you care for, it is my money. So calm yourself! I . . ."

She stopped, for he was coming toward her, with clenched hand raised. For an instant he stood in this threatening position, then drew back, and his hand fell at his side. "O most miserable creature!" he cried. "Go! Go, and take everything! I wish nothing of yours, nothing, nothing. Go! I drive you forth."

She went out slowly, never lowering her gaze, as an athlete retreats when defeated, but

Pastor Naudié's Young Wife

is still strong and collected enough to watch the actions of his antagonist. Left alone, Monsieur Naudié began to stammer a few words of prayer, but ended by breaking down into sobs and tears. He was forsaken, deserted.

CHAPTER IV

JANE carried out her plan of leaving Monsieur Naudié's house; and what a theme for conversation it furnished throughout the city, where few exciting events occurred! Not only the free-thinkers enjoyed discussing the flight of "the minister's wife," but everybody talked about it, wherever they met one another, in the street, at church, under the arcades, at the foot of the Duperré statue, in the restaurants, near the great clock of the St. Nicholas tower, or at the afternoon teas. Everywhere people discussed it, in low tones, and with a delightful sense of mystery.

The following Sunday, a young student, thin and pale, took Monsieur Naudié's place in church, and preached a sermon, constructed according to the best rules, to which nobody listened. When the congregation came out, there was a steady hum of conversation, as of a hive of bees greatly excited. There was still considerable uncertainty hovering in the air, regarding the exact facts. The good people who have great difficulty in believing anything ill, expressed themselves cautiously. Cynics

Pastor Naudié's Young Wife

and evil-minded persons, certain of the truth of the rumor, spoke boldly about the affair, and wore an expression of satisfaction and triumph. "It is certainly so. Positively! She has left his house. She will not go back."

Monsieur Merlin, much swollen with excitement, went about from group to group, seeking new details. "There is doubtless some cause? . . . Ah! . . . Somebody? Just as people said! Ah! . . . It is true, then?"

Nobody cared to make very open replies to his queries; the prestige of the Defos name was too great. A few ventured a remark or two. "Is it a divorce?"

"Oh, but a minister cannot obtain a divorce. It will be merely a separation, doubtless."

"Who knows?"

Monsieur Dehodecq dared to put a plain question, as a person in his position could: "What does Monsieur Defos say about it?"

Nobody knew. He had been in his customary place in church, seated between his wife and his son, with a more than usually arrogant air; and he had pushed through the crowd, coming out, returning greetings, but conversing with nobody.

"Madame Defos had a rather comfortable, self-satisfied air," remarked somebody.

Monsieur Lanthelme suggested, " That is, perhaps, for some other reason.   For instance, she may be expecting her son's return."

" Ah !   Is he coming home ? "

" He is coming home."   Some one said, and nobody knew exactly who it was, " Perhaps the affair will end in another marriage."

Monsieur Defos had not been at once informed of Jane's decision.   When he learned about it, it fell like a bomb upon him.   He had not suspected it.   He was at first angry ; he reasoned with his niece ; he pictured vividly to her the distress which must result ; but she would not listen to him.

Now, Monsieur Defos, despite his " Principles," was one of those who had great respect for facts, especially when they tended to enhance his own interests.   He soon freed his mind, after some inward tumult, from the " General question," which had baffled him, and now gave his attention to the " Particular questions," whose complexity he was very quick to perceive.   There was the honor of the family to be saved, there were the interests of the family to be defended, there was the unity of the family to be preserved ; and, inasmuch as his scrupulous honesty was not so much disturbed when there was no probable loss of money, he left his wife free to circulate her version of the affair, to direct public opinion, and to see that all blame was laid upon Monsieur Naudié.

Madame Defos, that "good woman," as she was called, who up to this point had manifested only a gentle apathy, now began to display an energy that was wonderful, considering her size, an activity which one would never have suspected. She was to be seen everywhere, giving her version of the matter, commiserating her niece, and enlarging skilfully upon the few favorable facts, which, like all calumnies and deceits that are effective, had a few grains of truth. "What could a young wife do, at close quarters with a girl of such a miserable character as Bertha, or with the evil nature of a boy like Abraham? Was the little vagrant not expelled twice from school, and would not have been taken back, except out of consideration for his father? Ah, if only the poor young wife, faced by such a burden of duty, could have had the assistance of her husband! But everybody knew the weakness of their pastor. He was such a selfish man, who let his own father die without hastening to his bedside. Had he not shown clearly how unscrupulous he was, in taking advantage of this young girl's romantic nature, and thus securing a fortune for himself; and that, too, without once considering his own age and profession and duties?"

It was interesting to see her, when she was speaking in this way, raising her little ferret eyes toward heaven, invoking corroboration from that source.

"However, I warned her, the poor dear child! All this which has come to pass, my dear friend, I foresaw. She has admitted it to me more than once, after she recognized her mistake. What could she do? Was it right that she should suffer, all her life? I myself counselled her to rise up and act, much as I stand for union and harmony in family life."

Shielded by such skill and influence as this, Jane shone forth like a saint, like a little martyr. "So young, so beautiful, so rich, and weighed down by a misfortune which might blight her entire life!"

"Fortunately," said Monsieur Lanthelme, "she has time to begin anew."

At first the town-talk turned chiefly upon the romantic and scandalous aspects of the situation; but, in a short time, people were learnedly and confidently discussing the worldly and material interests at stake. Where

would the money go?   Would Monsieur
Naudié sink back into the straitened conditions
in which he had lived before this marriage,
or would he find some honest, proper means
of retaining a little of this wealth, which had
cost him so much?

"The woman, in this affair, is entirely mistress of the situation," announced Monsieur
Merlin, who knew about the marriage contract,
having drawn it up with Monsieur Defos.

Then some good soul suggested, "Surely
she would never wish that he should sink back
into abject poverty."

"Women have no pity for men whom they
no longer love," said Monsieur Lanthelme.

Then another took it up: "If so desired,
she can be compelled to make over a certain
amount to him."

"Why?   He has had no children by her."

"Her own self-respect will compel her to
do it."

"Again, how can he possibly go back to the
old ways?   When one has become accustomed
to luxuries, it is hard to give them up."

While all these comments and discussions of
wiseacres were buzzing and droning on, Monsieur Naudié shut himself up in his house to
suffer alone.   The anger which Jane's conduct

had aroused in him quickly subsided. He was conscious only of his own distress, and of the invisible net of misfortune which had enveloped him. His children's joy, at being delivered from their enemy, they but poorly concealed. It seemed to mock him in his misery. And the consoling words of Esther and Angelica had little influence over his disordered state of mind. And what could they say? With that premature wisdom, so characteristic of her, Esther merely expressed her affection for him, though this was difficult for her, reserved creature that she was. Angelica, however, was more naïve, more candid, less accustomed to his ways; and she said more, whenever she felt confident of her words; but she made mistakes, often.

" She was all unworthy," said Angelica, rising to a height of indignation quite unusual with her.

And Monsieur Naudié responded : " She was my wife." Then his thought outran his words, and he reflected, " And I loved her so ; and perhaps do still."

" You have right and justice and conscience entirely on your side," said his sister.

He replied sadly, " I shall have public opinion against me."

Pastor Naudié's Young Wife

Angelica found it hard to believe that; but Monsieur Naudié knew which way people would lean; and it was like an additional wound to his heart to realize, as he did, that calumny would point her finger at him, and his name would be dragged in the mud by the very people who had great power over his life, yet who would carelessly or wilfully judge him and condemn him and scorn him.

"We cannot remain here," said he. "And what is to be done? It seems best to go away, and seek some other parish. Yet everywhere this evil slander will follow me. Methinks I can hear them now,—these new parishioners in the East, or in the North, over whom I may be placed. 'Pastor Naudié! Oh yes! Son of Abraham Naudié. He has been sent to us because he could not remain longer at La Rochelle; there was some bad affair in his family life.' Oh, may Heaven have pity on me!"

It was a part of the proceedings that Monsieur Naudié should have an interview with Monsieur Defos, in order to "come to some clear understanding" (as the ingenious euphemism of the councillor-general put it) "regarding the points raised." Accordingly, Monsieur Naudié, still hoping against hope, for some possible reconciliation, made his way at the hour named to Monsieur Defos's office; and as he stood before that august personage, he seemed like a criminal in the presence of a judge.

Monsieur Defos gauged his visitor's state of mind, with one glance. Then, seated firmly in his revolving chair, he began in solemn fashion: " It is a very serious matter which brings you and me together to-day, my dear sir."

Monsieur Naudié, with head bowed, assented, " Very serious indeed."

Monsieur Defos made him wait a moment or two, then cleared his throat, and said: " It falls to me — that is to say, circumstances lay the duty upon me — to try and find the best solution possible for this very difficult problem. There is one point upon which I am sure that you and I will be in entire accord. The one desire of both our hearts surely will be to avoid all scandal as much as possible. Is that not so?"

The clergyman did not reply immediately. Perhaps he had expected some other line of inquiry, some other solution; for, alas, the scandal was already abroad everywhere. He pondered a moment, then gathered his forces, and ventured to say, what he had hoped to hear Monsieur Defos say : " Very true !   But the thing which would be best of all, best for both sides, and most desirable as an example to the world, —this would be, would it not, a reconciliation ?   I still ask, Monsieur Defos, why my wife left me.   It is true that she spoke vaguely of a general incompatibility of natures, and a lack of mutual sympathy in tastes and ideas.   I recognize the truth of the claim ; and you are very well aware how little is left of that piety and devoutness which first drew us together.   Do these reasons suffice to justify the rash and momentous step which she has taken ?   Could not any slight misunderstandings be removed, by a little reciprocal care and an exercise of patience ?   At this very moment I find it impossible to believe that she has actually left me, once for all.   Cruel as were her words to me, when we last talked together, I am quite ready to overlook them. Will you not say that to her, please, and try to have her come back ?   Oh, if she would only return . . . . to-morrow !   Enter again my house, her house, and never let any question of separation again arise."

This very Christian solution of the problem, which Monsieur Naudié found in his own heart and religious faith, was precisely what Monsieur Defos himself would have welcomed, because of his veneration for propriety and good order. But Jane, with wilful determination, had rejected any such solution; and she was supported by her aunt, whose claws had enlarged the wound as much as possible, in the brief time at her command; she now was as insistent as was her niece, that no reconciliation should take place.

"Without any doubt, my dear pastor, this solution, which you suggest, would be the one approved by the best and soundest judges. It would harmonize, better than any other course, with your character and profession. Mutual concessions and forgiveness! How simple and beautiful that would be! Unhappily my niece will not listen, for a moment, to such a suggestion. She says that she has suffered much . . . "

"O righteous Heaven! Suffered? From whom?"

"I cannot judge between you, my dear sir. In affairs of this sort there is always wrong on both sides. Excuse me, then, from entering upon any inquiry into your respective sorrows. My task, I repeat, is to try and find some remedy, after impartially weighing the circumstances, and also after considering the wishes of my niece. Now her will is very decided. Her mind is fixed on gaining a divorce. I opposed this plan, as long as there was any hope of a reconciliation. Now I have given up this hope. There therefore remains a choice between divorce and separation. Taking everything into account, I incline to the view that the more radical of these measures would be the better, and I ask you to take notice that in the event of a divorce the questions of property are easier to manage."

Monsieur Naudié stood more erect. " These questions of property? I don't see any such questions. I wish for nothing that belongs to her."

" Yes, very well! But remember your children! "

" Their self-respect, my dear sir, is of more importance than their worldly welfare."

" But . . . "

" No more on that subject, I beg! And leaving out all questions of property, why, then, is a divorce desirable? "

His old-time jealousy awoke. It aroused suspicion of some secret understanding, some evil plot, which would result in the transferral to another man — quite in proper legal form, of course — of the woman whom he had so deeply loved. Indeed, a sort of adultery sanctioned by law; and, this time, the minister rebelled.

"The divorce, Monsieur Defos, will bring me dishonor; for it will be pronounced against me, not her, and, at the same time, it will set her entirely free. Well, I have been weak; I have bent my back under burdens of which you have no idea. Now it is over, I will arise, I will protect myself."

He raised his voice, he ceased to measure his words. Deep feeling convulsed his haggard visage.

"Let us look at the matter calmly, my good pastor!" said Monsieur Defos, emphasizing Monsieur Naudié's title sarcastically. "We are here to talk reasonably, not to recriminate. I agree with you, in a measure. Reconciliation would be best. I give you my word of honor, I have tried to effect that, but my niece was obdurate. She has a strong will, as you know. I have yielded to her, and it is in her name that I now speak. She asks for a divorce, no matter what I say to her. So there is the plain fact in the case."

"I will not consent," said Monsieur Naudié.

"Then there is the suit at law."

Pastor Naudié's Young Wife

"There must be one, whether I consent or not."

"Ah, but of a very different kind, my dear sir! It is one thing to obtain a divorce when both parties petition for it, and it is a very different thing when they struggle about it. A suit at law, my dear pastor, — well, do you know what that means? Your inmost heart opened before all eyes, your honor torn into shreds by the attorneys?"

"My life will bear inspection. I have no fear about that."

"But think of the calumny! It attacks you always; it undermines you. Already it has accomplished so much, aided by circumstances, that, as you know well, you will not be able to remain at La Rochelle. What will this calumny then become, when the speeches which are now whispered cautiously, in secret places, shall be uttered in full, clear tones on the streets and in the homes? You have children, daughters, and you are a minister of the gospel."

"This is outrageous, cruel, false. I have nothing whatever for which to reproach myself."

"An ordinary man, it is true, in your place would have little or nothing for which to reproach himself; but you are a clergyman.

Pastor Naudié's Young Wife

Have you not made a great mistake in the choice of a wife? — I confess I shared in that mistake, — but you made it, and for a man in your position it becomes a fault, a sin. Look into your own heart and reply to me! Your life is not yours alone; it belongs, in fact, to the little flock over which you are shepherd. And they have the right to hold you to account; for you influence them by your deeds, quite as much as by your words. And you may be sure that people will expect more from you than from an ordinary man. You have not remained simply a minister of the gospel, but you have joined in the affairs of the world; you have taken a wife, you have become a father. Why, then, should not the law deal with you as with any ordinary man? Remember, you would not, when I suggested it, have recourse to law, to recover your rentals. Why, then, should you have recourse to it to bring you back your wife, and to protect your fireside, after you have been unable yourself to protect it? Why ask the law to interfere, with all its array of attorneys and constables and sheriffs, especially in a case like this, where moral suasion ought to have been enough, and you have not had the strength of character to make use of it? Can you say that you have nothing with which to reproach yourself? More than that, I recall one of your sermons, which you preached, upon serving two masters. Well, then, allow me to ask you which you have been serving, these last eighteen months. And tell me if these concessions, which you have been making to Mammon, are not your fault! If you had served the other master, — I say it in all tenderness, — you would not to-day be expiating the faults which you are expiating."

Alas, they were harsh, cruel words, coming from the lips of a man who knew all about the compromises of life. Monsieur Naudié saw very clearly their force. But, at the same time, another voice spoke within him, — that natural voice, common to all men, which governs the actions of men when they are drawn into the vortex of strong human passions; and this voice rebelled, with all the strength gained by imposition and injury through many months, against this savage, remorseless hatred. Whether ordinary man or minister of the gospel, whether servant of God or of Mammon, how could he bring himself to deliver up to a successful rival, meekly and willingly, the wife whom he had loved and cherished, whose caresses were a tender memory, and whose love was his dearest treasure! This was the voice to which he listened, as he stood there leaning over toward Monsieur Defos, revealing by his tone of voice, even more than by his exact words, the deadly wounds in his heart.

" Are you sure, sir," said he, " that you are giving me the full measure of justice? Is there no hidden motive, no secret self-interest behind your words? Are you sure you are not serving an unjust cause, and abetting a wicked design? For — listen to me — why should she seek a divorce? For what end? Are you ignorant on that point?"

Doubtless, at the time when Jane left her husband's house, Monsieur Defos had connected, in his mind, that departure with Henry's confession to himself. But the mechanical, conventional character of his integrity had prevented him from facing the truth, and had made him listen to Jane's vehement protestations that his son had nothing whatever to do with her decision. The suspicion now touched him in his most sensitive fibre, namely, in his inflated sense of his family's respectability. He arose, slowly and deliberately, from his chair; and, standing erect, with face reddening, he said : " My son, sir? My son is not at all the cause of this. My son is incapable of entering into any such plot as this. I give you my word of honor for it. He has gone away to regain his strength ; he will not return, to be a party to any such infamy. If he could have entertained such a purpose, I would certainly have known it. Moreover, nobody can say that my interest in my niece has ever been tainted by any selfish considerations. I cannot allow any such suggestion of irregular conduct in my house. So, if it is some suspicion of this sort which makes you hold back, pause and reflect ! Reflect while there is time ! You will agree with me, I think, that in a condition of affairs like this, — they being such that there is no possible hope of a reconciliation, — some decision must be reached at once, some clear and final decision."

His convincing manner, his self-satisfied honesty, had their influence upon Monsieur Naudié, who could not find anything more to say.

" I will reflect upon it," said he, " I will reflect upon it." But, in his poor tortured heart, he added, " What good will that do ? What possible good ? I must submit to my fate."

CHAPTER V

THE trouble in the Naudié family was the theme on all lips. Comments and criticisms were rife. They were like a swarm of poisonous bees, whose evil buzzing was heard everywhere. Questions, replies, insinuations, explanations. "Who are their attorneys?" "What are the grounds for the suit?" "Incompatibility of natures! that will be as good a ground as any. It is general and very convenient." "Will *he* remain here? Will he marry his cousin? And the property! And the sister, recently come from Montauban! And the children!"

Thus the town-talk went on. Sometimes people were heard to say that Monsieur Naudié ought to be dealt with severely; sometimes wicked calumnies pictured him as a creature capable of every baseness. "*He* accepts the divorce, meaning thereby a rent-roll of two thousand dollars a year."

"Ah! I have heard it placed as high as twenty thousand."

"And *she* consents?"

"She must."

Pastor Naudié's Young Wife

" Well, money talks."

Thus the scandal spread, and grew larger
and more irritated. Thus the town threw its
web of infamous scandal around the Naudié
household. Negligences and insults and sins
were talked about openly; base, foul words
were rolled, like sweet morsels, under the
tongues of respectable people, who felt entirely
satisfied with their highly moral lives, because,
forsooth, they had never stolen a farthing, or
killed a fly.

Bertha and Esther dared not go out, because of the bold looks that followed them,
and the insulting words which they heard
around them. At first they had rejoiced over
their deliverance from their enemy; but they
saw the whole situation more justly now.
Jane's departure troubled them more than
her presence had done. A certain amount
of disgrace was somehow transferred to them,
to which they submitted, without quite understanding it. Their father's gloomy mood in-
fected them also, as an atmosphere of mourning will often do. In fact, the house would
have been a wretched scene of desolation, had
it not been for Angelica. Thoroughly accustomed, as she was, to wait upon the childish
needs of her aged father, she now found new

channels for an expression of the same old habitual watchfulness and self-sacrifice. The sweet influence, which emanated from her peaceful heart, chased away the bitter moods in the hearts around her. In a few days she had tamed Bertha, conquered Abraham, gained Zelia's adoration, and learned how to win her way into Esther's reserved nature. Her purity was like a dike, staying the flood of calumnies which often poured over the threshold, behind some tactless or malicious visitor. She stood firm in her belief that a day would come when justice would be done to the innocent. " They will subside into silence," she said to her brother, when he confided to her his unhappiness and his plans, "and they will admit that they have judged wrongly."

Angelica was quite right in her view. A reversion took place in public opinion later — perhaps all too late — when the resolution, which Monsieur Naudié had reached after severe struggles, was made known. He had decided to become a missionary, and go to Africa.

What surprise there was ! And what ingenious suppositions arose, as each person tried to explain this new development, in his own way ! There was much diversity, however, among these speculations ; and this was by no means strange, for, in order to understand a decision so much at variance with the usual outcome of life's dramas, it would have been necessary to read the characters graven in the very bottom of Monsieur Naudié's anguished heart. For this man was tossed about on the waves of many diverse emotions. There were his affections, as a father; and there was the harrowing consciousness of his wife's deceitfulness ; and the regrets which always made him cringe before his own conscience. There was the ardent hope of redeeming himself, in the eyes of the world, for his vacillations of soul and body ; and perhaps, at bottom, he felt a little of that eager martyr-spirit, which could lead him to face the arrows of savages, with their poisons, less cruel indeed than those which waste away the soul without destroying the body.

To understand the situation and Monsieur Naudié's decision, a person would have needed to know the terror which overwhelmed the children, as their father's purpose was revealed to them, and to have heard Angelica's gentle voice, as she said : " I will be with you, to take care of you. Let your father obey the voice of his conscience ! It never deceives. And who can know how to console, unless he has suffered ? "

There, also, was the exclamation of little Abraham, impulsive, affectionate, " I will go away with you." A cry of joy from his adventurous young soul, shut up in a routine of life which chafed him continually, a cry of hope, as he thought of that far-away country, which offered as much to his youthful audacity as to his father's despair.

Entirely in ignorance of this interior family-life, everybody — no matter how loudly and boldly he had lifted his voice in the discord-ant chorus of condemnation — was now com-pelled to acquiesce in the decision which had been reached.

We rarely appreciate the men who conse-crate themselves to great deeds. Their springs of action usually are hidden from us. We fail to understand how the heroic idea is born in them, grows, and culminates. But even if the mystery of the heroic eludes us, we cannot avoid the thrill which comes to us, as its fruit appears in full view of all men. Whenever a brother-man whom we have hastily misjudged, forswears all that seems to us worth having in life, and embraces dangers, privations, death, then our admiration rises and crowns him one of the princes of mankind. Before the man who sacrifices himself for country, race, or religion, we humbly bow. An inner voice tells us that he has chosen the path of righteousness. We may have shared neither his beliefs nor his illusions, we may not have possessed either his virtue or his valor; perhaps, also, we may not have committed any of the sins for which he seeks to atone; but what matters it, since light has come to him, since his path of duty is clear! And while we continue our existence among the common herd, cropping a meagre herbage, but avoiding the brambles, he rises up, catches visions of other horizons, and passes beyond our ken.

It was with some such feeling as this, faintly pulsating in their hearts, that a great congregation came together, one Sunday, Catholics, atheists, free-thinkers, and others, to listen to Monsieur Naudié's farewell sermon. For the last time the pastor climbed the pulpit steps, and seated himself, and they realized that his noble countenance never would appear there again. And, in the eyes which were focussed upon him, there was something more than the cavilling curiosity which had dogged his steps so long. Calmly and with dignity he

led them in the offices of devotion which preceded the sermon. The attention of all was
fixed, not on the liturgy, the psalms, the
prayers, but on his pale face, tranquil against
the green background of the pulpit; it wandered also to the five forms who were to be
seen in their accustomed place in their pew;
and here and there a whispered consultation
took place. "The sister has an air of great
courage . . . the eldest is weeping. . . . See
the little one! She is putting her handker-
chief to her eyes. And the son! is it really
true that he is going with his father?"

Reflections like these were exchanged among
the pews, during the earlier part of the service,
great care being taken to speak in subdued
whispers, and with considerable show of strict
attention to the service.

Then there was the closest attention, as
Monsieur Naudié announced his text: "A
portion of the eighth verse of the first chapter
of the Acts of the Apostles, . . . *Ye shall be
witnesses unto me, both in Jerusalem, and in all
Judœa, and in Samaria, and unto the uttermost
parts of the earth.*"

The preacher's little mannerisms faded, and
his oddities of rhetoric disappeared, as soon as
he had finished his exordium. Up to this

point he dealt, in the customary way, with the general duties devolving upon messengers of the Word. But soon leaving this style of address, he began to speak more freely, as man to men, regarding the truths which he held closely at heart. His discourse was by no means a confession, and still less an apology. It was a plain, simple lesson upon life; such as a person might be expected to give, who like himself was passing out from a sad and bitter experience. He spoke of that vain search for happiness, which sometimes scatters among the thorny paths of the world those who are naturally drawn toward God, and ought to find their greatest joy in him; he spoke of the serious mistake which such people made, and of the deep wounds which such mistakes brought them.

Entering thus into the deeper phases of his subject, he dwelt upon the sin of hypocrisy, and the evil effects of the habit of compromise, which keeps men hanging between heaven and earth, — nearer earth than heaven, — until sometimes a clear flash of light comes to them, as it did to Saul of Tarsus, and, while it blinds them, also enlightens them. In this flash of illumination, mingling salvation with sorrow, was manifested the divine wisdom and goodness. For, such is the peculiar quality of faith, that it ends by blessing the hand which has smitten it, and transforms the venom, concealed in its deepest wounds, into a balm of healing.

"Thus it is," said he, now returning to his text and to his own situation, "that one must not think to give only a half to the Master whom he serves. For a long time his voice has spoken to me, and I have not been willing to listen to it; and, in order that my ears should be unstopped, it has been necessary that his hand should be laid heavily upon me. It is only after having passed through the valley of the shadow of death, that I am able to reply to him, 'Master, here am I, thy servant is ready and waiting.' But what freedom from all bonds, brethren, in being able thus to speak these words! What comfort, in being delivered from the bondage of self, and of knowing that one belongs wholly to him, that in him are all one's hopes! What joy in being able to exclaim, with the Psalmist, '*Have mercy upon me, O Lord, for I am weak. O Lord, heal me, for my bones are vexed;*' and then those other words, '*I laid me down, and slept; I awaked, for the Lord sustained me.*' Having travelled the road which leads from the cry of despair to the cry of hope, I now place in God's hands, with entire trust, the remainder of my own life, and the lives of those who are a thousand times dearer to me than aught else on earth. Now I am about to carry his name to those who know him not; I am going to teach them that he is the source of all consolation, and that he is the seat and source of truth. Join with me, brethren, in asking his blessing on the whitening harvest fields, and on the humble husbandman who goes to labor in them!"

His voice never wavered for an instant. He continued firm and self-controlled, ending with a fervent prayer. When he had seated himself, after giving out the number of the closing hymn, the whole congregation, silent and motionless until then, showed signs of deep emotion. The organ played the hymn through slowly, solemnly; and little Zelia was seen to be in tears, holding out her hands toward her father; while Esther and Angelica leaned over her, and tried to comfort her. Then the choir sang, *Great God, we bless thee* . . .

Monsieur Naudié had opened his psalm-book, and tried to sing with the others; but the book fell from his hand. His glance had fallen upon that little group of desolate beings, so dear to him, yet whom he would soon leave forever.   He bent forward upon the pulpit; he leaned tenderly over toward them, and great tears ran down his cheeks.

THE END

www.ingramcontent.com/pod-product-compliance
Lightning Source LLC
Chambersburg PA
CBHW021721110726
47902CB00005B/1285